SO-AAC-731

# "You're the one who's in a rush to sell your grandmother's house."

Mandi picked up a paint scraper from the bucket and slapped it gently against her palm.

"Gray, all I ever wanted was for you to be honest and open with me. If you can promise me that, then we'll survive working together on this place."

Something shifted in Gray's face. He took the scraper from her and began clearing the cracked paint off the back railing.

"I'm an honest man, doing an honest day's work. Trust me, Mandi. Nobody knows me better than you do. And nobody ever will."

Was that an answer or a promise? A lump rose in her throat and she swallowed hard against it. Her heartstrings had tangled like wild, windblown hair the first day she'd met him, and it had taken her the past three years to loosen the knots. Grayson Zale was dangerous to her peace of mind. She wanted to believe him...but did she dare?

Dear Reader,

Welcome to Turtleback Beach! I hope you enjoy my new series set in a small, fictional beach town on the real Outer Banks of North Carolina's Hatteras Island. This series is filled with heartwarming animals, lots and lots of romance and a little mystery. I hope you join me for the ride!

The towns of Hatteras Island, including the famous Rodanthe, are small and quaint (no big hotels or crowds). This breathtaking island boasts quiet beaches and natural surroundings. The Outer Banks is also famous for sea turtle nesting grounds, wild horses, picturesque lighthouses and so much more. It's one of my favorite places to visit.

This first book of the series includes many themes, but one of the most significant is *secrets*—the life-changing kind. Often, what we're hiding is so serious or personal it keeps us from being able to embrace life, live freely, own our truth...or love who we want to love. Keeping that kind of secret is stressful, and might include lying to friends and family, but sometimes doing so can be a matter of life or death.

So, when are secrets worth the sacrifice? I'd love to hear what you think after experiencing what Mandi Rivers, a runaway bride, and Grayson Zale, who is in the witness protection program, must overcome in order to find love in *Almost a Bride*.

My door is always open at rulasinara.com, where you'll find my newsletter sign-up, social media links, information on my series and books and more.

Wishing you love, peace and courage in life.

*Rula Sinara*

# HEARTWARMING

## *Almost a Bride*

—

*Rula Sinara*

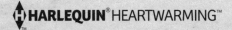

If you purchased this book without a cover you should be aware
that this book is stolen property. It was reported as "unsold and
destroyed" to the publisher, and neither the author nor the
publisher has received any payment for this "stripped book."

Recycling programs
for this product may
not exist in your area.

ISBN-13: 978-1-335-51071-6

Almost a Bride

Copyright © 2019 by Rula Sinara

All rights reserved. Except for use in any review, the reproduction or
utilization of this work in whole or in part in any form by any electronic,
mechanical or other means, now known or hereafter invented, including
xerography, photocopying and recording, or in any information storage
or retrieval system, is forbidden without the written permission of the
publisher, Harlequin Enterprises Limited, 22 Adelaide St. West, 40th Floor,
Toronto, Ontario M5H 4E3, Canada.

This is a work of fiction. Names, characters, places and incidents are
either the product of the author's imagination or are used fictitiously,
and any resemblance to actual persons, living or dead, business
establishments, events or locales is entirely coincidental.

This edition published by arrangement with Harlequin Books S.A.

For questions and comments about the quality of this book,
please contact us at CustomerService@Harlequin.com.

® and TM are trademarks of Harlequin Enterprises Limited or its
corporate affiliates. Trademarks indicated with ® are registered in the
United States Patent and Trademark Office, the Canadian Intellectual
Property Office and in other countries.

Printed in U.S.A.

www.Harlequin.com

Award-winning and *USA TODAY* bestselling author **Rula Sinara** lives in rural Virginia with her family and wild but endearing pets. She loves organic gardening, attracting wildlife to her yard, planting trees, raising backyard chickens and drinking more coffee than she'll ever admit to. Rula's writing has earned her a National Readers' Choice Award and a HOLT Medallion of Merit, among other honors. Her door is always open at rulasinara.com, where you can sign up for her newsletter, learn about her latest books and find links to her social media hangouts.

### Books by Rula Sinara

### Harlequin Heartwarming

### *From Kenya, with Love*

*The Promise of Rain*
*After the Silence*
*Through the Storm*
*Every Serengeti Sunrise*
*The Twin Test*
*The Marine's Return*

*A Heartwarming Thanksgiving*
"The Sweetheart Tree"

Visit the Author Profile page
at Harlequin.com for more titles.

## Acknowledgments

Many thanks to my eldest son for answering my questions (any errors are my own). Your passion for motorcycles inspired me, and the hero in this book loves them as much as you do.

And to my other kids for providing encouragement, support and inspiration. You never know what will make its way into my books!

And, as always, heartfelt gratitude to my editor, Adrienne Macintosh. I'm looking forward to working on this new and exciting series with you!

## Dedication

To those who devote their time to rescuing animals, whether wildlife or pets.
And to pets for rescuing us.

# CHAPTER ONE

GRAYSON ZALE BIT back a curse as he ducked between the weather-beaten posts that hoisted the pier at Turtleback Beach over the clawing surf. He crouched down, pulse racing, as he pretended to reach for a shell stranded by the low tide, and waited for the guy in the backward cap and sunglasses to finish taking a panoramic shot with his cell phone. The last thing Gray needed was to have his face plastered on social media and recognized by the wrong people. Or worse yet, what if this guy wasn't some random tourist? Not many tourists ventured this far south along the Outer Banks of North Carolina, and those who did usually stayed away from the areas roped off and marked as turtle breeding grounds. Most vacationers settled on staying in towns farther north of Hatteras Island, like Duck or Kill Devil Hills, where they could have their pick of hotels, amenities, shops and attractions, like the memorial where the Wright brothers took their first flight. Granted, Turtleback and neighboring towns, like Rodanthe or Avon, did get some visitors—usually more peace- and nature-loving types. It was just that being cautious and suspicious had become a twisted, unsettling part of who he was…like a leech or parasite, unwilling to let go.

Laddie, Gray's rough collie rescue, positioned himself stoically between Gray and the stranger. No barking or growling. That was a good sign, but getting caught in an online photo was a threat in and of itself. It was more than out of the question. It was a matter of life or death.

Sure, he was the town's veterinarian, which meant just about everyone had come to know him in some capacity or another since he'd landed in town five years ago. He was their pet's doc, a friend of a friend, the guy who grabbed his coffee and bear claw at the local bake shop the second it opened at six in the morning with Laddie ever at his side. He was the guy they'd wave to as he took off on a motorcycle ride down Highway 12. But as much as he'd integrated himself into the town, he'd also become adept at skirting photos, and he almost always wore his "Save the Turtles" ball cap and Oakley sunglasses when walking the beach during the busier summer season, just in case he did end up in the background of a tourist's photograph. He took every precaution to stay under the radar and live a low-key life.

Nonetheless, it was a tiny town. Everyone knew everyone and news traveled faster than the infamous riptides could suck a person out to sea and drown them. He was surprised he'd survived the gossip and sideglances when he was abandoned at the altar by Mandi Rivers, the town's sweetheart and former mayor's daughter, two years ago. As privately as he lived his life, having his heart shredded so publicly had been unbearable— not because of humiliation or pride, but because she must have known that having his personal life laid out for everyone to dissect was akin to physically stabbing him in the heart and leaving him to bleed out. Yet, she'd done it. She had deliberately hurt him. Sometimes he wasn't sure what hurt more… the pain of losing the only woman he'd ever loved and trusted, or the pain of knowing that she had cast him off like fisherman's chum and never looked back.

He glanced across the waves toward the horizon. It hadn't been the first time everything in his life had been cast away, but Mandi's leaving him would probably be the one loss he'd never fully recover from. He knew this because every time she entered his mind, a spot deep in his chest, beneath bone and heart, cramped and ached with pain and longing. And what bothered him even more was that he couldn't, in all honesty, place all the blame on her. He'd destroyed his own life. Every choice he made seemed to doom him—not that keeping that truth from her about his past had been a choice. But she had wanted more from him than he could give. Openness and honesty. And telling her that he honestly loved her clearly hadn't been enough.

The stranger's voice broke through the rhythmic cries of seagulls and crashing surf as he called out a name. A woman emerged from the tall grasses that flanked a narrow, sandy path leading from the road to the beach. Similar paths, some paved with weathered, wooden planks and some not, ran all along the Outer Banks. This one trailed over a short sand dune that masked the view of the road beyond. The young woman hoisted a toddler onto her hip and adjusted what looked like a baby supply bag that hung from one shoulder as she trudged through the sand toward the man, who belatedly tucked the phone camera in his back pocket and jogged over to give her a hand. He planted a kiss on her lips and took the child in his arms. Husband? Partner? Boyfriend? Whatever the relationship, one thing was clear. They were a family. Something Gray would never have again.

Laddie whimpered and began wagging his tail. He looked up pleadingly at Gray.

"Not this time. Come on."

The calming scent of salt water filled Gray's lungs once again. He tucked a shell in his pocket, stood and started for the lighthouse at the end of the beach. Laddie jogged alongside without complaint, distancing himself from Gray only long enough to skirt a log of driftwood strangled by seaweed. His ears perked at the sound of that toddler giggling in the distance, but he stayed on course for home.

The poor dog adored children, so much so that there were times when Gray could have sworn his expressive face and eyes seemed to say, "When are you going to get me some human kids of my own to look out for?" Yeah. That wasn't happening.

His past had ceased to exist five years ago, and the only people who'd come close to being family since then were Mandi and her grandmother Nana. His throat constricted and a sudden gust of wind slapped against his chest, forcing him to exhale. As of three days ago, Nana was no longer with them, a fact that still felt surreal. Nana was gone. There would be no more waving to her during his evening jog or stopping by for an afternoon cup of coffee. There would be no more deals or compromises where Nana would insist on his coming over for a home-cooked meal and he'd agree only if she let him pick up groceries for her. She would no longer be there to comb the beach for turtle nests with him at the crack of dawn— her favorite activity and time of day. As for Mandi?

Gray muttered a curse as he passed the white, two-story beach cottage that everyone knew as Nana's house. Raised on solid posts, like most homes here because of tropical storms and hurricanes, it stood much taller than a standard two-story and boasted just a touch of Victorian flair with gingerbread trim along the upper gable and around the small turret-style attic. That tiny space was more of a lookout and storage nook than a full room, according to Nana, who had always kept it locked. It was the window to the room just beneath it that caught his eye now. Nana had always referred to it as Mandi's room, even if she had technically lived with her father. That room beneath the attic space had been Mandi's spot, made cozy with an old sofa, painting easel and numerous canvases stacked against the wall. It had been her hideaway. The one place he knew he could always find her if her father had been giving her a hard time about seeing too much of Gray. Well, John Rivers got what he wanted.

Man, Gray had come so close—dangerously close—to giving up everything after Mandi had left him at the altar. His veterinary practice, his new life at Turtleback…

his fake identity. Everything, just to win her back. But doing so wouldn't have endangered only himself. It would have put anyone he cared about in danger, too…something the WITSEC—Witness Security Program—marshals had drilled into him with horrifying, gory visuals and stories about federal witness protection cases where cover had been blown—voluntarily or involuntarily. Ironic that revealing the truth had caused him to be sentenced to a life of secrets and lies. He was lucky that he'd been allowed to continue his career as a vet under a different name, but any record of his completing veterinary school through the US Army or serving as a vet with the US Navy Marine Mammal Program or even his very short time in the Department of Defense research division was essentially gone. That history didn't belong to Grayson Zale. Nor did any chance at a truly normal life beyond outward appearances.

He took to jogging the eighth of a mile from Nana's to the path that led to the old Turtleback Lighthouse and the adjacent one-story "ranger" cottage where he lived. Unlike other lighthouses along the Outer

Banks, this one wasn't a famous tourist destination. In fact, the powers that be made sure it was clearly marked as not open to the public. A metal sign hanging on a wooden post near the clearing welcomed wanderers with a firm warning that the landmark wasn't structurally safe, that it was undergoing restoration and that trespassers would be prosecuted.

There were no heavy security fences around the property. That idea had been nixed by WITSEC on the grounds that it would draw more attention to him than it was worth. Hiding in plain sight was essentially a more effective plan, which meant no added security fences that would only raise eyebrows. There was an old double-wide gate with a short, open-ended fence to either side where the main road led to the property, but it was nothing more than an entrance marker. Anyone could get around it, so he had a hidden surveillance camera on the property, just in case people got too curious. The few times he'd run into intrigued hikers, he'd told them he lived there as an authorized curator and guard, and then sent them off. As for townsfolk, they believed that lack of proper funding was the reason no major restorations had happened yet, including the high cost of relocating the lighthouse to a safer spot, farther away from the shore, as had been done with the Cape Hatteras Lighthouse. There would be no safer spot. At least not for him. There wouldn't be any major restorations either, because opening up the place to tourism was out of the question.

Laddie trotted up the steps to the cottage door and nudged the brass box that held mail. He could tell when it was empty or full and he knew the scent of the mailman wasn't a threat. Or it wasn't supposed to be, not just because of the Postal Service's reputation, but because, as Gray understood it when he first moved here, the delivery guy had been cleared.

He grabbed the mail, unlocked the door and waited for Laddie to follow him inside.

"Hungry?"

The dog responded with his usual half grunt, half yodel. Dog-speak. Gray chuckled as he poured kibble into the food bowl and put fresh water in the one next to it. He didn't know what he'd do without Laddie.

Having him around the past few years had made life manageable.

"We rescued each other, didn't we boy?" He scratched Laddie behind the ear and got a dog smile in return. "I still have you. It doesn't matter that Mandi will be here for the funeral. I can deal with it. Life's been just fine without her."

Funny how lying to himself had become just as natural as lying to everyone else. Or maybe repeating those words to himself had become more of a mantra. *Life's just fine without her.* God knew he'd relied on that mantra during Mandi's short and infrequent visits from up north to see Nana over the past couple of years. Most of the time, she had convinced her grandma to go visit her instead—a blatant avoidance of him.

He was guilty of steering clear of her too, though, down to not grabbing coffee at the local bakery whenever she was in town for a couple of days. He told himself he was avoiding gossip and proving to everyone in town that he'd moved on, but the fact was that one look at her and every stitch he'd tightened around the wound she'd left would unravel. He was strong and resilient, but there was only so much a man could take.

He glanced at the clock. *Sheesh.* Ten already? He scrubbed his hand across his face. So much for dropping by the office to make sure everything was under control. He needed to shower and change in time for the funeral. *She'll be there. You can't avoid each other this time.* Yeah. He knew that. A fact that had been gnawing at him for two days now.

As if having his life turned upside down when he'd been placed in the witness protection program, and again when Mandi had gone runaway bride on him, wasn't enough. Now Nana was gone. Nana…the one person who'd accepted him unconditionally…who'd treated him like a son and who'd taught him about rescuing endangered sea turtles by tending to their nesting grounds along her private stretch of beach and the sands that extended beyond the town limits. Nana was gone and the one person who understood and felt the depth of that loss the way he did was Mandi. But it didn't matter that a part of him wanted to reach out and console her or that he desperately needed to talk about

Nana and share memories about her with Mandi. No way would he open his heart, even a crack, and let Mandi in. He was a survivor. Burned once and all that. Others would be at the funeral, including Mandi's father, John Rivers, Nana's only child. They could console her and give her support. She didn't need Gray in her life. She'd made that clear long ago.

And he certainly didn't need her.

MANDI RIVERS EXAMINED herself in the tarnished silver mirror that hung in Nana's entryway above a rustic console table. Her eyes weren't any less puffy than they had been the five previous times she'd checked during the past thirty minutes. Why did it matter? No doubt, others in town had cried, too, when they heard of Nana's unexpected passing.

She scurried to the kitchen and chucked the cucumber slices that had proved useless into the trash bin. The fact was that she hadn't noticed what the nine-hour drive from New York yesterday—and the dam of tears that finally let loose once she'd stepped into Nana's home last night—had done to her face…until she had spotted Grayson down on the beach this morning. She wasn't sure if he noticed her peering past the sheer curtains. She had ducked back the second he glanced up toward the house, but the way he took off at a run seconds later made her wonder. Maybe he *had* seen her.

He had looked serious and irritated and so, so good. It was criminal to look that good with his dark brown hair all messed up by the ocean breeze and his favorite old T-shirt looking more worn than she'd remembered. Even from a distance, she knew which one by the faded blue color and tear at the bottom hem. It was the one that said "Save the Sharks" on the front. Heaven help her, she had a better chance of surviving a shark attack than surviving being around Gray this afternoon.

She closed her eyes and pressed her fingers against her throbbing temples. The last thing she wanted was for him to think she cared enough to spy on him. She had wasted too much of her life trying to get him to open up and share things about his history. She'd gone from having a crush on him when she was twenty, right about when he had first moved to town, to dating him and even saying yes when he had finally proposed on her twenty-third birthday. She thought that day would never happen, given how withdrawn and serious he'd sometimes get. As much as she had loved him and confided in him, he had been hard to crack. He was skilled at evading questions and switching subjects so smoothly that most people didn't notice. But she did. And it hurt that he didn't trust her enough to open up. She had thought being engaged and eventually married would make a difference, but boy had she been naive. She'd come so close to throwing away a chance at a master's degree and an incredible career for someone she'd never be enough for.

The last straw had been wedding jitters mixed with her father warning her that marrying Gray would be the biggest mistake of her life. The look on her dad's face when she stood at the altar had left her hyperventilating and sweating in her wedding dress. Her controlling father had been the one person she'd rebelled against and the last man she wanted to listen to, yet when push came to shove, his disapproval had carried weight.

The need for parental approval was one of those convoluted psychological things that latched itself to a person's mind even when logic shunned it. He'd made her second-guess herself. He'd made her second-guess Gray's love for her.

Wasn't it Freud who had written something to the effect that girls tended to fall for guys who were much like their fathers? God help her. Her father was a hovering, micromanaging, money-driven, controlling man who valued appearances and reputation above all else. He had made her teenage years unbearable. And then there was Gray, who had a compassionate side she couldn't resist, yet he had to maintain control of every conversation, and his explanations for mundane things, like why he never had visitors or why he didn't keep old baby or family photos, had frustrated her to no end. The thought of marrying someone remotely controlling like her father still made her nauseous. And there had been a part of Gray she couldn't figure out…a part he kept locked away with the key in his pocket. *Control.* That fact had kept her up every night the week before the wedding. It had driven her to choose control of her own life…and to abandon a love that was just too risky.

On one hand, she often wondered if her father's air of superiority and always having the final say in decisions had been the reason her mother had abandoned them when Mandi was still in grade school. Nana used to tell her that her parents had loved each other, but perhaps loving John Rivers had been too risky. Maybe the women in Mandi's family were simply doomed when it came to love.

But Nana also used to say that there were two sides to every relationship and every story, so a part of Mandi also wondered if her mother had had commitment issues and Mandi had somehow inherited that curse. Perhaps her mom had suffered from the same suffocating urge to leave Turtleback and travel or experience big-city life that Mandi had. What if Mandi was just like her mother? And what if maybe, just maybe, Gray wasn't at all like her father and Mandi had been fishing for excuses to run away. That would mean that she had thrown away the kind of love she couldn't ever imagine feeling again.

*Just stop it.* She groaned and clenched her fists as she headed for the kitchen. She was doing it again—overanalyzing and spiraling through pointless reasons for what had happened to her and Gray. She hated it when she slid into this pattern. It had taken months for her to regain her focus after leaving him and starting graduate school. She was *not* going to let seeing him weaken her resolve. She steeled herself against the slurry of anger and sadness that pooled in her stomach. She took a glass from the cabinet by the fridge, filled it with cool water and drank half before setting it down.

*No regrets.* Nana's voice swept through her mind with haunting clarity. The same words she would command Mandi to repeat like a mantra, whenever she was feeling down or torn about a decision. *Regrets are like steel anchors. They'll weigh you down and keep you from moving forward in life. Own every choice you make, and make it work for you.*

Oh, she'd made her choice work for her alright. She would never regret earning her undergraduate college degree on her own terms. Studying online may not have been the same as getting a degree from a university her father could brag about, but it had saved her money. It had been the affordable option, and her master's diploma from NYU was the one that counted now. Her father's insistence that she study prelaw out of high school, then attend law school—all because he felt his political aspirations would have gone far beyond town mayor had he done the same—had resulted in her taking a gap year after high school. He had given her an ultimatum that he would pay for college only if she studied prelaw, which she had no inclination toward or desire to do.

That gap year had really ticked him off, but not nearly as much as her decision to put herself through a four-year advertising degree online, while working locally to support her goals. Her father had been downright furious. Turning down his money not only stole some of the power he had over her, but that gap year had also stripped him of bragging rights. His only child was the only one in her senior class whose intended college wasn't announced at graduation. She had shamed him.

She never asked Nana for financial help

either, though there was a time or two she wished her grandmother would have offered. All Nana ever told her was that she had faith in her and that Mandi could accomplish more than she knew she could. And she had. She'd accomplished something significant, but her father had yet to express any pride or approval in her degree. Had she married Gray the year she earned her diploma and found out she'd been accepted into a master's program, she wouldn't be on the verge of jump-starting her career right now. She took a deep breath and rolled the stiffness out of her shoulders.

Gray had not known she'd gotten accepted into NYU, yet he had made it clear that selling his vet practice and moving was out of the question. If she'd trusted his feelings for her, maybe she'd have given it all up for him or maybe she could have figured out how to make a long-distance marriage work for two years, but that hadn't been the case. She didn't leave him because of the master's program. She left him because she couldn't see a life with someone who wasn't completely open and honest with her about everything.

*You don't regret leaving him. You're just feeling alone because Nana's gone.*

She opened the pantry and took out another box of tissues. This was so unfair. Nana hadn't said a word about being sick. Or had Mandi been so preoccupied with school and her career that she'd missed the signs? If she regretted anything, it was not being there for her grandmother.

She jolted when her phone alarm went off, then quickly silenced it and hurried to the guest room she was using while staying here. She glanced in the mirror and ran a comb briskly through her long, wavy hair. Her sun-kissed highlights were long gone and her face looked pale against the deeper brown. Unfortunately, her nose was as red and miserable as her eyes. She pinched her cheeks, then hurried to the sofa, where she'd thrown her purse last night. Years of avoiding a face-to-face with Gray, and now he was going to see her like this? She looked nothing like a successful graduate who'd just been offered her dream job with a top New York advertising firm. That was the impression she'd hoped to give. And why did that bother her so much?

She hated that one glimpse of Grayson on the beach had her worried about appearances and impressions...so much like her father. She just wanted people to see that she was okay and doing just fine for herself without Gray in her life. She didn't want her father seeing her as weak and doubting that she could make it on her own without his money or connections. She wanted everyone who had been a part of her life to feel at least a little proud of her for making it on her own...even Gray. But she knew Gray hated her and she couldn't blame him after what she'd done, yet a part of her yearned for him to wrap his arms around her and hold her until the pain of losing Nana became bearable. If it ever would.

She flipped the pillows on the sofa. Her keys had to be here somewhere. She distinctly remembered tossing them onto the purse. She shoved her hand between the sofa cushions. *Yes.* Her fingertips brushed against the pewter turtle that held the bundle of keys together. The doorbell rang. *No.*

She wasn't expecting anyone. The image of Gray standing in the doorway flashed in her mind. She knew it was him. She just did. Her instincts screamed it. Her stomach twisted and her pulse skittered at the base of her throat. This would be so like him… wanting to give her his condolences in private, away from curious friends and family. Public displays of affection had always made him uncomfortable. It didn't matter that this gathering was about loss. The fact that everyone in town knew their history practically guaranteed that behind all the sympathy would be curious eyes and gossip.

Gray was right. Getting this first encounter over with in private was the smart thing to do.

She shoved the keys in her pocket and took a deep breath as she went for the door and opened it.

"Mandi."

"Dad?"

Her gut sank a few inches, but she wasn't sure if it was relief or disappointment. Her father opened his arms and she complied. His embrace was anything but comforting. Maybe it was all in her head, but everything between them…even seemingly kind gestures on his part…always felt tainted with expectation or ulterior motive. Nonetheless, he was her father. Her only remaining family. That had to count for something. Mandi gave him a peck on the cheek and stepped back. He strode past her and stood in the center of the main room, his gaze darting around the place with purposeful efficiency.

"I thought we should drive over to the funeral together. Show how the Rivers are strong and will get through this together, as a family," he said.

And there it was. *Show.* Keep up appearances. Mandi folded her arms around her waist.

"I'm so sorry about Nana, Dad. I know losing your mom must be hard on you."

"Yes. Thank you. Same to you, sweetheart. I know you were close. And I realize that you were so young when your mother left, you probably don't remember what it was like having her around. It's different when you've been around someone day in and day out your entire life, like Nana, and then, suddenly, they're gone. I know she was old, but still. It hurts."

Leave it to her dad to put the color back in her face. It irked her to no end that he'd assume that she had no memories of her mother or that her leaving so abruptly hadn't left a scar. How many times had she, as a little girl, wondered if she'd caused her mother to leave, even if Nana had assured her that wasn't the case? Besides, Nana had been like both a mother and grandmother to her. More of a parent than John Rivers had been, for sure. He had always put his work first, whether it was when he was town mayor or, now, as a real estate investor. For him, life was about money and success. All he had ever cared about were Mandi's grades and future career.

Sure, he had given her a roof and had read her bedtime stories when she was younger, but when it really came to parenting, it was Nana who had stepped in and picked up the pieces after her mother left. Nana had been the one to offer emotional support through all her growing pains and the pitfalls of dating. She was the one who instilled confidence in Mandi, assuring her she was pretty during the awkward teen years, taking her clothes shopping or even just holding and comforting her when she had missed her mom and felt confused. Her dad had always been too preoccupied with work to realize

that parenting involved so much more than
providing food and shelter.

*It's different when you've been around
someone day in and day out your entire life
and then, suddenly, they're gone.*

Was he also trying to point out that she
hadn't been around Nana on a daily basis the
past few years? As if that would make her
miss her grandmother any less? She bit the
inside of her cheek to keep from lashing out.
It wasn't the time, or place. Nana wouldn't
want them fighting. She cleared her throat
and fidgeted with her keys.

"I miss her, too. I, um, was planning to
drive myself to the funeral home. In fact, I
was just about to leave. We can park near
each other and walk into the service together. I'd really like to have my car there,
so that I can go for a drive afterward."

What she really meant was that she
needed a getaway car if things got overwhelming. Nana used to lovingly call her
"my little hermit crab" because, for all her
talk about making it big in the world, Mandi
always needed downtime. She had the soul
of a hermit, Nana would say. Sometimes
she'd find her solace by reading upstairs

in her nook and sometimes it was a sandy spot, hidden by tall grasses, overlooking the sound side of Turtleback. Her mind flipped back to the lighthouse and the time Gray whisked her up the spiral stairs to the top and they sat for hours watching the sunset. He had been quiet enough for her to find peace, yet comforting, with his hand wrapped around hers and his special scent enveloping her. It had been the day after she had finished her online degree and her dad had not shown up to the "graduation" dinner Nana had made for her and a few friends. His only reaction to Mandi's telling him she'd finished her bachelor's was, "Good for you. Now figure out what to do with it." He had always dismissed her so easily, especially when she accomplished something that had not stemmed from his advice.

"Nonsense," he said, running his hand along an old, chipped bowl that was the color of the wet sand along the surf.

The piece of pottery had been passed down for generations. It had belonged to Nana's great-grandmother, who in turn had claimed it had made its way to her from a line of ancestors in the Algonquin tribe. Something about the way John Rivers touched it sent a streak of cold down Mandi's neck…as if Nana herself was protesting. No doubt that bowl was worth a lot, assuming it really was antique, but it needed to continue its journey through generations of family. Mandi's father wouldn't see the value in that. He glanced over at Mandi. He did look tired. She knew he loved them both. It was just that his love seemed so misguided at times.

"I really want you to come with me, Mandi. You drove all yesterday. Besides, didn't you used to hound me about the environment? Car fumes and fuel, etcetera…? Come on. Grab your purse or we'll be late."

He put his hand on her shoulder to ease her toward the door. She was too tired to fight him on this, as much as she wanted to.

"Fine. After you."

She followed him out, pausing only to close up behind her. A breeze tousled her hair over her eyes as she waited for him to unlock the car doors with his fob. She pushed the hair out of her face and stilled. There was Gray on his motorcycle, helmet turned so that he was undoubtedly staring right at her from the crossroad near the house. He turned away, revved his engine and disappeared down the road.

"Are you getting in?" her father asked, glancing back toward the road. He made no effort to mask his irritation. Mandi tipped her chin up and gave a quick shrug, as if the sight of Gray or the sound of his Triumph engine failed to stir anything in her.

"Yeah, sorry. The wind was blowing my hair and I was just thinking of getting a scarf, but never mind. Let's go before it's too late."

*Go before it's too late.*

That's what she needed to do. She'd stay for the funeral and then get out of town as fast as she could. Being this close to Gray was dangerous. She couldn't risk everything she'd worked so hard for—her independence, career…and finally getting over him. Being near Gray would only reawaken old feelings. Emotions had a way of confusing a person. She needed to stay on track. Grayson's life rested in Turtleback…and she simply didn't belong here anymore.

## CHAPTER TWO

FACES HAD A way of blurring at a funeral reception, especially at the rate Gray was moving through the crowd to exchange kind words about Nana Rivers. Everyone was there, from Darla, who ran the bakery, to Carlos Ryker, the town sheriff. Even the florist, who'd supplied the arrangements at all corners of the room, had lingered when her job was done. Nana would have preferred for the money to be donated to animal rescue foundations, rather than spent on expensive flowers. The baby's breath, however, she would have loved. It was the only flower she ever had in her home because she said it was the only one that didn't make her sneeze. Gray was going to need some fresh air soon himself. Between flowers and perfume, his eyes were beginning to itch. Animal dander never bothered him, but pollen and artificial scents he could do without.

He gave Nana's friend from the library his condolences and spent seconds too long trying to pry himself away from two young women he recognized as teachers at the local high school. He hated crowds, and the idea that anyone could have the nerve to flirt at a time like this nauseated him. The only saving grace of having so many townsfolk present was that it kept things civil when he shook hands with John to briefly pay his respects. He wasn't here for the man who'd almost become his father-in-law. He was here for Nana…and Mandi. Regardless of what had happened between them, he knew she was suffering right now. He knew firsthand how close she'd been to her grandmother.

He'd come so close to stopping by Nana's cottage earlier. If John hadn't been there, he would have already spoken to Mandi. Something told him that there wasn't anything random about her father getting there first. He wouldn't be surprised if John stuck by his daughter's side until she was back in New York, far enough away from Gray… the guy John had insisted was too old for her and not polished enough, as if six years' difference mattered when two people were meant for each other. It wasn't only about age, though. John was an elitist. A man of position, whether he held one or not. He would always look down his nose at Gray. Even now, Gray wasn't wearing a tie, a fact that was emphasized when he shook hands with John and the man smoothed his own. Gray hated ties. Nana knew it and wouldn't have wanted him wearing one on her account. She encouraged people to be themselves around her. But for John, he was too casual and too much of a bachelor. He didn't have what it took to be a family man or good enough husband for Mandi. And boy, did John hate Gray's love of motorcycles. There was just too much speed and freedom in a motorcycle ride for him to handle or wrap his head around. Motorcycles weren't stable enough…a direct reflection of Gray's character, apparently.

He scanned the foyer of the funeral home, but there was no sign of Mandi. Clearly, she hadn't lost her touch. He slipped through the group and stepped outside the massive oak doors that led out onto a raised decking with steps down to a walkway and the parking lot.

There she stood leaning over the railing at one end. She looked amazing. Even more beautiful than the selfie Nana had taken of the two of them during her last trip to New York about eight months ago. It was the photo Nana used on her cell phone lock screen, and he couldn't help but look at it the few times Nana had asked him to hold her phone for her.

Mandi's hair had gotten darker and longer but it still held loose waves, like the ones he used to run his fingers through. The wind kicked up, causing her skirt to hug the curve of her hip. She brushed the hair off her face and wrapped her arms around her waist as she watched clouds building up for a typical afternoon rain. Man, the sight of her made him long for the family they'd once talked about…like the one he'd witnessed on the beach that morning. He'd never wanted one with anyone else. He'd never wanted forever with anyone else. Only her.

He tucked his fingers into the pockets of his black jeans and walked over, bracing himself with each step. This wasn't about opening up an old can of worms. This was about getting the closure they both needed and making peace. Nana would have wanted that and it was the least he could do in the little time he had before Mandi left again. Chances were, without Nana to coax her into a rare visit, Mandi wouldn't have any reason to come back here again. Especially given the way she felt about her father and him. He hesitated when she tensed, clearly sensing his presence, then he stepped closer and leaned against the railing next to her.

"I thought I'd find you out here," he said, trying to sound cool and matter-of-fact. She simply pressed her lips together and nodded. A lump trailed down her throat as she swallowed. He could tell she was struggling to find her words. "You don't have to say anything. I just wanted to let you know how sorry I am about Nana. I couldn't find you inside. Besides, John would've found a way to intercept," he said.

That earned him a chuckle and she let her arms relax.

"You're right about that." She smiled softly. "Nana used to joke about how he needed a dog to help him relax but that he'd never get one because you were the only vet in town."

"That would have to be one biddable dog. I would think your dad would love having someone around who would obey his every command."

"Shh. He might hear you."

She stifled a laugh and looked over her shoulder. Gray shrugged.

"It wouldn't make him hate me any less."

"How's your dog? Laddie. Nana talks—talked—a lot about him," she explained. Laddie and Mandi had never been formally introduced.

"I usually take him everywhere I go when I take my truck, but he's at home right now watching a nature documentary. He's the best, smartest, most patient dog I've ever met, but I doubt he'd have the patience for your dad. *Everyone* has their limits."

"Don't make me laugh."

He loved her laugh. Her face relaxed and her dark brown eyes softened like warmed chocolate. He was letting himself fall into dangerous territory. But he had a safety net. She'd be gone soon.

"It's okay to laugh. Nana would want you to. She was all about celebrating life."

Mandi nodded, but her smile disappeared and chin quivered.

"She really was. I feel guilty about not being here. For not knowing something was wrong."

He reached over and put his hand over hers. For a fraction of a second, he thought she was going to pull away, but she didn't.

"You can't feel guilty. No one knew. You can't predict when an aneurysm will give, and she never told anyone she'd been diagnosed with one a few months ago or that the doctors told her operating in her case would be risky. It's probably the only time I've ever known her not to take a chance. It was her choice, Mandi."

This time, she did pull away. She covered her face briefly, then pushed her hair back.

"But don't you see? I used to go to her doctor appointments with her when I was here. I would have known. I could have convinced her to try surgery or something. If she had told me, I would have at least come down to be with her."

"Maybe that's why she didn't tell you. She didn't want you dropping what was important to you on her account."

Mandi's lips parted and she shook her head. *Oh boy.*

"That didn't come out right," he quickly added. "I mean that she knew you wanted to be out there following your dream. Maybe she didn't want to get in the way of that."

"I understood you perfectly. I prioritized what I wanted and left Turtleback. I left everyone behind, including you. Do you really want to go there now, Gray?"

"That's not how I meant it. I meant that she probably couldn't bear the thought of being hospitalized or anyone having to take care of her. Nana hated to burden anyone. She was too independent."

"Yeah. Maybe I got that from her."

Gray threw his palms up. This wasn't worth it.

"Forget I said anything. I'm expected over at the clinic, so again, my condolences. If I don't see you before you leave town, then—just drive safely and have a good life."

He turned on his heel and headed for his motorcycle as the first drops of rain hit the ground. He wasn't expected at work today unless there was an emergency, but as far as he was concerned, getting out of Mandi's hair qualified as one. He didn't care if he got drenched. He needed to get out of here. He put his helmet on and rode off without looking back, but he couldn't shake the hollow feeling that this was the last time he'd ever see her.

EIGHT HOURS SINCE Mandi had been dropped off at the cottage and she was still in a fetal position on Nana's bed. She glanced at the time on her phone, squinting with one eye to lessen the screen's glare, and slapped it back down on the bed. Three in the morning? She covered her eyes with her hand. Her legs didn't want to move any more than the rest of her did. Yesterday evening, without so much as a bite of dinner, she had wrapped herself in Nana's favorite crocheted purple shawl and curled up on her bed, dozing on and off for mere minutes at a time. At some point, she must have really fallen asleep, lulled by the faint, lingering scent of Nana's woodsy perfume on her pillow.

She stared up at the moon shadows that stretched across the ceiling. Her grandmother's energy still seemed to fill the room. It was both comforting and unsettling. Was

Nana passing away so suddenly all Mandi's fault? Had she brought on everything bad that had happened in her life, like losing her mother, grandma and even Gray? *No regrets.* That advice didn't make sense at a time like this. She *did* regret not seeing her grandmother at least one last time. She regretted not being there for Nana the way Nana had always been there for her. She regretted…

Gray's face flashed in her mind. No, she didn't regret leaving him. She had done the right thing not marrying him. Even Nana had consoled her through the ordeal, emphasizing that a person had to find themselves and master the art of self-love and self-respect before they could ever stand tall enough to lift others off the ground. Mandi had assumed that those who needed lifting referred to people—or even animals—around her in general or maybe future children and family…but not Gray. Nana couldn't have meant him, specifically. Gray didn't need anyone holding him up. He exuded confidence with every step he took and had his life exactly where he wanted it to be, from his thriving practice to his work saving endangered turtle hatchlings on the beach. Grayson Zale knew exactly who he was. He simply could not bring himself to share every part of him with Mandi, and that wasn't good enough for her. Or maybe she hadn't been good enough for him. Whatever it was, she deserved more than to settle for a life with someone who didn't trust or love her enough to be completely open with her. Neither of them would have been happy.

She rolled off the edge of the bed, flicked on the side lamp, gave her puffy eyes a moment to adjust, then began folding the shawl. The open, floral-patterned stitching on the bottom left corner snagged on the nightstand's knob, pulling the loose drawer slightly askew. She freed the shawl and set it carefully where it had been, near the end of the bed, then turned to straighten the drawer.

*Open it.*

She pressed her hands to her cheeks and sucked in the corner of her lip. Going through all of her grandma's drawers and belongings was inevitable. She would have to face it sooner or later, but the fact that she was actually curious about what Nana kept in her nightstand felt wrong. She had never been a snoop. She had always respected people's privacy because she wanted the same for herself. That was probably why she'd never made enough headway with getting Gray to share more about his past with her. She wasn't aggressive enough. Her father was aggressive and she made a point of trying not to be like him. She fingered the knobs.

"I'm sorry, Nana, but I get the feeling you'd want me to make sure there aren't things tucked away you don't want my dad seeing."

Nightstands were very personal spaces. What if her unabashedly wild-at-heart grandmother kept secret love letters or sexy romance novels hidden in there? Did she want to know? Did she dare look inside? She opened the drawer, supporting the side with the broken runner with her left hand. A five-by-eight notebook with a recycled paper cover adorned with pressed flowers lay next to a few pens, a very old camera, a rather large multi-tool camping knife, a colorfully woven, empty change purse that looked like it had been made somewhere in South America and the remains of a small ball of yarn with a crochet needle stuck through it. Leave it to Nana to have such an eclectic collection of items.

Mandi picked up the journal and did a quick flip of the pages. They were yellowing around the edges and one had what looked like coffee stains. "Journal #2" was written inside the cover, but there wasn't another notebook in the drawer. Apparently, Nana had another tucked away somewhere. What was odd was that this one was mostly empty. There were only a few entries, the first of which was dated a couple of decades ago, around the time when Mandi's mother left town. She held Nana's difficult-to-read cursive scribbles up to the light.

*I haven't written in many, many years. Not since returning to Turtleback. But I thought it was time to try again. I haven't been able to write since I lost the two most important people in my life. The only trusted, loved, closest friends I've ever had and ever will. That pain still lingers in my chest and haunts me in the early morning hours when I walk the beach. They would have loved this beach. They would have understood my need to protect the turtle nests...to save lives. Lives hidden secretly beneath the sand, waiting for the chance to break free and truly live. But some secrets can never surface. They would have understood that, too.*

*After they died, writing about my days didn't seem as important as returning home, picking up the pieces, building a new life and figuring out how I was going to raise my unborn child. I had survived the worst in life and knew I'd survive this, but I didn't know I'd fail at it. I failed my only child. I spoiled John when I thought I was giving him everything I didn't have. He has never learned the true value of life... and love. Audra left them last night. She left John and her sweet little girl without warning. I sensed it would happen sooner or later. It makes me so sad to know that Mandi won't have her mother around. I love that little girl with all my heart. I'll be there for her. I'll do my best and hope that this time, I won't fail at parenthood. My hope for her is that she will someday experience love as deeply as I have and that it never leaves her behind.*

Mandi wiped her face on her sleeve, but the tears kept falling. All she'd ever been told was that her grandfather had died at war. Nana had never expressed or shown in any way just how heartbroken she was, nor had she mentioned this other friend in her life. What secrets was she talking about that could never surface? Did everyone have secrets they were keeping from her? Like Gray?

Mandi grabbed a tissue and blew her nose. Her grandmother didn't say anything specific about why Audra had left. All she'd ever told Mandi was that it wasn't because of her. And her father had declared the subject off-limits more than once, during her teen years.

She turned to the next page and double-checked the date. This entry was only written about two years ago. That was strange. It seemed that her grandmother's attempt to start journaling again hadn't worked out. Why? There weren't any entries made during the years since Mandi's mother, Audra, had abandoned them. The only other entry was on the day Mandi had almost become a bride. It was a little shorter and the handwriting slightly messier, no doubt a reflection of Nana's age and arthritis.

*I failed again. Mandi did find the kind of love I had wished for her, but I had asked for it to never leave her. Love didn't leave Mandi. I know this because I saw the pain she left in her wake. She was the one to abandon love. Maybe her father was right, for once, in saying that she was too young. He and Audra had been too young. I hope that someday Mandi embraces her inner strength and confidence and proves to herself that she can achieve anything she puts her mind to. I hope she finds success and understands the true meaning of it. And, most importantly, I hope she learns to love herself.*

Mandi closed the journal. She had no more tears. Instead, she suddenly felt empty and cold. She'd never known anyone to exude confidence like her grandmother. Nana had been her rock. Yet, these two entries mentioned failure and loss. They were tinged with disappointment. Why hadn't she written about the good times, when Mandi was growing up? Had she been too busy helping to raise her? Did she only write about bad times? If so, that made Mandi wonder even more what her secrets were and where the first journal was hidden. Maybe it had answers. As for Mandi's finding success, she hoped Nana had seen that happen over the past couple of years. Maybe that's why she hadn't written another entry. All was good and she felt Mandi had picked up the pieces of her life and was on the right track. She *had* told Mandi, during her last visit to New York, that she was proud of her.

Mandi shut the drawer and quickly rummaged through the opposite nightstand, top shelf in the small closet and dresser drawers. The other journal wasn't in the room, but she'd find it. Not this minute—for all the hours she'd spent trying to sleep, her body and mind felt wrung dry—but she would probably find it while sorting through Nana's belongings. She turned off the light.

"Nana, if you can hear me now, know that

you didn't fail. You were always amazing and so important to me. I won't fail you. I'll prove you did everything right. I will be strong and I'll continue to prove I can be successful. I promise."

She would. As soon as she wrapped things up in Turtleback, she was more determined than ever to put all her drive and energy into her new job She'd make that advertising company wish they could clone her. She'd make other companies in New York wish they could have her. She'd channel her grandmother's strength and show the world what she could do.

Her stomach growled and she pressed her hand against it. She didn't actually have an appetite, but maybe the lack of food had something to do with how weak she felt.

She walked over to the window and peered out. The beach was dark and quiet with nothing moving but the moonlight skipping on the water. She closed the blinds and went to the kitchen. Maybe a cup of tea would be enough to shut her stomach up and open up her appetite. And going through emails might get her mind off things.

She turned on the kitchen light, set the

water to boil and checked messages on her phone while her laptop booted up on the breakfast table. A few messages were from new acquaintances at work letting her know about where they were planning to meet for Friday night happy hour. She ignored them. One was from Lana, her college apartment roommate and friend sending her sympathy from New York. She'd met her through the same master's program. Mandi sent her a quick reply. She scrolled down and almost missed the one from a name she recognized as Nana's lawyer and old friend.

She had forgotten all about that part of dealing with a loved one's passing. She was supposed to meet him this morning at nine regarding Nana's will. He was confirming the time. She'd be there, but she dreaded it. Hearing Joel read off Nana's will would only grind in the reality that had hit her today at the funeral.

She stared at the message for a second. Nana's will. She knew she would have to help sort through her grandmother's personal items, but in her mind, she pictured the house and everything in it as staying the same forever. But for what? Her father? He'd likely inherit it, but he had his own place on the sound side and never really cared for the cottage. He claimed that it was a money pit in need of too much restoration and repairs, especially after hurricanes. True, the salty air and frequent storms had weathered the place and it needed constant upkeep, like most homes along the Outer Banks, but it had charm and told a story, like the lines on the face of someone who'd experienced more than their share of life. Someone like Nana.

But Mandi wouldn't be able to argue with her dad if he wanted to sell it. He never listened to her anyway. She certainly couldn't care for it herself, not just financially in terms of repairs—she was still new at her job and had tons of college debt to pay—but logistically, too. She wouldn't be around. A sadness enveloped her. This cottage held a lot of memories. Memories that hadn't been captured in Nana's journal. Sometimes a person didn't have a choice in life. Letting go was a part of living, wasn't it? That was one lesson she'd learned in life, so far. And if she wanted to honor her grandmother's wish and find success in life, she'd have to let go of this place, too. She closed the lawyer's email and held the phone to her chest. She didn't care what was in the will. It didn't matter.

She didn't want to gain anything from Nana's death. She just wanted her back.

THE LAW OFFICE of Joel Burkitt occupied a space on the second story of what was the original Turtleback volunteer fire station. The station had been moved to a more accommodating space fifteen years ago, partially funded by the sale of the original. The ground floor housed a yoga studio that most people in town claimed stayed afloat only because Joel, who owned the building, was sweet on the instructor.

Mandi noticed her father's car parked along the street in front of the yellow building. Joel hadn't mentioned having them both show up together, although it made sense since Nana didn't have any other family in town. Mandi figured Joel would just give her a copy of the will, review any mention of her in it, and that would be it. That's what she'd hoped would happen. Nothing formal or staged like in the movies. She pulled up behind her dad's car and went inside, noting the studio had only two students in it, currently in mountain poses. She climbed the steps to the Burkitt Law Office and knocked before entering.

"Mandi, thanks for joining us. I'm sorry that I didn't catch you yesterday at the service," Joel said, waving her in.

"No worries. Hi, Dad." She shook Joel's hand and sat on the empty chair next to her father.

"Mandi." John nodded his welcome, then motioned around the room. "Hard to believe you could have been sharing this practice with Joel by now. A shame, really."

"Seriously, Dad?" She couldn't believe he was embarrassing her by bringing up the fact that she had refused to go to law school and, according to him, had thrown away an opportunity he'd set up for her to work with Burkitt and eventually take over his practice when he retired.

Joel cleared his throat.

"Law isn't for everyone, John. And not everyone makes it in," he said, barely raising a brow as he looked over at her dad. "Although, I'm sure if Mandi had wanted to and had applied, she would have been accepted."

Wow. Had her dad been rejected from law school back in his day? Why hadn't she heard about that? Did Nana know? Or had her son applied without telling her…in case he didn't make it in. It would be just like him to go about things in a way that allowed him to cover up failure and save face. John dropped the subject. That said something.

Joel took a third chair from the corner of the room and placed it next to her. Mandi frowned. Her father uncrossed his legs.

"Is someone else joining us?" he asked, sitting straighter.

"Sorry if I kept you all waiting," Gray said, as he entered the room without bothering to knock.

Neither Mandi nor John said anything. Joel greeted Grayson by his full name and motioned for him to sit. Why did Gray's being here surprise her? Of course Nana would have left something for Gray to remember her by. She had treated him like family and he'd been good to her. Mandi would always be grateful that he had been a good neighbor to Nana and had kept an eye out for her. It was just that… Mandi hadn't expected to see him today. Seeing him did things to her. It shook the ground beneath her feet. Gray's eyes met hers and she quickly looked away and focused on Mr. Burkitt.

"What's he doing here?" John asked, not bothering to mask his disapproval. Joel shot her father a professional smile.

"Everyone here is mentioned in the will and, although I had intended to meet with Dr. Zale separately, I realized late last night that your mother had specifically requested a group reading. Dr. Zale was kind enough to adjust his schedule this morning at the last minute. Today is about your mother's wishes, John. Not yours. And now that we're all here, let's get started. This shouldn't take long." Joel shuffled through some papers, straightened the ones he needed, then began reading the initial formality and a list of animal and children's charities she had bequeathed money to. "For you, John, your mother left you the sum of ten thousand dollars."

"Ten?"

Mandi and Gray exchanged looks. Her father wasn't shocked in a positive way. Nope.

His face turned a purply shade of red. The sum total Nana had given to charity was more than twice what she'd give to her own son.

"That's what it says, John. As for you, Mandi, you now own half of her house and all of its contents, including—your grandmother has specified—the antique pottery bowl handed down from her side of the family and all of her jewelry."

The color rose in her father's neck and his expression tightened. Direct mention of that bowl was a definite dig on Nana's part. She knew her son well and he'd nagged her one too many times about getting it appraised and possibly selling it. After all, a chunk of pottery didn't really serve a purpose in his eyes. He didn't value history. He only worried about the future.

"I assume, then, the other half of the house is mine," John said. He seemed mollified enough. Half a house softened the blow the measly ten grand had given him.

Mandi didn't understand him. She never would. Ten thousand would make a huge dent in her graduate school debt, not to mention credit card. Not that she'd take it even if he offered. Money gave him control. She *did* learn from history and she wasn't letting him ever have a say in her future.

"Actually," Joel said, nudging his glasses higher on his nose, studying the document for confirmation, then looking up at Gray. "It says here that the other half of the house belongs to you, Dr. Zale. And that the property cannot be sold or leased without both parties agreeing to the arrangement."

"What?" The question shot out of her father and Gray simultaneously. Mandi had no words. She couldn't wrap her head around what had just been said. Gray owned half of the house? They *shared* Nana's house?

"This isn't happening," she muttered, sinking in her chair. She clutched her purse and closed her eyes. *Why, Nana? Why?* Her father stood up and braced his hands on the edge of the desk.

"Are you sure? She was old. Were you there when she wrote this up? Was she coherent? Was she of sound mind?"

"Oh, for goodness' sake," Mandi said.

"Sit down, John. And yes, I'm sure. And for the record, I've never known your mother to be anything but sharp and sound minded."

John sat, shifting his weight to one side and grinding his jaw. Gray pinched the bridge of his nose and hung his head for a moment, the way he did whenever he needed to gather his thoughts. Mandi would bet her life he wasn't comfortable with the situation. She knew him well enough to know he didn't want or expect anything from her grandmother. He took a deep breath and let it out, then leaned forward in his chair.

"Does she explain why? Like, what I'm supposed to do with it or what she wants done with it?" Gray asked.

"There is a little more. A note. It says, *To Dr. Grayson Zale, I leave you half of my property, to be shared with my granddaughter, Mandi Rivers. I hope you can carry on our work protecting the beach and saving the turtles. You were like a grandson to me and we were more alike than you'll ever know. We cared about the same things in life, you and I. Keep it all close to your heart.*"

There was a moment of silence as Joel linked his fingers.

"That's all she has, apart from stating that

anything not mentioned specifically should be assumed to belong to Mandi."

"I share a house with Gray." It was all she could say. It was surreal. Cruel. Nana wouldn't do that to her.

"If you're done, then I'm leaving," John said. He scowled as he stormed out of the room, but Mandi saw his eyes beginning to water and his chin quiver when he thought they could see only his back. Her heart went out to him. The man had his faults, but he was human. No doubt he was upset about the money, but his pride and feelings had been hurt, too. They had to have been. Was this Nana's way of trying to teach him what mattered in life? That it wasn't about money and possessions?

"These are for the two of you." Burkitt held out two copies of Nana's house keys.

Gray had a key to the house.

She really needed to go back to bed.

## CHAPTER THREE

GRAY CROSSED THE street and headed for the used bookstore, Castaway Books, where he had dropped Laddie off for reading time. The kids loved sitting around him just as much as he loved the attention, but more important, his presence had a positive impact on their attention span. Plus, what kid wouldn't develop a love of reading if they associated books with spending time with a dog like Laddie?

The place was nestled along a row of shops lining the only main street in town. Each storefront sported a different color, from pale blue to shades of yellow or tan or even red. Turtleback was a quaint place, he had to admit that. It was sad, however, that so many of these shops struggled to recoup their losses after the damage incurred by hurricanes. Like many of the buildings in town, Castaway Books was raised on short stilts and reminded him of a coffee shop he used to frequent by the wharf when he lived on the West Coast…a fact that no one knew about him and no one ever would.

The small string of shells with a bell on the end announced his entrance when he opened the door. Eve glanced up and smiled without missing a beat, as she read the last page of a storybook that looked, from where he stood, like it had a shark eating a carrot on the cover. Laddie sat right in the center of a group of five kids—a pretty good-sized group considering most folks were on the beach by the beginning of June. He looked back at Gray, swished his tail and smiled. Some might have mistakenly thought he was opening his mouth the way dogs did when they panted, but Gray knew from the way his face lit up that it was a dog smile down to his canine core.

Eve finished reading and told the kids they could browse her book treasures until their parents were ready to leave. The place was laid out as though it had once been a house, and each room had a designated sub-ject area. He'd been upstairs a few times, where she had a collection of reference books, including cooking, military history and gardening. He suspected many of the parents were up there. Downstairs included two rooms that held everything from mystery and general fiction to romance, as well as a dedicated kids space decorated in a whimsical manner with paper fairies and dragonflies hanging from the ceiling, pictures of wizards and dragons on the walls and comfy beanbags in every corner.

"Thanks for letting me borrow Laddie," she said, setting the book she held back on the shelf. Laddie wagged his tail harder as he joined Gray near the entrance.

"Good job, boy." Gray rewarded him with an ear scratch, then looked at Eve. "I'm the one who should thank you. I hate leaving him at home alone unless I have to and he adores being around kids. Looks like you had a good group today."

"Pretty good. I luck out in the summer when people want something to read on the beach. Not everyone has an e-reader they can use in the sun. I sold three romance novels this morning alone to two women who were headed down to Cape Hatteras

as part of their vacation. Are you planning
to browse today?"

Eve was single, though he wasn't sure
why, other than the fact that she put a lot
of time into keeping her business afloat.
She was cute with her pixie haircut, bright
green eyes and sweet personality, and she
had asked him out for drinks once, though
he had declined. Gray wasn't interested in
dating anyone, and Eve was a good enough
friend to understand why without his having
to spell it out. She wasn't the only woman
he'd put up a wall with dating-wise the past
couple of years. Nana had teased him a few
times about being one of the few eligible
bachelors around. It was the nature of living
on a barrier island, with only one road leading in and out of town and, eventually, connecting them to the mainland via bridges.
The odds were in his favor, but he certainly
didn't feel eligible. He knew he wasn't. He'd
learned how impossible relationships could
be in a situation like his. He often wondered
if the whole "small town small pickings"
thing was the only reason Mandi had dated
him and agreed to marry him. It would have
explained why she ran off the minute she'd

gotten her graduate program acceptance letter. She had made her choice: him, or the world out there. The same world he had been forced to leave behind.

He quirked the corner of his mouth apologetically. He knew every sale mattered to her and he always bought books from her, as opposed to a big chain, unless she couldn't get her hands on what he needed. Today, however, he didn't have the time or desire to browse. Not after what had just happened in Joel Burkitt's office.

"Nah. I need to get to the clinic. I've already lost time the past few days and I've got a few spay surgeries scheduled today. Maybe next time." He put his sunglasses back on and patted his thigh to let Laddie know to follow, then opened the door. Eve held it open and waved as they headed down the street.

"See you around, then," she called out.

Gray gave her a thumbs-up and picked up his pace. His vet clinic was only a quarter of a mile away. The walk would be good for Laddie, not to mention Gray himself. He needed time to process what had happened regarding Nana's will.

"We own half of a house, buddy. With Mandi, of all people." Laddie's ears perked at the name, as if he recognized it from talk around town or maybe from Gray muttering it in frustration. Laddie hadn't been around back when Gray was dating Mandi. He had found him through a rough collie rescue organization on the mainland shortly after Mandi had deserted Turtleback. Laddie's owner had been killed in a car accident. So basically, he and Laddie were perfect for one another. They'd each lost someone they had loved. The two of them had formed an instant, tight bond the second they met.

Laddie had loved Nana, too. He had been like an unofficial therapy dog, hanging out with her whenever Gray couldn't take him to work or wherever he was headed. Only, Gray made sure never to refer to him as a therapy dog around Nana. She was too independent and proud and wouldn't have liked it. From her perspective, she was the one looking out for Laddie when Gray wasn't around. In fact, she had been the one who had suggested to Eve to invite Laddie to reading time and she had been trying to get the local elementary school to get on board with a dogs-for-reading program. Unfortunately, the idea had yet to be accepted because of some kids with allergies.

They passed the outskirts of town and made their way a little farther down the road and through the small parking lot of the Zale Veterinary Clinic. He went around the backside of the one-story clinic to the Employees Only entrance he usually used. He held the door open for Laddie to follow him in, then waved down the hall to where two of his techs, Gavin and Nora, were prepping the intake and surgical areas. He had a small office near the back end of the clinic where Laddie could hang out. He was up to date on his vaccines, so Gray wasn't too worried about his ever catching anything. In any case, Laddie never had direct contact with clinic patients. However, his dog never lacked attention when he came here, given that Gray's receptionist and tech assistants adored him.

"Doc, I just got word on a successful trapping of those two feral cats that have been hanging out behind the Ocean Organics Mercantile. They should be here in the next ten minutes," Chanda said. She had been his receptionist since day one and he had never met anyone more organized and efficient.

"Perfect. I'll be ready." He tossed his keys and sunglasses in his desk drawer, gave Laddie his favorite toy and headed down the hall. He did free spay and neuters once a month as part of a trap-and-release program for feral cats. It gave the cats a purpose and allowed them to live out their lives, while preventing new litters. Places like the mercantile area or the bakery and seafood restaurants would have been battling mouse and rat problems if it hadn't been for the feral cat program. All they had to do was supply an outdoor shelter, food and water, and the cats would earn their keep. "What else do we have today?"

"Not a whole lot, actually. But I just checked in a walk-in. I figured you could see them before you start surgery. A couple on vacation with their dog. Something stuck in his paw, or possibly a sting. It happened while they were playing on the beach. Room one."

"Thanks."

It had to be a different couple from the

one he had seen on the beach yesterday morning. He hadn't noticed a dog with that family. It seemed like Turtleback was getting more and more tourists trickling down this year from more popular towns north of them, like Nags Head and Kitty Hawk. She handed him a file and went back up front.

He took a deep breath. He needed to clear his head and focus. Figuring out what to do about Nana's house could wait. He needed to forget about his inheritance and concentrate on work. But he couldn't shake the irony. Had he and Mandi gotten married when they were supposed to, they would have already been living together right now, under the same roof. And here they were, further apart than ever with no future in sight for the two of them, yet they each owned half of the same house. Go figure.

*We cared about the same things in life, you and I. Keep it all close to your heart.*

What had Nana meant by that? The house? The turtles? Mandi? Had she been trying to urge him to hang on to the house and not sell it? For the sake of the beach and turtle nests? Or had she been referring to their both caring about Mandi? He couldn't keep her in his heart against her will. Unless Nana's words implied keeping silent. Close to the heart, close to the chest. Same thing. Was she was warning him to keep his feelings for Mandi quiet…like everything else… like his secret past?

No, that wasn't it. Nana didn't know about his past, any more than anyone else in town did, save for Sheriff Ryker. But the sheriff was a locked chest. He never once mentioned the classified information, not even the few times they shared a beer at the local pub. It wasn't talked about within earshot whatsoever. The marshal who'd set Gray up with a life here had let him know about the sheriff as a contact, in case of an emergency relocation. Nana must have meant that she didn't want him interfering with Mandi's career. But then why would she not have had the note delivered privately? She knew John and Mandi would be there at the reading. She must have wanted John to hear what she'd written so that he would understand the decision to give Gray the house had been hers and hers alone.

He scratched the back of his neck, then

cranked it to one side to release the tension before reaching for the exam room door. He'd survived worse. He'd survive this. Nana was only being the kind, generous person she'd always been. She wouldn't have purposefully turned his life upside down. Unless…unless she'd intended to do just that. Maybe keeping it all close to his heart had indeed included her granddaughter.

"You sneaky woman," he muttered.

Maybe old Nana was giving him a second chance.

MANDI HUNG UP with her soon-to-be supervisor at the advertising firm. The woman had sounded understanding, unless she was faking it out of professionalism, but Mandi couldn't shake the fact that delaying her return to New York had left the worst possible impression. She'd gone out of her way, during her interviews with the advertising group, to assure them that she had nothing keeping her from applying herself fully to whatever projects they would have her working on. She had told them her schedule was flexible. She had even—in her desperation to land the job—volunteered taboo information, like the fact that she had no family obligations—aka she was single—and was totally dedicated to her career.

Yet, here she was, less than a week from her agreed start date, having to ask for a few more days so that she could deal with matters related to her grandmother's passing. They couldn't blame her, but in a cutthroat, competitive market, she was sure her supervisor was being polite and tolerant and that she wouldn't hesitate to cut Mandi loose if it affected the bottom line and her own reputation in the company.

Mandi looked around the living room. She couldn't believe her father didn't inherit the place. A part of her felt relieved, though another part felt ashamed, knowing that, in the end, she'd be letting her grandmother down, as well. Before the reading of the will, she had been ready to criticize her father if he sold the cottage, but it was now in her hands and she was guilty of the same plan. She had no choice but to sell. It wouldn't be as bad as her father selling to strangers because, in her situation, Gray could buy her out. He had always liked the place. He already owned half of it. And as Nana had pointed out in her will, she wanted her work with the turtle nesting grounds to continue. That would be that. Problem solved. At least she'd know the house belonged to someone who cared about it. She barely had time to go through Nana's things, but she'd get everything packed and shipped to New York. She'd have to put most of it in storage, though. The only place she could afford in the Big Apple was barely large enough to fit one or two pieces of Nana's furniture, let alone all her personal belongings.

Man, there was so much to go through. Some of it could be donated, no doubt. Things like clothes, though Mandi knew of a few vintage pieces she would never be able to part with. The rims of her eyes stung. She couldn't do this right now. The lawyer appointment had sucked the energy out of her and seeing Nana's things made her want to cry all over again.

She headed outside, closed her eyes and lifted her face to the sun. It felt so good against her skin and the warm decking soothed her bare feet. She opened her eyes and scanned the beach. The sky was clear and the breeze was low and steady. Seagull cries pierced the air with boisterous excitement that only the spotting of a school of fish could trigger. She made her way down the deck steps, across the sandy path and to the water's edge. She could see a few folks with their beach umbrellas set up in the distance, but for the most part, no one "camped out" on the private strip in front of Nana's house. The signs she and Gray set up every year, marking turtle nesting grounds in the low dunes, served as a deterrent.

The lighthouse looked down upon her from the south side of the beach. She opted to head north, walking along the wet sand, relishing the way it sifted between her toes. Salt water splashed gently against her calves, a comforting reminder that everything— even a turbulent ocean—finds a way to settle down. Things would fall into place. She had to believe that.

"Mandi?"

She spun around, not recognizing the voice at first. Water lapped her ankles, then sucked her feet deeper into the sand as the wave retreated. Her stomach went with it.

"Hey, Coral." The nickname was over the top, in Mandi's opinion, considering they were a seaside town, but it was the name the real estate agent insisted on going by. Coral knew Mandi's father all too well, or so it had always appeared to Mandi. She had department store beauty—always done up to the last lash—and she had to be at least fifteen years younger than John. Funny, considering how he disapproved of Gray being older than Mandi by far less. Still, Coral supported John's love of real estate investments and had worked on several deals with him, including the purchase of the renovated bungalow he currently lived in. At least he had someone in his life.

Coral ran up and took a second to catch her breath.

"Mind if I join you? I tried calling after you when you didn't answer the door and I spotted you heading down the beach."

Mandi kept walking. She didn't respond. She didn't need to. Coral was going to join her regardless.

"I needed some fresh air." *Alone.*

"I can't blame you. I'm sorry about your grandma."

"Thanks."

"Speaking of her, John mentioned that she left you half of the cottage."

And there it was. She *knew* this was what the interception was about. Her father hadn't wasted a second after leaving Burkitt's office. She gave Coral a flat smile.

"Yes, she did."

"I know you no longer live here, and John seems to think this inheritance is only going to burden you."

"Why isn't he talking to me about this himself? It's kind of a private family matter."

"Of course it is. And I wouldn't have dreamed of coming here had he not asked me. He's really distraught with losing his mother and needed to get some rest. But since you weren't planning to stay in town long, he wanted to be sure that you knew we're here for you. He said he'd be interested in coming to an agreement regarding your half."

Mandi stopped walking and crossed her arms.

"An agreement? That sounds fishy, Coral." Now that was bad, but Mandi couldn't resist the pun. The fact that her father had sent this woman after her had her pulse pounding loud enough to drown out the sound of the surf and gulls. Coral returned the fake smile.

"Mandi, he's your father. He wouldn't hurt you. He's trying to help. He has no need for another property right now, but he said that if it helps, he'll scrounge up the funds to purchase the place."

An immediate sale. Exactly what she wanted, only she wanted Gray to buy her out. Nana didn't do anything without thinking ahead and having a purpose. She didn't leave the cottage to her son for a reason. That alone gave her pause. Besides, Gray lived in Turtleback and had no plans to move and he already owned half the house. Hopefully, he'd soon own the whole thing. Besides, the will stated they'd both have to agree to a lease or sale, and she couldn't imagine any kind of agreement happening between John and Gray. Nana had probably predicted that John would try to pressure Mandi about the house. Had she given half to Gray so that he could act as a buffer between Mandi and her father, since Nana wouldn't be around to do so?

"I'll think about it but I'm not making any

decisions today." She just wanted Coral off her back.

"But aren't you leav—"

"I'll handle my own schedule, thank you. You can tell my father that if I'm interested, I'll talk to him in person."

"Oh. Okay, then. I'll let him know." Coral squared her shoulders and cocked her head. "You take care. Enjoy your stroll."

She stalked off, leaving Mandi ten times more stressed than she was when she had left the cottage. So much for fresh air. She trudged across the dry sand, rinsing her feet at a spigot along the wooden path leading to the street, almost half a mile from the house. She put on the sandals she'd been carrying and continued in the direction of the one place she knew no one would find her.

Within five minutes, she was hidden from the road by reeds and the ruins of a half-washed-away fishing shed where wire crab cages and rods for hand-lining used to be stored. The small dock where she and Gray used to spend summers dangling their toes in the waters of the sound or catching themselves a fresh crab dinner still stretched over the edge of the bank. It had, surprisingly, survived every hurricane that had ravaged the area. Nana used to say that her grandmother believed everything had a spirit and with some things the spirit was strong enough to withstand anything. If something was meant to be, it would be.

She made her way to the dock, treading carefully to make sure it would hold her weight, then settled down at the edge. Near her fingertips, to the right, the initials *G & M* still lay there, carved deep into the splintering wood. If something was meant to be, it would be. And some things simply weren't…like her parents' marriage…or her and Gray's.

She set her flip-flops over the initials and started to lower her feet, but the sound of crying on the breeze had her jumping up to scan the area. Her heart raced. Was there a lost child? What if some tourist's kid had wandered here all the way from the beach?

She heard it again. It was more than one cry. Not human, but they were cries of distress nonetheless. She put her flip-flops on and tried not to think about the dangers of walking through the grassy, marshy area with no foot protection. There was a good chance there were snakes and other creatures slithering around. She hesitated, but the cries got louder as she approached the old shed. She quickly looked around for any obvious sign of danger, then picked up a nearby piece of driftwood and used it to push the door to the shed open. Her heart sank.

"Oh God. How could anyone do this?"

Three kittens, mewing helplessly, tumbled over one another inside one of the old wire crab cages. They weren't born here. Someone had to have put them there, as evidenced by the locked trap with no mama cat in it. Whoever had done this had probably figured a predator would have an easy dinner and the litter of unwanted kittens would no longer be a problem. Thank goodness they had not drowned the babies.

She wanted to cry, but anger took over.

"It's going to be okay. I've got you."

She opened the trap and scooped each terrified baby out. She wasn't sure how old they were…old enough for their eyes to be open and for them to be clamoring at the cage to get out. They couldn't have been here that long, though they looked starved. The summer temperatures had dipped down to seventy-five last night and then there was yesterday's rain. She doubted they would have made it through the night had they been left here yesterday.

She tucked her T-shirt tightly into her shorts and slipped the kittens inside the V-neck one by one. Yes, she knew she'd probably end up with flea or tick bites, but it didn't matter. The babies needed some warmth and there wasn't anything in the shed that would do.

She cradled her arm under them from outside her shirt as she rushed back out to the road. They squirmed against her belly and had surprisingly sharp claws for such tiny paws. She ignored the pain and reached into her back pocket for her cell phone, as she headed toward Gray's clinic. She had deleted Gray's number after leaving him at the altar, but the clinic's info was on its website. She kept walking, knowing that her phone would pick up service the closer she got to town, and dialed the second the website page appeared on screen.

"Chanda? It's Mandi. Is Dr. Zale around?"

"Mandi! It's so good to hear your voice again. You have to stop by and visit while you're here. He's in surgery right now. Almost done, though. Did you want to leave a—"

"Listen, I'm coming down the side of the road and halfway to you with a litter of kittens I found, left for dead, by the old dock."

"What? Oh, no. I'll be right there to give you a ride the rest of the way. Leaving now." Chanda hung up without wasting another second. She was a no-nonsense woman with a heart of gold and zero tolerance for animal abuse or neglect.

Mandi kept walking, wincing when one claw got her good, but at least the mews had softened a bit. Within five minutes, Chanda's blue hatchback slowed down on the other side of the empty, two-lane road and made a U-turn. Mandi climbed in, carefully adjusting her position so as not to squish the kittens.

"Chanda, it's so good to see you."

"I want to hug you—for saving those kittens and for seeing you again—but I'll wait until we're back at the clinic," Chanda said.

"You'll be getting that hug. Thanks so much for picking me up."

"Are you kidding? You're an angel for saving them. It kills me to know that someone out here would do something like that."

"It could have been anyone. An out-of-towner. Cousins visiting cousins. Sometimes schoolkids with issues and too much time on their hands in the summer do things without stopping to think first. Who knows. I can't imagine anyone I know doing this."

Chanda parked in her usual spot behind the clinic and unlocked the back door for Mandi. The odor of alcohol mixed with what was definitely a potty accident in one of the kennels in the clinic's recovery and holding area took her off guard. She hadn't been here since she left Gray. She'd avoided the place—and him—during her few visits to see Nana. But she recalled the hours she used to volunteer during her free time, helping with kennel cleaning and taking pooches outside for breaks, like it was yesterday.

"Dr. Zale, you have a patient pregnant with kittens," Chanda called out.

Mandi's cheeks warmed and the expression on Gray's face was priceless, when he found Mandi, of all people, standing there with a stomach bulge.

"I'm going to pretend that dear Chanda here did not just embarrass the life out of me," Mandi said.

She could read everything Gray probably wanted to say, but didn't, on his face. Like the fact that, had their lives gone as planned, she'd be standing here right now pregnant with his child. Not three fur babies.

"Pregnant with kittens." His tone was laced with humor, but just enough bitterness to confirm what she'd suspected. He came over but stopped short. "Um…maybe you should do the delivery."

"Yeah, maybe I should," Mandi quickly added. Chanda smothered a laugh with the back of her hand. Gray and Mandi ignored her.

"Here. Stand close to the exam table and release them slowly. Chanda, would you mind passing me three of those towels from the warming stack? Gavin and Nora have their hands full."

He took the proffered towels and set them on the table next to Mandi's waist. His cheek was close enough for her to brush her lips against, and he still smelled of soap from his morning shower. She shook the thought, gathered herself—and the bottom of her shirt—and gently freed the first kitten. Gray caught it in his hands and nestled it in the warm wraps. The kitten started crying for its siblings, who soon joined her.

"Congratulations! You have triplets!" Chanda quipped. Her deeper, intended meaning wasn't lost on either of them. Mandi let out a breath and Gray gave his receptionist a pointed look.

"Thank you for your help. But if you don't mind, I think I hear the phone ringing up front."

Mandi was pretty sure she didn't hear any ringing, but Chanda had to stop with the jokes. Bless her heart, she had been so supportive of their wedding and had, according to Nana, cried for two weeks after Mandi had left. But still. Now wasn't the time.

"Okay, okay. But this time, I don't think I'll be able to resist adopting one myself. I mean, the story behind how they got here and Mandi the heroine and this delivery…"

"You adopt one and you're forgiven," Gray said, as he examined each baby carefully. "But first, let's see if they make it and then we'll determine if separating them is a good idea. They may be bonded, especially with what they've been through."

"I can't take all three. Not if I'm keeping them inside with my other cat. Trust me. I wish I could," Chanda said, leaving the room.

"Let's just make sure they're okay. They have to be," Mandi said, cradling the tortoiseshell, as Gray checked the largest of the three, a black cat with citrine eyes. The third and smallest of the litter was also black but with white paws and a tuft of white on her chest. Mandi was already falling for those golden eyes, but no way was she in the market for a kitten. She'd gotten them here. She'd done her part.

A vet tech she hadn't met before entered the room and immediately bolted into action when he saw what was going on.

"Gavin. Mandi," Gray said, motioning between them with a nod of his head. "Gavin is my right hand. You'll see Nora in a second, too. They started here after Madison decided to go to vet school. I couldn't run this place without them."

She remembered his assistant Madison. Gray used to have a high turnover rate with assistants. Mandi had once recommended that he pay more for someone highly trained and devoted to being a vet tech.

He placed a stethoscope against their little chests and listened.

"They sound okay, considering. Let's get them hydrated, do a fecal float, blood draw for viruses—FIV and FeLV etcetera… You know the protocol," he told Gavin, who looked like he'd already organized three groups of testing supplies on trays.

"They must be starving," Mandi said.

"No doubt. We'll get a starting weight and put them on formula." Gray took the tortoiseshell from her hands. "We need to do a few quick tests first, like checking for internal parasites. Do you want to name them? It helps us mark their charts. I prefer names to numbers. Names help them get adopted. Why don't you do the honors?"

"Me? I don't know."

"Two girls and a boy. Where's that creative mind of yours?"

Her professional, competitive side kicked into gear. It sounded cold, but creative advertising was what they needed to get the kittens adopted. The right names would make a prospective family feel connected. Drawn in.

"How about Sandy, Windy and Storm?"

"All tying in to the beachy feel. I like that." He did a double take at her shirt. "Are you bleeding?"

Mandi frowned and looked down. A small dot of blood had seeped through her shirt. The kittens must have scratched harder than she thought they had. She peeked under without lifting her hem too high. Gray took one look and shook his head.

"Mandi, we need to get those scratches treated. You don't want to know what organisms these poor guys could be carrying," he said.

Nora walked in and blubbered at the sight of the kittens, but quickly joined Gavin with equal efficiency to get the litter worked up.

"Nora, I don't think you've met Mandi. She's…an old friend. Could you take over cleanup with Gavin?"

"Got it."

"Thanks. Mandi, follow me."

This clinic was his kingdom. He was in

boss mode and she didn't work for him, but she trailed after him without complaint. She glanced over her shoulder and was astounded at how quickly and efficiently everyone moved. Gray's team knew exactly what they were doing. Watching them work was a beautiful thing. Seeing those kittens being loved and cared for was beyond beautiful. This was what Gray did. He saved animals. Her chest pinched at the reminder of why she'd fallen for him all those years ago. But that was then.

"Here we go." He pulled out a box filled with wound cleaner, antibiotic ointment, gauze, bandages...you name it. "Just lift your shirt enough."

"I could just go home and shower. I'm sure Nana has antibiotic ointment lying in a cabinet somewhere."

"Mandi, you can do that, too, but we really should take a few precautions here. Bacteria multiply faster than you can imagine."

She bit her lower lip.

"Seriously?" Gray asked. "I've seen you in a bikini. You don't have to take the shirt off. Just lift it. Or here, take this stuff into that bathroom there and treat yourself. I just don't want those cuts getting infected. And regardless, if you develop a fever, you need to get seen and let them know what happened."

A fever? How bad was this? Fine. He was right. She had probably spent more time around him in a bikini than in jeans. She knotted her shirt at the bottom edge of her bra like a halter top and held it in place. Her lace bra didn't come close to qualifying as a bikini, but he didn't need to know that.

He grimaced at the sight of mini slashes all over her waist.

"It was worth it," she said, eyeing the little cuts. Most weren't deep enough to bleed, but they still left red, slightly raised lines. Two cuts to the left had definitely broken skin.

"Yeah. Thanks for saving those kittens and bringing them here," he said, as he cleaned the area, apologizing when she jolted at the sting. His touch was gentle and almost made her forget why she'd gotten mad at him earlier. He looked up at her as he grabbed a new gauze pad. "My only worry is those kittens have fleas and you have broken skin. Fleas are a vector for a certain bacteria, *Bartonella*, that can get in open wounds and cause cat scratch disease. I'm sure you'll be fine—I've never had a case here and we've had plenty of scratches occur—but like I said, watch for fever, malaise or swollen glands over the next few days to two weeks. Just be aware." He applied ointment and put bandages on the two deeper ones.

"Great. I think you might have just triggered the hypochondriac in me," Mandi said, lowering her shirt. All she needed was to get sick on top of everything else.

"You'll be fine. I can't put a number on how many scratches I've personally suffered and not one ended up getting infected."

"If you say so. Thanks. Um. I'm going to head back to Nana's—my—I mean our—place." That sounded so strange. Awkward, to say the least. Something shifted in Gray's face.

"We need to talk about that, but not here," he said.

"Agreed. You can stop by later, but I can tell you now, I need you to buy me out. It's that, or agree to putting the place on the market. My father didn't lose time in expressing an interest."

Gray's jaw hardened and his eyes darkened.

"I can tell you now, none of that's happening."

## CHAPTER FOUR

JOHN RIVERS PACED across his newly built deck that overlooked the sound, but neither the picturesque scenery, nor Coral's somewhat annoying consolation, settled his nerves.

"What do you mean she told you off?" he asked.

"She brushed me away. Wouldn't even listen. In fact, she was kind of rude. I'm telling you, that girl certainly didn't inherit your business sense." Coral took his hand in hers and gave it a squeeze. "Don't worry. I'm sure she'll come around. It's too soon after the funeral to talk about it. Emotions are still raw."

He felt more than raw. He'd been reduced to feeling inconsequential…practically nonexistent. The whole town would eventually find out that his mother had put a stranger—an outsider—ahead of him. They would talk. Gossip behind his back, just like when he was the kid in school with no father… Times were different back then and bullies highlighted things like that. Even adults had a tendency to zero in on a person's vulnerability and bring it up, like when Audra had run off and left him. People had talked about it ad nauseam.

He hated pity. But it didn't matter what he did or what he achieved in life, it never seemed to be enough. He loved his family, but he would never understand why his mother wasn't prouder of all he'd achieved. He had loved Audra, but she had made it clear she didn't love him anymore. If she ever truly had. Marrying so young had been the biggest mistake of his life. His mother had warned him about rushing into marriage when the two of them barely knew each other. He had ignored her. And Mandi… all he ever wanted was to protect her from making the same mistakes in life he had made. At least she had come to her senses about marrying Grayson. That man was no more right for Mandi than Audra had been for him.

Mandi tended not to listen to him, though. She may not have gone into law, as he'd wanted, but he'd be damned if she took another wrong turn and threw her career away on account of seeing Gray again. He needed to make sure the man didn't take advantage of her feeling vulnerable right now.

He downed the glass of brandy Coral had poured for him and went inside. He could hear her closing the sliding glass door behind her. He wished she'd close the front door behind her, too, but he didn't want to be rude. Every ally mattered when your own family was against you.

"Maybe you're right," he said, turning his laptop on and opening the documents page. "In the meantime, find out exactly how much the property is worth. I also want numbers on at least two adjoining homes."

"Big plans?"

Did he ever. He'd spent his life making a name for himself, not only in Turtleback but along the entire Outer Banks. People didn't live forever. Life was short and this was his chance to leave a permanent mark. The location. The proximity to a historic lighthouse. It was all too perfect. So long as that vet didn't get in the way. But everyone had a price. He shrank the file with old notes he had on Zale from back when he'd convinced Mandi to marry him and opened a new online search.

"My dear, you should know by now. I only deal in high stakes."

GRAY HADN'T DEALT with such a confusing barrage of emotions since the day WITSEC US marshals had facilitated his new life in Turtleback. He hated anger as much as he hated people who lacked morals and ethics. He also hated those who lacked compassion—for all life—and honesty. Yet, here he was, angry and living a lie.

*But you did it for the greater good.* He lived every day reminding himself that the truth got him here but the sacrifice had been worth it. Just like Mandi insisted that the injuries she'd suffered in rescuing the kittens were worth it. He loved that about her. But love wasn't enough. Was it? Keeping the truth from her had to have played a part in her leaving. She had sensed that he was holding back and they had argued about it more times than he cared to remember. She was digging; he was denying.

But his truth would only endanger them

both. He couldn't draw that kind of danger to this quiet, unsuspecting town. His sacrifice would have all been for nothing.

That a person would knowingly endanger someone else blew his mind, but he knew people could be bought. He'd never given much credence to the saying that everyone had a price, until that day, when he had made the conscious decision to let his life get mixed up with the criminal world.

There was no price when it came to keeping Mandi and every other person and thing around here safe, including the turtle nesting grounds. He didn't trust Mandi's father when it came to preserving nature. Nature didn't make bank deposits. John was too shortsighted to understand why protecting those nests was so important. It didn't make sense that Mandi would even consider selling out to him. Had she really been gone so long that she'd forgotten what this all meant? The house…the beach…helping to protect and save endangered species like the Kemp's ridley sea turtles? Had she forgotten how many turtles had been lost to cold shock farther up the East Coast the last winter she'd spent here? Or how many hatchlings never made it to the water because of people who didn't care? People like John. How could she not consider what Nana had valued in her life? Both of them had stopped discussing the subject at the clinic when Chanda had stepped into his office with another chart. She had raised her brows to indicate their voices had been carrying.

He climbed the wooden steps to Nana's place—he'd always think of it that way—with Laddie at his heels. *Nana's place.* Her hummingbird bird feeder hung empty from its hook above the front porch railing. The afternoon rains had kept the flowers from dying in the garden beds along the side of the house, but weeds were beginning to sprout everywhere. He'd never noticed the paint chipping along the railing before, probably because he usually approached the house from the beach side. The back porch was Nana's favorite place.

He knocked because it was the right thing to do. It didn't matter that he had a key. He'd never actually lived here before, even if he'd spent plenty of hours in the house helping Nana with minor repairs when he could.

A small gasp escaped Mandi's lips when she opened the door.

"You're such a stunning, handsome boy."

Gray's ego skyrocketed for the fraction of a second it took for him to register that she wasn't looking at him. She went down on her knees and began petting Laddie. The dog wagged and sniffed. "So, you're Laddie. Your mane is something else."

"Yep, this is my sidekick. My wingman." *The little traitor.*

"I saw him from a distance on the beach." Mandi hesitated as if trying to take back her words. Had she been watching them? She cleared her throat. "But he's even more beautiful up close."

Laddie gave her palm a lick and gave Gray a look of approval.

"He's an amazing friend. Needs a good brushing every week to keep his coat from matting but it's good bonding time, and when he sheds, I find the longer hair easier to clean than the shorter, needlelike type."

"You are so beautiful and calm," she said, running her fingers through Laddie's rough coat.

"Patient. Loves kids and animals. And

very smart. He knows this place. He used to keep Nana company."

"I know. Sometimes, when I called her on the phone, she would tell me your dog was hanging out with her."

"Can we come in?"

Mandi's eyes widened.

"Oh gosh. I didn't mean to trap you in the doorway. I got distracted. Can you blame me?"

"Nope. Happens to me on walks all the time."

He closed the door behind him and noticed her keys sitting between a conch shell and her purse on the console near the door. Something stirred in his chest. The pewter turtle. She was still using it? He fingered the matching turtle key chain in his pocket. He'd given it to her on her twenty-first birthday. He had assumed she'd gotten rid of everything related to him after she'd called off the wedding. Interesting. No doubt Nana had noticed, too. Nothing escaped her. That woman could have spotted a flea trying to hide in a pile of sand. She could read between the lines, too. He was beginning to believe more and more that it had something to do with this whole house-sharing situation. Maybe she really was trying to give him a second chance with Mandi. He certainly wasn't throwing that away.

"Make yourself comfortable. After all, it's your place, too," Mandi said. Her words sounded rehearsed and defeated.

"Mandi, I didn't put her up to this. You must know that. I was as surprised as you were when Burkitt read her will."

"I never said you did." She frowned at him and shook her head. "Gray, in the past, I may have accused you of being a locked box, but I never thought you were manipulative."

More like Pandora's box.

"Thank you for that. The manipulative part, at least. Besides, we both know Nana can't be manipulated."

That earned him a chuckle. Mandi sat on the floor cross-legged and patted her knee. Laddie lay down beside her with his head on her lap.

"Nope. Nana was too strong for that. I think that's why my dad was always frustrated with her. And she with him."

"We can make this work, Mandi." Gray sat on the sofa and rested his elbows on his knees. "Just because you live in New York doesn't mean we have to sell. Most folks only get to dream of having a beach vacation home."

Mandi closed her eyes briefly, as if carefully planning each word.

"I can't keep it, Gray. With Nana gone, there's nothing left for me here…at least nothing that warrants me coming back enough that I'd need a house, including if I ever visit my dad. Not that he has ever asked me to. I need the money more and I probably won't have the time to come down here anyway. And before you criticize me for that or accuse me of being like my father, remember why I worked so hard to put myself through college. Remember that I refused to let my dad pay my way. And you of all people know how much that accomplishment meant to me. Especially getting into graduate school."

"Trust me, I know. I believe you left me for it."

She stopped petting Laddie.

"That's not why I left. Not entirely, and you know it. I'm not in the mood to fight about that. Please. Let's put that behind us.

I just want to sort out this situation. Look, the fact is that graduate school left me with a whale-sized debt, and on top of that, there's the cost of living in New York, which—don't get me wrong—is worth it because my new job is the kind of opportunity most people only dream of. If I prove myself to them, I can work my way up the ladder and find myself in a position where I'd get to travel for business, expenses paid, and see places I've never been. Maybe someday, I'll have enough free income to donate regularly to charities the way Nana did. I've worked hard for this, Gray."

He did know college costs were astronomical. That's why he had gone the army route. The only catch was having to work for them a few years postgraduation. That's what led him to the Navy's Marine Mammal Program and the rest was history. Or, the erasure of his.

"Isn't this new big-city job of yours paying enough?"

She raised an irritated brow at him.

"Not everyone walks out of college and starts earning a doctor's salary. It's one of the most prestigious advertising firms on the East Coast. I'm starting at the bottom like all newcomers. Look. I don't want to rent this place out, because I've seen what renters can do. Besides, there'll be times of the year when there won't be business, especially this far south along the Banks. And I didn't think you'd want to share the place with strangers. Hermit that you are."

"Agreed. No renting. I don't like that idea either."

The idea of college kids partying and puking in here or people bringing dogs that weren't trained like Laddie and letting them loose bothered the heck out of him. They'd destroy all the turtle nests. But he also had to consider the strangers who'd be coming and going. People he'd have to deal with as a landlord if he chose to keep living at the lighthouse and rented the cottage. Considering his witness protection situation, it wasn't a safe choice, or one his WITSEC contact would approve of. Nope. Renting was indeed out of the question.

The corners of her mouth sank. Not that he was staring at her lips…or her brown eyes and the faraway look that settled in them.

"You're my first choice, Gray."

Wow. That had so many layers of meaning to it; it left him torn between hope, loss and bitterness. They were each other's first true loves. They'd chosen each other. And now she was basically choosing to break the link between them and leave a second time.

"I assume you mean for buying you out." He didn't bother hiding the bitter edge to his tone.

"Yes. You know that's what I mean."

Laddie whimpered.

"I can't afford to and you know it."

"How would I know it? You have a thriving practice and haven't put a dime into restoring the lighthouse place. I'm sure you could get a loan if you needed to. At least the house would be cared for by one of us… the way Nana had intended."

"I should get a loan so that you can pay off yours?"

"I didn't mean it like that."

"Well, I can't afford your half. It takes a lot of money to get a practice up and running the first few years. Whatever I don't put back into it or need to live off of, I donate to various wildlife and animal rescue groups or environmental and humanitarian causes, because what's the point in life if I don't. It's not like I have a family to take care of."

"That was low."

She was right. What had gotten into him? He was going to run her off instead of convincing her to at least stay in touch with him. If not more. He raked his hair back.

"Sorry."

"Gray, I'm just trying to come up with a solution that doesn't involve—"

"Selling to John. You absolutely cannot sell to him. Stand your moral ground, Mandi. He doesn't care about the history of a place. He'll want to raze it and build something bigger and better, all for the money. He'd try to use his connections to get the town to let him build a small hotel or something. He's into real estate and development. Forget quiet beach or saving endangered species. That's not in his mind-set."

"I don't want to and, trust me, I've thought about all of that. But he's interested. And he *is* family. I may have always had issues with him, but he's my father. We can't put it on the market and ignore him. Can you imagine what his reaction would be like if we blew off his offer and accepted another? I wouldn't be here, but he'd make your life a living hell. Why do you think I want you to buy me out? That said, you heard the will. We'd both have to agree on any sale."

"I told you I can't buy you out and if you open the door to the idea of selling at all, he'll hound me endlessly. Your father has tunnel vision. He doesn't stop until he gets what he wants. He got in the way of us, didn't he?"

"Okay. You want to make this about us? Let's put it all out there, because clearly, it's eating away at you. I didn't leave because my dad ordered me to. I'm an independent woman. I make my own choices. I left because a marriage is built on trust and you didn't trust me enough. You wanted to be in control instead of being equals. You want to be in control now, too. Listen to yourself. You gave me an order not to sell to my dad."

"You know that wasn't an order. It was passionate desperation. And what on earth are you talking about me not trusting you? I respected and trusted you."

"Respected, yes. You're a good, kind man. But trust? Gray… I still don't know how your parents died. Just that they did and that you don't want to talk about it. When I wanted to talk about traveling and seeing the world, you told me you had a fear of boats and planes. Then I caught you sailing with Sheriff Ryker. And the night before the wedding, when I suggested we adopt a dog, I asked you what name you liked and you said, I quote, 'Bently, like my first dog.'"

"You canceled the wedding because my first dog was named Bently?"

"I distinctly remember you once telling me that your first dog, a golden retriever, was named Bailey. We were up in the lighthouse watching the sunrise and I had baked you banana muffins. I know I'm not mistaken. It was the little things like that, Gray. They piled up. I really did love you, but in my gut, I knew it wasn't right between us. Maybe we hadn't known each other long enough. Or maybe you were traumatized as a kid and it affected your memory. But that's the point. You never shared things with me the way I did with you."

Had he mixed up names? He'd been advised to change pet names but he had used something similar, hoping it would help him remember. It was hard to keep some experiences and tweak them just enough to make them different, without confusing his old reality with his new one. Planes, he didn't really have a problem with. As for boats, he really did hate them. Specifically, the smaller kind that could easily capsize. He did okay on larger vessels back when he worked with the Navy's Marine Mammal Program. But even then, he'd preferred being on the choppers helping with dolphins being transported, or working with animals in aquatic holdings near the main facility. There had been plenty of other staff willing to go out into deep waters, especially when they'd witnessed his anxiety attack after one excursion in turbulent conditions. His parents had died in a boating accident off the coast of Maine. He had been the only survivor and the accident had made it in the local paper, along with his middle school picture, which was why it was one of those parts of his past he wasn't allowed to mention. However, Carlos had wanted to check on him and out at sea was the only place no one would overhear their talking. That had happened once. It wasn't safe to get too comfortable mentioning his past self like that. One never knew who might be watching with binoculars or lip-reading, assuming there wasn't a hidden mic somewhere.

"I went out on that boat on a dare. My male pride was at stake. And you read too much into the name thing. I've had many pets and was confusing names the way parents confuse their kids' names. What can I say? I like dog names that start with the letter *B*. Laddie here was already named, since he wasn't a puppy when I got him."

The dog's ears perked as he dozed off against Mandi's leg. Mandi took a deep breath and held it for a moment before blowing it out.

"Whatever. That's in the past. My life isn't here anymore and yours is. That's the bottom line. Along with the fact that I need to sell the house. I loved Nana more than anything and this place is sentimental to me, but I have to be realistic."

Her eyes glistened. He could tell she didn't want to let go, regardless of what she was saying. This place meant something to her. He needed to remind her of that. He stood up and walked to the glass doors that led onto the back deck. He opened it and slid the screen door in place. The crash and fiz-zle of waves against sand and Nana's wind chime singing on the breeze filled the room. A royal tern spread its wings and took off over the water as a boat dragged a parasailor through the air like a child flying a kite.

*Keep it close to your heart.* The house or Mandi? Maybe meeting her halfway would stretch the time he had with her. He'd have more time to remind her of what this place used to mean to them…what they meant to each other.

"Even if I agreed to help you find a quick buyer—a family interested in a house…not a businessman like your father—and agreed to selling, we'd have to do a lot of work to this place before putting it on the market."

"You're overthinking. There's not that much to do besides packing. It's move-in ready. Nana lived here, didn't she?"

"When you live in a place that long, you let some things slide that a buyer won't. If someone sees the chipped paint, rotten wood, water damage from storms, the roof, and several other things that need fixing, you won't get what a beachfront property out here is really worth. I might be willing to consider selling, but not if it means throwing money away. Money you claim you need for debt or charities. More would make a bigger dent in both, don't you think?"

Mandi's brow furrowed and she eased up so as not to bother Laddie. He jumped up anyway and stuck to her side as she slid the screen open and stepped into the sharp sunlight. She shaded her eyes with her hand and looked up at the roof and the rest of the house.

"See what I mean?" Gray said, pointing toward spots in need of repair. She didn't say anything. Her arms fell to her sides. She took the steps down to the beach. Laddie wagged his tail and looked up at Gray pleadingly.

"Go on, you fool."

Laddie chased after her. Gray took his time getting there. She was mulling over the idea. At least that was a step in the right direction.

He was halfway to her when she turned around.

"So, what if I convince my dad not to demolish the place? I could have Burkitt write up a legal agreement or something."

"Not going to work. And I won't sell to him because I know nothing good will come of it. Remember, you need my agreement."

Her lips curled in.

"How much is all this that you're talking about going to cost?"

"A lot less if we do some of the work ourselves. You know your way around with a brush. Nana still has your high school paintings hung around the house. There's the inside, too. I can't do all the work alone and see patients and do surgeries."

"Except that painting a landscape isn't the same as painting a house and I'm only here a few days."

"You'll catch on. Just don't start painting murals on the walls. And explain to the powers that be that you need more time. At least a few weeks."

"They'll fire me before I start!"

He scrubbed his jaw. He wasn't trying to destroy her life. He just needed to buy time with her.

"Talk to Burkitt and see if he can help in terms of the contract you signed. Maybe there's leeway in the starting date."

"I already got a few days so that I could come for the funeral."

"These are extenuating circumstances. Your grandmother died. Maybe the company will let you trade out time, like working through the holidays when others want to take off. Look, I know it's easier said than done. I'm not trying to get you fired before you start. I don't expect you to throw your life away. I just want to do what's right and settle things the smartest way possible with the least chance of harm coming to Nana's beach and the nesting grounds."

Laddie ran circles around her, slowly moving her in Gray's direction. Mandi seemed unaware. That dog had definitely retained his herding instincts, minus the excess barking.

"Fine. I'll call and see what I can do, but they'll want a date."

"Give us two weeks."

*Give me two weeks. Give us a chance.*

"They'll never agree to that. I'll be embarrassed enough asking for one."

"Okay, fine. See if they'll give you ten days and we'll take it from there."

"Ten days and we find a family for it," Mandi said, extending her hand. He shook it.

She'd taken the words right out of his mouth. She just didn't know that he already had a family in mind. And he was looking right at it.

## CHAPTER FIVE

MANDI HOISTED ONE of two boxes of books from the back of her car and carried them into Castaway Books. Eve, who had graduated two classes ahead of her in high school, was crouched on her knees organizing books on a shelf near the front desk, which consisted of the same live-edge wood counter Mandi remembered her insisting on when she took over the family business. Eve turned as the shell and bell chime clanged.

"Mandi Rivers?" She dropped what she was doing and wiped her hands on her jeans as she helped Mandi set the box down on the counter. "I knew you were in town but I didn't know if I'd see you. If you need anything…" She placed her hand on Mandi's arm, leaving the rest unsaid.

"Thank you, Eve. You look wonderful, by the way, and I like what you've done with the sign out front." The sign was new and played on the castaway theme. The carved font had a rickety style and ended with a logo consisting of a palm tree on an island and a broken, washed-up boat filled with books. It was cute, like Eve. Totally her style.

"Oh, that. I decided I needed something catchy when I put the store online a year ago. I think it's paying off."

"I like it. Listen, I'm going through Nana's things and was wondering if you'd be interested in any more books. I have another box in the car. Mostly thrillers and mysteries, plus a few classics."

Eve started rummaging through the titles.

"Ooh, I've read this one. It's really good. Are you sure you don't want them? I can figure out how much I can pay you for them if you have a few minutes. It won't be much. Around five dollars a box?"

"No need." Ten bucks wasn't going to break the bank. Getting them out of the way was payment enough right now. "I read most of them long ago and I'd be happy if someone else gets the chance to enjoy them. If you find any you don't want, feel free to pass them along to the hospital or library."

"This is wonderful. Thank you so much. I lost some inventory during the last hurricane. I didn't have enough time to move everything before evacuating. These castaways will be loved."

"Perfect. I'll get the other box."

"I can help. You must have a lot to do. Word around the block is that you and Gray now share a house," Eve hedged, as she held the shop door open for Mandi.

Word had made it only around the block? Not through the entire town yet? Amazing.

"Yep." She lifted the second box.

"Sooo…does that mean you're moving back?"

"Nope."

"Oh." She looked a little perplexed but had the decency not to pry further. "Well, I hope everything will settle down for you soon. If you come across any other books you don't want—"

"I'll let you know. I appreciate you taking these. I have to run, but enjoy your day, Eve. It was good to see you."

"You, too." She waved and bounced back inside, the door creaking behind her.

Mandi moved her car to a small gravel

parking area near the town's very short
boardwalk to get it out of the way, then suc-
cumbed to the decadent aroma of freshly
baked sweets and coffee wafting from the
local bakery. A handful of tourists—including a man with a wicked sunburn—walked
past her, likely on their way to lunch along
the boardwalk. There was only one full-
service seafood restaurant down there,
but several smaller eateries had managed
to stay open, despite economic ups and
downs, mostly by overcharging for beer,
wine and especially frozen mixed drinks.
None of them opened until lunch, but they
stayed open well into the night, taking advantage of folks hungry after a long day on
the beach.

She waved to a few familiar faces down
the street, town residents who had come to
the funeral, then she ducked into The Saltwater Sweetery. For a moment, her eyes
closed involuntarily and she couldn't move.
All she could do was inhale the sinful scent
of pastries and saltwater taffy being made in
the kitchen. Come to think of it, she hadn't
had anything to eat but her morning coffee and an apple for breakfast. Her stomach

rumbled and she approached the glass cases filled with rows of storybook confections. Bins filled with a rainbow of saltwater taffy flavors lined the far-left side of the counter area. It was sensory overload in the most delectable way.

"What can I—Mandi!" Darla came scurrying around the counter and hugged her like a long-lost puppy. "I've missed you, girl. I can't believe those big city bakeries satisfied you enough to forget about mine."

Mandi wrapped her arms around her old friend. She needed that hug more than she had realized. She swallowed hard and willed away tears before letting go.

"Not possible. I gain twenty pounds each night eating here in my dreams. Luckily, I toss and turn enough to burn off the calories by morning. How've you been, Darla? Apart from your delicious social media posts. I've seen those."

Darla didn't spend much time on social media, other than to update her website and such. There just weren't enough hours in a day considering how early she had to start baking every morning. And for the most part, Mandi restricted her own use to minimal necessity…school or work related. She had learned the hard way how addictive social media could be when she almost failed a class her first semester in grad school because of time spent online instead of studying. On one hand, she needed to analyze current advertising, but it was so easy to get sucked into looking at online sites and not realizing how much time had passed. There was also the issue of how much it had interfered with her quality of sleep and anxiety levels. She had never really used it before leaving Turtleback on account of the fact that Gray hated it. He wasn't on any social media sites, other than a pet advice blog he maintained as part of his office website, and since they had been hanging out together, she never had the need to waste time on it. She had spent enough hours online for her undergraduate classes. She had craved fresh air and time with Gray after that, not social media.

"I'm good. Come sit. What can I get you?"

"Everything?"

Darla laughed.

"How about coffee and a crab claw?" Crab claws were her version of bear claws.

Darla gave them little crab shapes the same way her thumbprint cookies with jam on top were shaped like little turtles, in honor of the town.

"No complaints here." She grabbed a seat in the corner and Darla joined her with her treat and a steaming mug. Her assistant, who looked like a high schooler, took over helping a customer and Darla sat down.

"I needed a break. Your timing is perfect," she said. "Make sure you take some taffy before you leave."

"You don't have to convince me," Mandi said, biting into the pastry. "Mmm. So good."

"When do you head back?"

"Twelve days. I was supposed to leave sooner but, due to circumstances, I was granted two work weeks before starting my new job. That includes a weekend, so essentially twelve days, but I need a day for traveling back to New York. I'm sticking around because there's work to be done on the cottage so that we can sell it. Keep that to yourself for now. I don't want my dad butting in."

"You're selling?"

Mandi cocked her head and shrugged. Darla leaned back into the chair.

"I guess I was holding out hope that you might move back."

"And do what?"

"I'd hire you to run my website and marketing."

"I can't live on one client, Darla. Besides, you know I'd give you free advice anytime."

"What about Gray? Doesn't he want the house?"

Mandi was going to go on the assumption that the entire town knew the details of the inheritance by now, but she wasn't about to discuss Gray's finances. Darla was a good friend, but Nana had taught Mandi to never say too much to anyone. There were some things that stayed within the family circle. Mandi had also not spoken to Darla in a long time. It hit her that she really had distanced herself more than she realized over the past two years…not just from Gray, but from everyone.

"We came to an agreement of sorts. Look, Darla, forget about me. I need a major sugar binge and to hear about you."

"Okay. Not much to say, though. Always

busy, busy." A hint of color tinged her cheeks and she paused, as if mentally filtering what she should or shouldn't share, then gave her head a subtle shake. "Gray comes in here every day. Brings that gorgeous dog of his and buys an entire box of whatever's fresh out of the oven for everyone at his clinic."

Mandi was glad she'd just taken a huge bite. She chewed and nodded like the information was no big deal. So what if he came here on a daily basis? It was classic Gray to think of his staff and bring them breakfast. It was the way Darla blushed that made something flutter in her stomach. She washed down her bite of pastry with hot coffee and tried to look as nonchalant as possible. What did she expect? For Gray not to have a social life over the past two years? Darla had been Mandi's friend since high school, so she had also met him back when he first moved to town. She just didn't know him as well as Mandi did. At least Mandi didn't think so. Maybe they'd gotten to know one another better in her absence. Maybe he had opened up to Darla about things he'd never shared with Mandi. He hadn't mentioned seeing anyone, but then he was good at keeping secrets. Mandi shuddered visibly.

"Oh my gosh talk about a fast sugar-caffeine high," Mandi said, wiping her mouth and hoping to change the subject. She was losing her mind. Since when was she the jealous type? Never. This was stress induced. The funeral, feelings of loss, the house, seeing Gray again…it was having a negative effect on her. "I'm talking about myself, but I'm sure Gray's staff get it, too, whenever he picks up pastries for them."

"The secret is in the sea salt," Darla whispered. "It brings out the flavor in everything, and between salt and sugar, I have everyone's cravings covered."

"You're no better than a drug dealer. I'm surprised Sheriff Ryker hasn't taken you down yet. Is he still single?"

Darla flipped her thick blond braid over her shoulder.

"He's always in here, too. Coffee, no cream, and a cinnamon pecan muffin. He says the cinnamon and nuts balance the sugar and hold him over till lunch."

"You're brilliant. You know that, don't you? You can stay in one spot all day and the men come to you. The marketer in me thinks you should rename the place The Sugar Trap."

They broke down laughing, drawing the attention of customers on their way out, and the assistant, who acted like he'd never heard his boss laugh before.

"Trust me, I'm not dating the sheriff. Too serious about everything. Even his muffins."

"If you say so. Darla, I could sit here all day but I have so much to do," Mandi said, scooting her chair.

"I'll box one of everything for you. On the house. Just promise me you'll find time to hang out with me before you leave."

"I will." She stood and looked at her friend. Darla was a genuine person. Who was Mandi to get in the way of her happiness? Or Gray's? Doing so would be selfish. She really did want them both to find happiness. "Just so you know, I'm okay with it if you and Gray are interested in—"

The bakery's door chimed and Gray stopped in his tracks.

"Darla and I are interested in what?" he asked.

Her friend's eyes widened.

"Interested in going to a bonfire she's holding on the beach tonight," Darla blurted. "Mandi was checking to see if we'd help set it up."

What kind of cover-up was that?

"Um, yes." Mandi shot Darla a look and scrambled to fall in step. "A small bonfire. Old friends. And a toast in honor of Nana."

Gray's eyes narrowed and skipped between the two of them.

"Sure. Count me in."

PEOPLE WHO COULDN'T comprehend why anyone would live on a narrow strip of land dangling in the Atlantic Ocean and practically beckoning for hurricanes to unleash flood and fury on it had never visited the Outer Banks. If the soft sands, egrets peering above tall grasses, bold lighthouses and the wild horses farther north in Corolla— endangered descendants of Spanish mustangs—weren't enough to make up for the hurricane threat, being able to see the sun in the west, dripping its last rays over the sound, while at the same time watching the moon rise over the Atlantic, was more than enough.

Gray added another log to the small fire he started and brushed the sand off his hands. He could see Darla heading over, carrying what were probably leftover bakery items from today, and a few others, Carlos included, were close behind her. Laddie ran over to help round them up and guide them to the fire.

Mandi unfolded a fourth camping chair. Her dark brown hair, glistening with red highlights from the sunset, fell across her face. He pretended not to watch as she tucked it behind her ears. Her cheek was damp and she swiped it with the back of her hand. She was having a moment. He had been having them, too, ever since Nana's passing. Moments where he seemed to forget she was gone and half expected her to walk out onto her porch. Mandi wiped her other cheek, conscious of the crowd nearing the campfire. He wanted to hug and comfort her, but it would only spread rumors. She'd hate him for that.

"I think we're set. Hopefully others will bring chairs…and ice. I didn't get ice," she said, a hint of panic in her voice.

"Mandi, breathe. It's a casual gathering.

It's all good. I've got plenty under the drinks in the cooler. If we need more, I'll run back to the house."

He could have meant either place, his lighthouse caretaker's cabin or Nana's. They had set up midway between the houses and the town's boardwalk, to make it convenient for everyone. She nodded and pressed her lips together, then left the campfire circle to greet the others. Laddie stuck by her side. That dog had an incredible sense of who needed his support. He had also probably picked up on the energy between Gray and Mandi and knew that Gray would want him to look out for her.

Gray moved the cooler a little out of the way to make more seating room. The weather was perfect and the breeze had died down, allowing the fire smoke to twirl straight up into the dimming sky. Personally, he preferred sitting on the beach at night as far from town as he could get to escape the artificial lights. There was something spiritual about sitting beneath an indigo sky with no light except that of the moon and stars. But whenever turtle nests along the beach closer to town were due to hatch, he stuck close by. The town lights made his presence more critical. For years now, he had been keeping a log and reporting found nests to a local nonprofit organization that specialized in tracking, counting and testing eggs for the type of endangered or threatened turtle—hawksbill, Kemp's ridley, green, loggerheads and leatherbacks. Nests were typically laid high up on the beach, closer to the dunes that led to beach cottages and town boardwalks, leaving baby turtles with quite a journey to the shoreline after hatching. The organization had volunteers to help watch for hatchlings when they were due, usually around two months, give or take, after laying. He was one of those volunteers, just as Nana had been, and he knew that some of the nests he had marked this season were due to hatch within the next few weeks. The problem was that the town lights, and lights from beach houses, were prone to disorienting the baby turtles, but he had never been successful in trying to get businesses along the boardwalk to shut down at a reasonable hour. Money was the bottom line and this was their busiest season. They catered to visitors wanting a place to hang and have a late meal or drinks. Not to turtles.

In the past, during hatching, he had always left Laddie at home. Even friendly dogs were a bad idea with hatchlings crawling everywhere. Gray then did his best to help the babies—naturally wired to head for the brightest horizon, which was usually the moon and starlight reflecting off the ocean—make it to the water's edge safely. Town lights had a way of confusing their sense of direction. The light pollution also stole their prime protection from predators—darkness. They needed to stay in the shadows, much like Gray was destined to do, in order to survive. But no one whose livelihood relied on keeping their business in the black was about to turn away customers—a fact of life that frustrated the heck out of him.

"Hey, Doc. This one's on me." Carlos slapped him on the back and handed him a beer, before sitting down and popping open an orange soda. "Cheers."

"No beer?"

"I'm taking the night shift in an hour. Can't stay long."

The rest of the group set down their food and drink contributions, said their hellos and headed straight for the water, leaving him alone with the sheriff. Mandi lagged a little behind them, hands tucked in the pockets of her shorts and Laddie still at her side, although he did glance back at Gray once or twice, as if to admonish him for sitting around instead of looking after her.

Mandi didn't want or need looking after.

The group neared the water's edge and a few began wading in.

"Hey! Sharks like this time of day!" Gray called out after them.

"What happened to that shirt you wear with the vegan shark on it? You lied to us," Darla called back.

"Me, lie? Haven't you seen that meme that says the ocean gets its saltiness from the tears of misunderstood sharks who just want to cuddle?"

"Who wrote that?" Mandi asked.

"I don't know, but it's all over the internet," Eve said. "I've seen it before and respect the sharks, but don't plan on cuddling with any."

"Good choice," Gray said.

"Don't worry. We're only going ankle deep." Darla gave Gray a reassuring smile.

"You were born a mother hen, Zale." Carlos chuckled as he watched everyone kicking up water, then he took a swig of soda.

"Says the man who stays up all night watching over this sleepy town." Gray stoked the fire, pausing to let a cluster of sparks escape into the night, before turning one log.

"We're a pitiful pair," Carlos said, stretching his legs out. "Bachelors acting like parents, yet unwilling to take the plunge."

"At least I gave a serious relationship a try," Gray countered. "You? I don't dare call a sheriff chicken, but I call it as I see it."

"You're skiing in shark-infested waters, buddy. I'm *not* afraid. I'm just too smart to go down that road again."

"So, there *was* someone?"

Carlos took a long drink and shrugged. He'd never mentioned a past relationship before.

"A very, very long time ago. It didn't end well. Let's leave it at that."

He could respect not wanting to talk about

one's past. He jerked his head toward the waves.

"Darla's a nice person. I'm sure she'd add doughnuts to her menu just for you," Gray said.

Carlos finished off his soda in one gulp, crushed the can and chucked it at him. Gray laughed and caught it midair.

"This is war." Carlos grinned, then sobered and shook his head. "Nothing against Darla, but I'm just not in the market. Besides, I'm pretty sure I'm not her type."

Mandi and the others jogged over, kicking sand up in their wake. Everyone took their drink of choice out of the cooler and gathered around. Most ignored the chairs altogether and plopped down on the sand.

"Thanks for calling off the sharks, Dr. Dolittle," Darla teased.

"The powers of communication that come with being a vet. What can I say?"

Mandi's face twitched when she looked over at him. Okay, fine. She had made it quite clear during their relationship that he had communication issues. At least when it came to her. Obviously, he did better with animals. Then again, pets were loyal. They didn't abandon their loved ones.

"Hey, guys. Room for more?" Chanda asked. Nora and Gavin were with her and Nora was carrying a box that looked like it had flowers in it.

"Absolutely. How are the kittens doing?" Mandi asked. She'd asked him the same question only an hour ago.

"They're little troupers. Gaining weight already and doing much better," Nora said. She pulled out a small wreath and passed around the box of loose flowers and pieces of driftwood and shells. She handed the wreath to Mandi. "This is for you. It's completely natural and biodegradable, made with things from my organic garden. No glue or foam. Just reed grass for tying. I thought each of us could add a flower, driftwood or shell to it, while remembering something we loved about Nana. Then, maybe in the next few days, you and Gray could take it out far enough in a boat and release it."

Mandi's nose turned red and the rims of her eyes pooled. Gray's eyes stung and his chest tightened. He noticed that Mandi didn't bring up his supposed fear of boats.

"I can't express how thoughtful and meaningful this is, Nora," Mandi said. "You made it? You're incredible."

"This is really kind of you," Gray said. "You spend so much time working at the vet clinic, I don't know how you manage to create stuff like this and keep up with that garden of yours."

"It's just a hobby," Nora said.

"She's super talented and overly humble," Darla added. "You guys remember that wedding cake I made for the Delcatos? Guess who put the flowers on it?"

"You're not quitting on me and opening a flower shop, are you?" Gray asked, only half-serious.

"Never. I love helping animals too much. They keep me coming back even when my boss is being an ornery pain in the butt."

Everyone laughed at Gray and he conceded the barb by raising his bottle in a self-toast. Mandi got up and gave Nora a hug, then the group quieted as the wreath began making its way around the circle. Mandi insisted that Nora begin the ritual. Nora took a sprig of lavender from the box and tucked it into the wreath.

"Nana was generous…"

"…and wise. Always giving needed advice," Darla said, taking the wreath from Nora and tying a shell to it. She passed it to Gavin.

"She believed in charity and random acts of kindness," he said, adding a sand dollar.

"…to all living things. Not just people," Eve added on her turn. She fastened a yellow carnation in place.

"She was pretty spunky and hilarious, if you ask me. Always said laughter was medicine. I agree with her." Chanda added a miniature sunflower and tied a bow around it using a reed grass.

"She was a bit of a daredevil, too. I'm not even sure if she knew how to knit, but she sure could parasail and she was ruthless on a Jet Ski," Darla chimed in, even if she'd had her turn and wasn't holding the wreath. "Not exactly what you'd expect from most women her age. But who am I to say? She told me that yoga class kept her young and fit, but I don't know. I do yoga but have never been able to jet ski successfully."

"You're right in that she was unexpected," Carlos said. "Kind of like Mary Poppins.

Full of surprises." He added driftwood to the wreath. "I can't remember how she talked me into a bet, but she beat me at target shooting once. And I trained in the military and for police work. I never wagered a bet with her again."

"Where'd she learn to do that?" Gray asked.

"Said she used to hunt before she went vegan."

"Seriously? Did she ever take you hunting when you were a kid, Mandi?" Gray asked. Mandi had never mentioned hunting.

Mandi shook her head. "Nope. She was a vegetarian, and later vegan, during my lifetime."

"Well, as good a shot as she was, she must have done quite a bit of shooting before you were born," Carlos said.

"A woman of many talents and a big heart," Nora said, bringing the box of flowers and shells closer to Mandi and Gray. Mandi took out a red rose and slipped the stem between the twigs that made the wreath.

"She just wanted everyone to love themselves," Mandi said in almost a whisper. "And to be loved…"

Gray took the wreath from her, his fingertips brushing hers. He hesitated, then tucked in a sprig of baby's breath. He knew it was his imagination, heightened by fire and memories, but he could almost feel Nana's spirit prodding him…daring him to say it.

"…and to love each other."

He didn't dare look directly at Mandi to see her reaction. He simply handed the wreath back to her.

"Amen to that," Darla said.

Everyone voiced their agreement, then silence blanketed the group. For several minutes, the only sound was that of the crackling fire and fizzling surf. Mandi was the first to break the silence.

"Thank you for this. All of you. And for the wreath idea, Nora. I can't express how special you've all made this evening. I'll take this out to release it first thing tomorrow morning. Early morning was Nana's favorite time of day."

She spared Gray a quick glance before standing up as Carlos did, since he needed to leave for his shift. Gray knew exactly what she was thinking—whether he had been telling the truth about his fear of boats or not. She was waiting to see if he'd join her at sea in the morning. She had him. She knew he felt strongly about anyone going out on a boat alone, especially at the crack of dawn when no lifeguards were on duty. The other time of day sharks loved.

Shark advocate or not, he wasn't planning on having any showing him their love. But if there was one thing he feared more than boating, it was Mandi being out there on a boat alone.

MANDI STOPPED TO catch her breath, then continued to haul the two-person sea kayak that had been stored beneath the cottage decking to the shoreline. Gray hadn't shown up yet. She had told him, last night before leaving the fire, the exact time that she was planning to head out. He had nodded without giving her a firm answer. She left the kayak near the water but far enough for it not to float off and jogged back to the house to get the life vests—an extra in case he showed up—and the wreath. She had tied a piece of twine to it that she planned on using to secure it to her vest or the kayak so that it wouldn't float off before she was ready. She needed her hands free to paddle and would have to get just far enough past the surf for the wreath not to immediately wash up on shore.

She headed back to the kayak, disappointed that Gray still hadn't shown up, and began putting on her vest. The sound of his motorcycle approaching had her looking up. Why hadn't he just come down the beach from his place? He emerged from around Nana's cottage and hurried over.

"I almost left without you," Mandi said.

"I went to the marina. I assumed you were renting a boat. You never said anything about kayaking."

"I said I was going to leave from Nana's. You know we have a kayak here. What difference does it make? If you were willing to show up at the marina to take a boat, then why stare at this kayak like it's any different? They both float on water. They're essentially the same thing." Was he lying about his fear? Overplaying it at his convenience?

"Are you kidding me? That thing is a whole lot smaller and it puts you pretty much level with the water's surface. If a shark mistakes its silhouette for prey, you're in big trouble."

"What is it with you and sharks? It's like this weird love-hate relationship."

"It's called respect for their ways."

"I see. So it's not about the actual boating or kayaking?" She held out the vest she had brought for him. He took it reluctantly.

"Yes, it's about that, too. I told you, the only reason I had gone out with Carlos that one time was because he had essentially forced me to."

"Forced. Right. Because of that male-ego, save-face thing? If you can do it for that, you can do it for Nana's wreath."

He didn't respond. He stretched his neck, then put the vest on, all the while working his jaw.

"I'm not forcing you to do this, Gray. I'm quite capable of going out there on my own. There's no wind and barely any waves right now. You can stand here and watch and call for help if a megalodon decides to have me for breakfast."

"Not funny. And no, I can't stand here and let you go out alone. You know that. And a two-seater would be harder for you to control alone."

"Then help me push this in," she said, going around the kayak and shoving it closer to the water.

Gray took to the other side of it and helped. They needed to put the kayak mostly in the water to make their launch possible. She got into the front seat and secured the wreath before picking up one of the paddles. He looked out over the water, curled his lips in, then got in the backseat and took his paddle in hand. They pushed off the sand and began rowing in tandem. She had forgotten how much arm muscle it took to counter the current. Had she really gotten that out of shape since leaving Turtleback? Too much studying and desk work?

The sun had cleared the horizon and the effect of the blood-orange sky reflecting off the water was magical. A shallow wave rolled beneath them and they floated over it, then kept gliding out. She glanced over her shoulder at Gray and frowned at how pale he looked. Her stomach sank. Oh boy. He *had* been telling the truth about boats.

"Are you okay back there?"

He didn't answer. She looked back again. He was still rowing and gave her a terse nod, but his lips were practically fused together and his back looked stiffer than it had been back when she had told him she was sorry right before fleeing their wedding.

"Gray, I'm sorry. Since you had gone out with Carlos, I really thought this was one of those things you weren't being up-front with me about. I didn't think you were really that scared of boating…or kayaking."

"Just hurry it up, would you." His words were strained, like someone anticipating a tetanus shot.

"We can turn around."

"No. Just do it."

"Okay. Okay." They were almost as far out as they needed to be. She paddled another minute, then balanced her oar in front of her and untied the wreath. "We love you, Nana. We'll never forget you."

She glanced over at Gray but he didn't add anything. He simply gave a stiff nod. He looked a bit pale.

"You okay?" she asked.

He gave her another unconvincing nod.

They watched for a brief moment as the

wreath floated away, then Mandi leaned her weight to start turning the kayak as they resumed paddling. She didn't bother talking to Gray. He was paddling, but the look on his face and the way he'd stopped saying much gnawed at her. He really didn't do well out on the water. She should have believed him. She just hoped he didn't pass out before they reached the shore.

As soon as the tip of the kayak hit sand, she got out and started pulling it in. Gray actually scrambled out of his seat and began helping, the color back in his face as if nothing had happened. He set the oars on the beach, then sat on the dry sand and lay back with one arm across his eyes. Mandi went and kneeled next to him. She put her hand on his other forearm.

"Hey, I'm really sorry. If this fear of yours is that bad, why'd you do it?" He didn't answer because the answer was obvious. He had done it for her. He had tried telling her that before they launched. "Okay, you don't have to speak to me. Thank you for coming out there with me…for me and for Nana."

His chest rose and fell. He took a second, then sat up. She brushed the sand off the back of his head with her hand. His hair felt good between her fingers. She used to play with it all the time when they were dating and engaged. A part of her missed that intimacy.

"I'm fine now," he said.

"I don't get it. You love wildlife and nature and you work with sea turtles and drive a motorcycle like you're hooked on adrenaline. What's up with going out on the water?"

"I just don't like it. Everyone has something they're not into."

"Not into? Gray, you looked like a ghost out there."

"I warned you."

"You did. But can you blame me for not believing you?"

"I was being honest with you, Mandi. I don't see why I have to give a reason for everything I do or don't do. I spent the past two years without any explanation from you."

He had her there. She pulled up her knees and wrapped her arms around them.

"Leaving wasn't easy for me. It was something I knew I had to do. You don't understand how hard or scary it is to leave everything you have ever known behind to try to start a new life on your own. But I did it and it took courage. It took courage to leave you and to survive missing you."

"I do know what that's like. But you have no idea what you put me through. I'm not talking about dealing with all the attention around here. I'm talking about ripping me apart, Mandi. You were everything to me."

"Was I? Then why didn't you want to share our engagement with the world? Why wouldn't you let me put our photo and announcement in the newspaper?"

"Because I'm camera shy."

"Give me a break. There you go again."

"It's a fact."

"How is it that you know what it's like to leave everything behind? What did you leave behind when you moved here? *Who* did you leave behind? Did she break your heart? Clear your bank account?"

"For God's sake, no. I've been as honest as I can be with you, Mandi. I told you that I've never loved anyone the way I loved you. What we had was real. And I would never have dreamed of holding you back. I always supported and encouraged your online studies and would have waited for you if you had told me you'd been accepted into that graduate program."

"Except that I never thought I'd actually get in and when I found out that I did, I knew it wouldn't be worth it to earn that degree only to come back here. I wanted more. A full career and life out there, and you made it clear you'd never move for me."

"You know, the world out there isn't all it's cracked up to be. You used to love it here. I don't know what changed. You used to talk about getting your degree so that you could help businesses in town and along the Outer Banks. You never mentioned wanting to live permanently somewhere like New York."

"Have you been there? Because if you have, you'd understand. There's a driving force there. An energy I can't quite explain. Incredible architecture. Old mixed with new and people from all around the world. It has everything."

"Never been, so I guess I'll never understand."

GRAY BIT THE INSIDE of his cheek. That *was* a lie. He'd been to New York, all right. He was born there, though his current birth certificate listed Denver, Colorado, as his birth city and state. Man, he hated lying to her.

"Why won't you leave Turtleback, if only for a road trip?"

"Work."

"So, if a vet from a nearby town was willing to exchange practice coverage with you so that you could take vacations, you'd do it?"

She was going to start running him in circles, the way she used to when they were engaged. He took a bracing breath.

"I didn't say that. I'm not having anyone else mess with my things at the office."

"I see. You get to pick and choose when I'm worth the risk. You just kayaked for me, but you were never willing to travel with me, even if you knew I was dying to explore new places with you."

He stood up, took off his life vest and began moving the kayak toward the cottage.

"That's very typical of you. That's the reason behind my giving up on us. When you don't want to answer or discuss something, your solution is to switch subjects or walk away."

"Maybe you should learn the art of backing off. It might come in handy when you're pitching advertising plans to those big client contracts."

"Not funny. I know boundaries and when to back off." She unbuckled her vest and picked up the oars, then trudged after him. "This conversation's not over. You can't just walk off like that."

"Watch me." He left the kayak under the house decking and started walking down the beach toward the lighthouse. She dropped the oars by the kayak and hurried after him.

"For once give me a straight, believable answer."

She was relentless, but he knew just how to end this. He turned on his heel and gave her a twisted smile.

"I'm heading home to shower," he said.

That's all it took. She stopped in her tracks and her face flushed the moment she realized that maybe she should stop following him.

"I didn't realize you were heading home.

Your Triumph is parked in front of the cottage," she said, trying to recover.

"I'm covered in sand. I'll come back for her later. No way am I risking a scratch on my girl."

His girl. The one on two wheels. Not Mandi. Not anymore.

# CHAPTER SIX

JOHN PARKED OUTSIDE the four-foot-high picket fencing and gate that ran across the front of Grayson's place. A sign nailed to the gate read Private Property, to keep tourists from thinking the Turtleback Lighthouse and corresponding caretaker's cottage were sightseeing attractions, like the lighthouses in other towns along the Outer Banks. Lighthouses that drew tourists, thereby boosting the town economy. This place was being wasted.

He grunted at the gate and started to walk along the fence until it ended abruptly against an oleander tree. It served as nothing more than a deterrent for passersby and would be the first thing he'd get rid of. He didn't care if the Historic Lighthouse Preservation Act allowed for private ownership or that the town board had approved its sale and restoration plans, submitted by the good vet. This place should be open to the public. The town deserved it. It needed it. And the one board vote that had made the difference had been his mother's and she was no longer here.

Getting on that board himself was on his to-do list. But he needed to plan carefully. The first order of business was to convince Mandi to listen to him for once. He knew what was best for her. Mandi would give in sooner or later and agree to sell the cottage to him, especially if Coral managed to...discourage...any other interested buyers. Then would come Grayson's share. He needed to do some digging. Oh, he'd done it before, back when the man had the nerve to propose to Mandi, but nothing had come up. His connections had reported that Grayson didn't have a criminal record, not so much as a speeding ticket, no past marriages, and held a legitimate veterinary license. All the usual stuff had checked out. But there was something about the guy that John didn't like, apart from the fact that he had convinced Mandi to marry him at too young of an age.

Grayson Zale was a player. Ever since

Mandi left, John had seen him with just about every eligible girl in town—hanging out wherever they worked, the bakery, bookstore, gas station and the grill. He probably had something going on with those ladies at his office, too. John would prove Zale was a lying cheat, even if it meant seeing how far Coral could get flirting with him. Mandi would find it all very interesting. He wasn't doing this to hurt her, though. He was doing it to protect her. He didn't want her throwing away her chance at this career in New York for someone who might someday leave town as quickly as he had appeared. Just like Audra had done to him.

He had a few more contacts. It was handy having people beholden to you—the perfect reward for doing small favors over the years. Being nice just for the heck of it was a load of bull. It was an art. As a business-minded man, he knew full well that everyone had an agenda. Having people owe him favors didn't make him greedy. It made him smart. People who believed folks did things for them without payback in mind needed to get their heads out of utopia. That kind of behavior had never gotten him anywhere. He had served in local politics. He knew how life worked. The difference in how generous people had been toward him while he was mayor versus after his term ended had been blatant. Even as a kid, not being aggressive in school had only gotten him bullied. Over the years, he had been generous to his classmates, townsfolk, his wife and, of course, to his mother, but had nothing to show for it. He didn't have many close friends, other than Coral. His wife had left him. His mother had always been critical of him, then went and humiliated him with her will. Even Mandi, his own daughter, rarely called him or visited. But that would change. He was going to make sure she knew that her father was the only person left in her life whom she could truly trust and count on.

He passed under the tree, scanned the property and started for the 150-foot black-and-white tower. Grayson's motorcycle was parked by the keeper's cottage, but his truck wasn't anywhere to be seen, nor was that dog of his barking. It wouldn't hurt to look around. He might come across something that could help him figure out the best way to get Grayson to sell his share of Nana's house. He had no doubt that once he was the owner and his plans for the cottage and surrounding beach were under way, the noise and traffic alone would help him to pressure Grayson into letting him take this pitiful place off his hands, too. After all, with all those animals to take care of at his clinic, he'd never be able to find the time to invest in restoring the lighthouse. This place was a burden to him. Grayson Zale would understand that soon enough.

GRAY THRUMMED HIS fingers against his mug of coffee as he watched the security camera feed on his monitor. John Rivers jiggled the locked knob on the lighthouse, grimaced and headed straight for the caretaker's cottage, covering the one-hundred-foot distance at a brisk pace.

Gray shook his head, then gave Laddie, who was staring at the screen, ears perked and ready to charge, a reassuring pat on the head.

"What do you think, boy? I call out 'intruder' and you channel enough Cujo to make him wet his pants when he tries to walk in here and finds us waiting? Or should we go on out and get entertained by whatever excuse he has for prowling around?" Laddie went over to the door and waited. "You're right. Outside intercept. Less floor cleanup. And be nice. I was kidding about 'rabid hell dog.'"

He took a swig of coffee, set the mug down with purpose and was at the door in two long strides. He hardened his face, then swung the door open fast enough to catch John off guard. The older man's expression was priceless.

"Grayson. I didn't know you were home. I mean, I was hoping you were. Your truck wasn't here, but since your motorcycle was, I thought I'd check."

Right. His truck was getting inspected at the gas station, but that was beside the point. And nobody's business. Laddie positioned his body in front of Gray.

"John." Gray cranked his neck to one side till it gave a pop, then squared his shoulders and stood akimbo, blocking his doorway. "You got sand in your shoes getting here. Must be important."

John frowned and looked down at his shoes.

"Oh. You mean because the gate's closed. Yes, yes. I assume it always is to keep out intruders. I knew you wouldn't mind *my* going around the side of the fence and knocking on your door. After all, we *were* almost family."

Gray raised one brow and folded his arms.

"Almost. What can I help you with? Finally gave in and adopted a dog or cat?"

"Heck no. I mean, it wouldn't be fair to them. I'm not home enough."

It wouldn't be fair to them for a host of other reasons. The disgusted look on John's face said enough.

"Well. There's that. Besides, what was I thinking? You would have come to my clinic. So what gives? Missed me? We both know there's no love lost between us, so this can't be a social call."

John gave Laddie a look.

"It's not. I came by to let you know that Mandi wants to sell me her share of my mother's house—she's pretty relieved about getting it off her hands. I know you need to agree to the sale and I'll pay you the same price for your share. I'm sure you want what's best for Mandi, and you know she doesn't live here anymore. It would behoove you both to sell. After all, you have this place to take care of and you must be overwhelmed with the restorations as it is. In fact, I don't see much work being done around here."

"I like to work from the inside, out. After all, appearances aren't everything." He was sure the insult flew over John's narcissistic head. The part about his daughter bugged him, though. "When exactly did Mandi agree to your offer?"

John looked quickly over his shoulder before answering.

"Recently," he muttered. "So, I take it you're interested, then?"

Gray examined the sky. There were quite a few clouds building up today. Temps were nice. His jaw itched. He scratched it. Much better. He squinted at John and shrugged.

"Nope. Not interested."

"Don't be ridiculous, Grayson," John said. The creases on his ruddy, sun-damaged skin deepened with each breath he took. "I'm paying market value. Have you no financial sense? Maybe if you had any, you'd have been able to afford a better lifestyle and vehicle…and a nicer clinic."

"I'm pretty happy with how things are. Goodbye, John."

"But I need both—"

Everything was always about what John needed. The world revolved around him. That was his biggest mistake in life, but he was so fixed as the center of his world that he was no different from people long ago who couldn't comprehend that Earth wasn't the center of the universe. He had yet to learn that accumulating wealth and satisfying his material desires were akin to trying to fill a black hole. A person's life and everything in it could disappear in a flash. Gray knew that all too well. Which made giving—rather than greed—the only worthwhile way to live one's life, while they had it. He only wished he could truly give Mandi what she needed and wanted from him.

"It takes two. You're right about that. Now, either I can show you to the gate, or my dog would be happy to."

John huffed, scowled and marched off. He bypassed the gate when he remembered it was locked, stomped through the sand around the tree and slammed his car door shut with more force than necessary.

Gray let out a long whistle and let his shoulders relax, though his jaw ached. Just how recently had Mandi spoken to her dad? Before or after Gray had agreed to help her fix the place? Or had John been bluffing? Playing one against the other. That was certainly his style.

"Come on, boy. We have some painting to do."

MANDI TOOK DOWN the painting she'd done back in eighth grade of a quiet marshland with a storm rolling in. She never understood why her grandma had bothered to frame it and hang it in her breakfast nook, but it had been there all these years. Until now.

She leaned it against the wall in the living room, then hung a dry-erase board she'd found at the local hardware and house supply store in its place.

"Perfect." She had this. Efficiency was her middle name and her knack for plotting and planning was the reason why she'd finished college with awesome grades and had landed her first job as if it had been waiting for her. She uncapped a dry-erase marker and went at it, switching colors according to each task.

A tap at the balcony door had her jumping and streaking a line of green right across the board.

"Look what you did."

Gray stood with Laddie at the glass and shook his head as he slid the door open.

"I must say, that's some work of art." Gray scratched the side of his nose and failed to hide his smile.

"Very funny." Mandi gave Laddie a pat on the head before taking a washcloth to the streak. "I'll have you know my methods work."

Gray pointed to a bucket of tools and paint scrapers he'd left outside.

"So do mine. It's called getting to work."

"Having a plan and a list makes the actual work go more smoothly," Mandi insisted.

Gray walked up to the board and cocked his head.

"It's not done yet," Mandi said. She'd gotten the days of the week, time of day and the to-do list for two of the days written in. The rest was still blank.

"What happens if it's raining over here

where you have 'paint front porch' down on Wednesday at ten? Or the power goes out on Saturday at two, when you plan to vacuum floors inside?"

"Then I'll switch two tasks to accommodate the situation."

"Or you could skip all this and dig in. Play it by ear."

"There are these funny things called forecasts you can check online. I'll adjust the schedule as needed."

Gray laughed.

"You really have been gone a while if you've forgotten how unpredictable the rains are around here. We haven't had an accurate forecast in… I don't know…ever?"

"You're right. I've been gone so long I've forgotten how annoying you can be."

"Come on, Mandi. It's obvious what needs to be done. Writing a plan isn't going to accomplish more than digging in will."

"Creative advertising is a big part of selling a house. I have a degree in that field, and drawing or plotting out a plan and ideas is fundamental to success. The place needs to be cleaned up and staged to appeal to buyers. This was all your idea. You said you wanted top dollar and I'm trying to get us that. Plus, I only have a little over a week here, so I need to be sure to get things done. We can't take our time doing this the way you can with your place. Your other place, I mean."

"I see. Funny how John commented on the same thing. Was my property and how slow it's coming along the topic of conversation with your father earlier today? When you promised him the place?"

"What? I haven't promised him anything. The last conversation I had about this house was with you. What did my father say to you?"

"Don't worry about it. He was obviously trying to manipulate us. Caught him snooping around my place and when I confronted him, he tried convincing me to sell to him."

Mandi closed her eyes briefly. Of all the nerve. She set down her marker and walked outside. He joined her.

"I assure you, Gray, I won't make a deal with anyone unless you're present, and I'd hope you wouldn't either. Can we agree on that?"

"I have no issue with that. You're the one who is in a rush to sell."

She picked up a paint scraper from the bucket and slapped it gently against her palm.

"All I ever wanted was for you to be honest and open with me. If you can promise me that, then we'll survive working together on this place."

Something shifted in Gray's face. He took the scraper from her and began clearing the cracked paint off the back railing.

"I'm an honest man, doing an honest day's work. Trust me, Mandi. Nobody knows me better than you do. And nobody ever will."

Was that an answer or a promise? A lump rose in her throat and she swallowed hard against it. She wanted to believe him but did she dare?

She kept scraping, wondering if she should tell him about the journal she had found. Maybe not. Considering what he'd said about boundaries. Maybe sharing Nana's journal with him would be disrespecting hers.

"How long are you free to work on the house today?" she asked.

"Most of the afternoon." He set down his scraper and shaded his eyes as he looked up at the second story. "I'll be right back. I know Nana has a long ladder. I should get a lot of the scraping and prep-work done on the second story while I'm here. If we're lucky and have time, we can start some painting. You can start prepping the ground floor."

"Is that sexist? I'm not afraid of heights."

"I don't care if it is or isn't. I'm not having you fall off a ladder from the second story. Let's just say you're more stable on water than you are on land. You were at the helm with the kayak, so we can call it even."

"Fine," she said, but she was willing to bet he was splitting up and doing the upper story because it would be harder for her to prod him with questions when he was up there. She opened up the smaller A-frame ladder and set it up so that she could scrape the upper part of the casing around the balcony door. Gray returned with the other ladder and extended and secured the moveable section until it reached high enough for him to strip and prime the trim near the eaves. They kept at it until the trim on both levels was ready for paint. He filled two small containers from the first gallon can she had bought and handed her one. "This will save you from having to go up and down your ladder to load your brush." He grabbed a brush and started to climb.

"I know."

She took the other brush and started up her A-frame, snagging the tip of her sneaker on the third rung from the bottom and losing her footing. She yelped and caught the nearest railing to steady herself, just as she heard something clatter against the decking and felt Gray's arm wrap around her waist. He set her down rather quickly, but the touch of his hands lingered.

"And that's why I don't want you on the extension ladder," he said, looking back at the mess he'd made. She had managed to keep her hold on her paint container and brush. Gray, on the other hand, had dropped his in order to "save" her. The decking where his supplies had fallen didn't look so good.

"I was about to catch myself on the railing. I would have been fine. It could have happened to anyone, even you."

"You're welcome." He shook his head at the mess.

"Thank you. Really." She set her paint and brush down. She wasn't trying to be ungrateful. He had always been attentive and chivalrous in the past, but it had been so long since they'd hung around each other like this, his protective reaction was unexpected. She didn't know how to react given they weren't a couple anymore. "I'll get some rags and clean up."

"The wood will still hold the color. We could paint the balcony floor the same as the railing, after we finish with the trim, just in case you end up catching me next time," he added, for good measure. She smiled and shook her head. As if she'd be able to support his fall, although the thought of having an excuse to wrap her arms around him was nice.

Her heartstrings were beginning to tangle like her wild, windblown hair the first day she ever met him, and it had taken her two years to loosen the knots. Grayson Zale was getting to her. She blamed her loss of footing on being distracted by him. He was dangerous to her peace of mind. Dangerous to her freedom. Like moments before a lightning strike, there was a charge in the air whenever she was near him. But she knew that letting herself so much as wade in shallow waters with him was as good as diving in deep with sharks. Because when it came to a man like Grayson Zale, it was all or nothing.

## CHAPTER SEVEN

MANDI YAWNED BUT pain stopped her mid-stretch. Her upper arms felt like she'd been punched in each. Who knew scraping and painting could be that much of a workout? She let her arms flop back down on the bed and winced as she rolled over onto her side. How much more painting had she listed on her dry-erase board for today? She moaned.

Painting in and of itself wasn't hard. It wasn't anything like creating a scene on canvas, but the easy rhythm of sweeping the brush back and forth was meditative. And the almost instant impact of a fresh coat of paint on a banister, trim or wall was gratifying. However, when it came to holding one's arm overhead, like when she was scraping trim she could barely reach using the A-frame ladder or when she painted the ceiling of the front porch overhang, it amounted to lifting free weights all afternoon.

The dawn sky filled her bedroom window with energizing shades of watermelon tourmaline. She eased out of bed and made her way to the bathroom. Man, she really didn't realize how much studying and desk work had melted her muscles away. She used to be fit. Walking just about everywhere in town and jogging daily on a beach, with sand giving way with each step, had built muscles in her thighs she didn't even know she had back when she lived here. She'd taken that exercise for granted. It didn't feel like exercise with the waves crashing and salty breeze blowing around you. She had access to a gym in New York, but motivating herself to go work out in a closed-in, crowded space like that had proved impossible. No wonder Nana had lived well into her eighties. She woke up to this sun and beach every day. It was life-giving.

She splashed cold water on her face but what she really craved was a rich cup of coffee. No bells or frills. Just the coffee Nana used to brew, which was so good anything added to it would have been sacrilege. It was a specific bean she came across once on a trip to Africa. Something about volcanic soil.

The sun was now peeking over the watery horizon, shooting a beam of light across the living room that reflected off the wall mirror. Mandi stood on a chair and rummaged through the cabinet above the coffee maker. An unopened bag of coffee sat behind a container of loose tea. She took it out and stepped down from the chair. Kenya. That was where Nana had said she'd gotten her coffee.

A dog barked once, just as Mandi set the machine to brew. She looked outside the deck door. Laddie was trotting after Gray, who was carrying nest-marking supplies.

Turtle nests. She used to go in search of them with Gray on mornings like this. It had been her favorite time of day. Quiet. Peaceful. The two of them alone or with Nana along for the search.

She sucked on her lower lip and tucked her hair behind her ear. A part of her wanted to join him but she wasn't sure she'd be welcome with this whole knowing-her-boundaries comment from him. Things had changed over the years. She'd be an intruder now. She didn't belong down there with Gray and his dog...feeling the cool sand beneath her feet...experiencing the exhilarating excitement of spotting a new nest and the pure joy of setting up stakes and tape to mark a safe area around them, knowing you were doing something so pure of heart there were no words for it. Saving a helpless life.

She rubbed her arms and went to fill a mug. The first sip eased down her throat and warmed her chest. It was pure sin. Two sips later and she could feel it in her veins. She glanced outside again, not because she was spying on Gray, but because the sunrise was beautiful. She took another sip. *You're such a liar, Mandi. Just go. You can ask him about the kittens if you need a reason.*

"Okay, fine. This is stupid. I can drink coffee and walk outside on a beach in front of my house without it having anything to do with Gray being out there."

She stepped outside and took a deep breath, not because of nerves but because her lungs demanded it. The air here couldn't be denied. No fumes or smog or trash odors emanating from the alleys behind restaurants.

"I hope Laddie's bark didn't wake you," Gray called out, as he finished taping off a nest area.

It hadn't taken him long to spot her. Had he been eyeing the place? Maybe even hoping she'd come outside?

"Not at all. I was up and making coffee. Want some?"

"Definitely. Thanks."

She went back in and hurried to find a mug. Why she was hurrying, she didn't quite know. Coffee sloshed onto the counter as she tried to steady her hand while pouring. *Chill, girl.* It was just a cup of coffee for goodness' sake. She paused to ground herself. *Your heart's not racing because of Gray. It's from the caffeine in Nana's special coffee.*

Yeah. That was it. Totally.

She took both mugs outside and made her way across the thirty feet of sand to where he was at a leisurely, carefree, relaxed pace.

"Thanks," he said. His hand touched hers as he took the mug and every nerve end-ing that made contact triggered a flood of memories.

"Sure. It's nothing. Just coffee."

"Thanks anyway." He gave her an odd look.

Laddie circled her twice, then stood in front of her wagging his tail. She kissed the collie on the head and scratched his neck.

"He's good about not eating the eggs? Or hatchlings?"

"I trained him on leash at first. He was well trained, but I had to teach him the nests were not toys. He actually sniffs them out for me now, without disturbing them. He wouldn't harm a fly, but when hatch dates come around, I keep him inside. It's to avoid excitement for him and stress for the babies. He'd probably try to round them back up to the nests while they're headed for the water. I have had to post signs for tourists to keep their dogs on leash, though, because of the nests. Most dogs would destroy them."

"Makes sense," Mandi said.

Gray drank some coffee, and the way his eyes closed briefly said it all.

"Wow. You found Nana's stash. Takes me back," he said.

"I did. And it does."

"You remember doing this?" He motioned toward the nest he'd found.

"Yes, I do. I kind of miss it."

"Well, while you're here, you're welcome to join us."

She smiled without giving a definite response. She wanted the invite, didn't she? Reassurance that she wasn't an intruder? Then why did his saying it suddenly put her on the spot? She followed him farther down the dunes, looking toward the sand for more signs of nesting.

"Have the past few years been good in terms of nest numbers?" she asked.

"They've been okay. The town lights are still an issue and I can't cover all the nests around here alone. We had a shortage of nest-sitters in general all along the Outer Banks last year. And then there were a few cold-stunned adults at the beginning of last winter. The cold hit too soon and they hadn't made their way to warmer waters fast enough."

"All you can do is your best."

This time he didn't respond right away.

He let her fall in step and they kept walking in silence while sipping coffee.

"I suppose that's all anyone can do at any given time," he said.

They walked a little farther. Mandi wanted to ask more but was afraid he'd put up a wall if she said the wrong thing.

"Why a beach town if you don't like going out on the water? Why did you decide to set up shop here?" she finally asked.

He took a sip of coffee. She should have kept it to one question.

"The people." She'd never heard that from him before. "This town is like one giant extended family. I mean, look at how our friends were so quick to gather in support the other night. And the thoughtful gestures. There's a lot of heart in this place. Nana said that to me shortly after my move here, and she was right. As for the turtles, they're here and I'm here. I've always loved them, ever since I was a kid. The way most kids like dinosaurs. Sea turtles are extraordinary, beautiful and fascinating. That migration they take? Taking off on that journey, hundreds or even thousands of miles, from foraging to nesting grounds the way they do. Surviving on instinct. It's really something else. The more I learned about them the more I wanted to help. I care about all species preservation, but this is where I can try to make a difference."

He actually mentioned that he had loved them as a kid. Maybe she could ask him about—

"I should head back. I have patients to see this morning, but I'll help with the house this afternoon. Don't go climbing the long ladder."

The man must have read her mind and decided on an escape. She rolled her eyes at his ladder remark.

"Seriously, Mandi. And I didn't mean that as an order. You know that. I simply don't want you having an accident. Okay?"

"I'm not going to have an accident. Why are you always so paranoid about accidents and danger? Ever since we met, in fact."

"Please, Mandi. Can you just give me that peace of mind?"

"Can't you ever give me a simple freaking answer without me having to pull teeth?"

"Yes," he said, with more force than necessary. "I've known people who suffered severe accidents. I don't want that happening to you. Is that simple and clear enough?"

His tone warned her not to ask for specifics.

"Okay. There's plenty to do that doesn't require heights."

"Good. Guess I'll see you later. Thanks again for the coffee." He handed her the mug and she made sure their fingers didn't touch this time.

"Sure. Later."

She watched as he hurried off with Laddie. She'd almost said "anytime" but caught herself. There would never be "anytime" between them. Less than two weeks and she'd be gone, trading the relaxing sound of ocean waves for city taxis honking their horns impatiently. She'd be grabbing coffee at a street-corner kiosk on her way to work. Her dreams would be coming true very soon. She needed to remember that.

"OH, DR. ZALE. I've been looking for you. I stopped by the clinic and they said you'd left for the day." Coral had one of those voices that made Gray's eardrums ache, not because it was particularly high-pitched, though she did hit rather grating notes and had a way of singing words that weren't meant to be sung. Like his name.

He put on his professional face before turning on the sidewalk in front of the bank to face her. She walked with a slight limp but managed to reach him on a pair of strappy heels that, given the sand and old streets around town, had *bad idea* written all over them. She fanned the low neckline of her blouse and looped her arm in his the second she reached him.

"Coral. I'm kind of in a hurry. Anything important?" He looked around uncomfortably and held his captive arm away from his body but she still managed to close the gap.

"I'm so sorry, but I think I hurt my ankle in these shoes while trying to catch up to you. Can we sit for just a minute? I won't keep you long."

He reluctantly guided her to the closest street bench, about two shops down. At least if she sat, she wouldn't be clinging to him.

She crossed her legs, dangling the injured one in his direction, and rubbed her hand up and down her calf. Gray hadn't felt this uncomfortable around a woman since that college professor in his freshman year who'd flirted with him enough that he ended up dropping the class. At the time, he had been too young and inexperienced to know how to handle the situation.

"If you're really hurt, Dr. Bayar's office is only two doors down. I'm not the kind of doctor you're looking for."

She slapped his arm playfully.

"I know that, silly. I'll have you walk me there in a moment. But first, I was up in Duck today showing a condo to a guy looking for a vacation place. He wasn't sold on it, but then I mentioned that there might be a property coming on the market in Turtleback and he said he'd be interested in checking it out."

"I see."

"Do you? Oh, good. I mean the house you just inherited would be perfect for him."

Gray tried to add a little distance between them.

"Half of a house. And I never said I was selling. Besides, we're a long way from Duck and we're a very different kind of town. Why would this guy want to come down this way or get a Realtor this far south?"

The whole thing made the hairs on the back of his neck prickle, but he knew he was overreacting. People looked for homes along the Outer Banks all the time and Coral wouldn't have an income if she limited her zone to one tiny town.

"Well, John mentioned to me that Mandi wanted to sell, so—"

"Now, *that* I do find interesting. I thought John wanted the place for himself, so why would you of all people want to bring in competition?"

Her cheeks flushed and she uncrossed her leg.

"I was only trying to be nice and give you options. Think about it and let me know."

"As I said, I'm in a hurry, but thanks for the info." Gray stood and she followed suit, without the help of his arm.

"You have my number." She headed down the street to where her red convertible was parked…right past Dr. Bayar's office and without a limp.

Gray scrubbed his face with one hand, then raked his hair back. None of this felt right. Not some guy interested in a house that wasn't even on the market yet. Not

Coral undermining John. And especially not Gray himself letting Mandi think he was on board with putting the house on the market, when the fact was that he was trying to get her to change her mind. The more time he spent with her the more he realized that, even if she left and never returned again, he couldn't sell the house. It held too many memories and he couldn't in good conscience put the nesting ground at risk. No one could guarantee that new owners would take the same care Nana had. No one. That was why he had just checked in with the bank to see what kind of loan he'd qualify for if Mandi still insisted on selling and he had no choice but to buy her out. So much for being forthright and honest with her.

She didn't want diamonds and rubies in life, though the ring he'd almost put on her finger still sat in his safe at the bank. *Honesty.* What she wanted didn't cost a penny, yet it was priceless. And he couldn't afford to give it to her.

MANDI WAS PRETTY sure she was part hound when it came to sugar. She knew when Darla was pulling out a fresh batch of cream cheese kolaches from the oven, and resistance was futile. Besides, she both needed and had earned a break. She'd gone through most of the closets and all of the kitchen cabinets—none of which contained the first journal—and then she delivered a huge load of clothes and household items to a drop-off center for a women's and children's shelter. There was so much she wanted to keep and she did hang on to the most sentimental items, but she knew in her heart of hearts that her grandmother would have wanted her belongings to help others.

She closed her eyes and strained to keep from crying. *Not now. Not again.* As empathetic as Nana was, when it came to crying she had one rule: if it involved self-pity, she had no time for it. She would be telling Mandi to suck it up, right now, because this *was* self-pity. She missed her grandmother, and every other box or cabinet she'd gone through today had triggered an overwhelming heaviness, as if she was getting sucked down to the bottom of the ocean by a whirlpool. She was exhausted. She needed to sit and eat sugar with a friend. Bad stress-coping habit or not.

She dried her eyes, blew her nose and opened the door to The Saltwater Sweetery.

"Hey, girl. I didn't think I'd see you so soon," Darla said from behind the counter.

"I knew I smelled kolaches. If I gain weight while I'm here, it's all your fault."

"Come to yoga class with me. It's how I cope with temptation and self-control. Do you have any idea how dangerous it is to be in a bakery all day?"

"You have the willpower of a saint. I'm not even going to pretend that I do. That said, I'll take two of those. Make it three. One for tomorrow morning. No wonder I used to run every day when I lived here. I had to."

She pulled out a chair and waited for Darla to join her.

"Trust me. You have nothing to worry about with that figure of yours," Darla said. "Listen, I'm glad you stopped by. I was hoping I could talk to you about the last time you were here and I told Gray we were planning a bonfire. I was under the impression that you were thinking I was interested *in him* and had to cover up when he walked in."

"I was. Aren't you?"

"No! Rest assured, I'm not."

"I don't need assurance. It would be fine with me. I mean, we're not together anymore."

"Mandi, I'm not interested. But you're here and I wanted to talk to you about—"

The store chime rang and, of all people, Mandi's father waltzed in. The corner of Darla's mouth twisted.

"We'll talk later. I'll go bag your third kolache. Hi, Mr. Rivers. Can I get you anything?"

"No, no. I saw Mandi through the window and needed to have a word."

He took one of the two pastries on Mandi's dish, without asking, and bit in.

"Mmm. This is good."

Mandi simply smiled and exchanged looks with Darla.

"What's up, Dad?"

"Let's sit outside."

"It's really hot out right now and I just sat down. Why don't you pull up a chair?"

"Mandi, I'd like to sit outside. Join me." His mouth was set firm and she suddenly felt like she was in middle school all over again. Darla frowned at her from behind the counter.

"Sure. After you," Mandi said, slinging her purse on her shoulder and picking up her plate to carry out to one of the bistro tables Darla had lining the sidewalk.

"It's not that hot," John said. "Sunshine like this feeds the soul. I hear folks don't get enough of it up north. They end up with seasonal affective disorder or something like that. Fancy term for depression." He put his sunglasses on and sat down.

Mandi had an urge to tell him she was less depressed up north than when she was around him.

"Sit."

For goodness' sake. She wasn't a dog. She was in the process of sitting. She literally had one hand on the back of the iron chair and the other was setting her plate down on the table. If patience was inherited, it had clearly skipped a generation.

"What's up, Dad?"

"I wanted to see how you were doing. I know the funeral had to have been hard on you."

She wasn't in the mood to share feelings. "How are you holding up?" She deflected his question with the skill she'd learned from Gray.

"I'll be okay. When a parent passes a certain age, it becomes a matter of time. Each day is a blessing. I knew I'd have to face losing her sooner or later."

The guilt that had been gnawing at her for not being around Nana more before she passed away suddenly switched gears. She had always gone out of her way to avoid spending too much time with her father. He was judgy, overbearing and made her feel "less than." Who would willingly stick around a toxic relationship? But he was right. He was her father. The only close family she had left.

"Plenty of people live well past the century mark. Nana was thriving and healthy the last time I saw her. How can you make it sound like no big deal?"

"That wasn't my intention. You asked how I was doing and I told you. Maybe the way I think about it is how I deal with it. Logic and reality. We all know none of us can live forever. My clock is ticking, too."

Her head did a quick spin and she sank back in her chair.

"Are you sick, Dad? This whole clock-ticking thing. Is that what you're trying to tell me?" Her mind backtracked the minute the words came out. If he was dying, then why would he be so determined to buy the house?

"No, sweetheart. But it means a lot to me to see that you care. I'm not getting any younger and you're all I have left. A person reaches a point in their life when they realize that not that many people have their best interest at heart. Everyone out there has an agenda. Trust becomes a luxury."

She wasn't sure where he was going with this but she lost her appetite and nudged the plate away.

"Why do you want to buy Nana's house so badly?"

"To keep it in the family. You know I never trusted that veterinarian of yours."

"But Nana did."

"I have no idea what she was thinking, unless he played her like he plays all the women around here," John said, with a deliberate look of disgust on his face. "No one can manipulate *me* like that. You, Mandi, are my sole inheritor. I know you can't handle the property right now, with your new career on your hands, but I'm experienced at all this. If I own the house, it stays in the family. I die, and you inherit it. The entire place. Not just half of it. And by then, the value will have gone up. It's called thinking smart and planning right. If I buy it now, you'll make money on it later." He slapped a hand on the edge of the table and gave her a smug nod. He'd made his point and had the final word. In his mind, there was never any hole in his logic and no one could outsmart him.

She chewed the inside of her cheek and picked at the drop of dry paint on her jeans. It irritated the heck out of her when he made sense. He had upped his game since sending Coral out to talk to her after the funeral. She knew he was playing psychology and wanted to convince her to sell, but he was also right. He was laying out a financially brilliant plan, one in which he technically wasn't loaning her money because he knew she'd never take it. But the whole thing betrayed Gray and went against Nana's wishes.

Gray's concerns with John buying the place were well founded. Her dad had a track record for bulldozing old places and rebuilding in the name of profit. What sounded financially prudent also made her feel like a selfish traitor. It would make her no different than her father, putting money above all else. But making more profit would also mean having extra money to donate to wildlife causes, as Nana had done. Assuming her father didn't betray her and sell the cottage or develop the plot once he had it under his control.

"How would you assure me that you'd leave the place as is?"

"We can put it in writing. Trust me on this, Mandi."

"I don't know. I need to consider why Nana wrote her will the way she did," Mandi said.

"I'll tell you why. First, because she never believed in me. Her own son. Second, because, like I said, that Grayson has always had a slick side to him. He proved it when he thought it would be okay to date you when you were only twenty"

"Twenty is more than old enough to date."

"He was six years older. That's a big gap when you're only twenty and you haven't even left town for college. And then marrying only three years later? I tried to warn you about it. You finally came to your senses when you called off the wedding. I was so proud of you for standing up for yourself that day. And when I saw how he was when you weren't around, I knew you'd made the right choice."

Her father, proud of her? John Rivers acknowledging her strength?

"What do you mean how he was?"

"I mean how he enjoyed the attention of other girls in town. That chick at the bookstore. Even your friends. He never went after you. If you had really meant everything to him, he would have gone after you."

"The way you went after my mother when she left?"

His neck reddened. She felt sick to her stomach. Was her dad making things up? He could manipulate. She knew that. But even she had seen the way some women around town looked at Gray. Was her dad being honest for once?

"Don't be disrespectful. You were too young to know what really went on between your mother and me. I tried to get her to stay…to not leave us. I offered her the world…a house, money…everything she wanted."

*But not what she needed.* Unless Mandi had made wrong assumptions. Relationships did take two. She accepted her own role in her failed relationship with Gray. She had been the one who needed more…the one who left.

"Sorry. I know that." She did because she trusted Nana and she knew from her that he'd also tried to get her mom to come back after she left town. That was the reason why Mandi had never contacted her mother. She had zero desire to know where she was or what she was doing with her life. If she had cared enough about her child, she would have returned, if only to visit. Gray, however, had never come after her. Only, she couldn't blame him after the very public way she'd left him.

"You've got to be kidding me." Her father glared right past her about five shops down on the other side of the street. Mandi started to turn around. "Don't look, sweetheart. You'll only get upset."

She spun around in her chair.

What in the world? Gray was walking with Coral, who was practically plastered against him with her arm in his. They sat on a bench and she was caressing her leg in front of him. He certainly didn't seem to mind. Mandi turned back and gave her dad a sympathetic look, though her stomach roiled and her head buzzed. She couldn't believe he'd gone to this length to manipulate her, but she felt even more unsettled by the fact that seeing Gray with anyone—even if she knew this whole this was a setup—bothered her.

"I'm sorry you had to see that, Dad. I was under the impression that you and Coral were dating. I see what you mean about trust." She waited for him to pick up on her sarcasm. This…this was why Nana had never trusted him.

"Exactly." John did a double take and pursed his lips the second it dawned on him that she hadn't mentioned Gray. She'd turned the table on him, but he persisted. "I mean, no. I'm upset for you. Don't you see who she's with, Mandi?"

When was she ever going to learn? She'd taken some psychology classes for her degree with the intent of better understanding the mind of a customer, but she had also learned that even as adults, people had a deep-seated need for parental approval. Everyone was in a constant search for unconditional love and trust. It didn't matter that she could process all of that on an intellectual level. Her dad could still get to her on an emotional one.

She stood and picked up her plate and napkin off the table.

"It was nice talking to you, Dad. I really have to go now, as soon as I take this in to the trash." She wished she could delete their entire conversation from her head…trash it like junk email.

"But wait. If you're upset about seeing Gray with someone and need to talk, I'm here for you. And think about what I said regarding Nana's—"

"For the record, Gray and I broke up long ago. I don't care who he dates and he couldn't care less if I have ten boyfriends up in New York. I know it must be harder for you, though, seeing Coral over there…considering your clock is ticking and all that. And from a financial standpoint—I did take a few classes in that subject area. Actually, I got a minor in it. I think I'll keep the house and rent it with Gray. That way, we can make money while we wait for the market to go up. I'll see you later. Take care of yourself. Make sure you're keeping your blood pressure under control. I hear that having a dog or cat can help with that."

She left him looking like he wanted to ground her for a week and disappeared into the bakery. She knew he wouldn't dare follow her in. Not unless he didn't care if everyone in the shop heard him carrying on. Obviously, she wasn't planning to rent. Renting wasn't a consideration, based on her initial conversation with Gray about not wanting the place to suffer at the hands of summer college kids, plus his aversion to the whole rental idea. He hated the idea of strangers living so close to the lighthouse all summer and invading his privacy, and she certainly wouldn't be around to deal with anyone who caused problems. But she couldn't resist putting her dad in his place.

She dumped her plate in the trash and went to the cash register, where Darla was finishing up with a customer.

"Hey, you don't look so good," Darla said.

"I'll be fine. Can you break a twenty? I don't have anything smaller to pay for the kolaches."

"You know I hate charging you. Don't worry about it."

"I insist. You already treated me and I need something to keep me from binging. I need the change anyway."

Darla took the twenty, handed her the bag with the extra pastry and made change.

"Why do you always do that, Mandi?"

"Do what?"

"Bow to his command. It's like you're a high schooler again. He insists on eating outside and that's that."

"I'm not that bad," Mandi sighed. "Maybe a little, but only because I pick my battles. I do call him out on things when necessary. I just did, in fact."

"But if you keep bottling up all that irritation and frustration, it's going to make your hair fall out. It's bad energy. Pushes each follicle from inside to out."

"Right. You take your yoga seriously. I still have my hair. I'm gonna run. Thanks for the comfort food."

"Anytime."

Darla came around the counter and gave her a hug before she left. Mandi shielded her eyes from the sun and tried not to look like she was scoping the street. Her father was gone and the bench where Gray and Coral had been sitting was vacant. She took long strides toward her car and wasted no time in turning the key. She couldn't handle seeing anyone else today. Not even Gray over the house reno.

She knew Coral was the last person on earth he'd start a relationship with. Mandi knew him that much and knew exactly how Coral got on his nerves. What scared her was the fact that seeing him with anyone at all had more than bothered her. It stirred something inside her that she didn't want to acknowledge. No way could she care that much. Caring that much and lying to her dad about it could only mean one thing. She'd never truly gotten over Gray.

# CHAPTER EIGHT

"I'M SO RELIEVED these kiddos made it through." Gray cradled the tortoiseshell kitten named Sandy. She climbed up his scrubs and nuzzled his neck.

"She's the one I'm taking home," Chanda said. "Consider us bonded. You can't separate us."

"Hear that, Sandy? You've got a home." He put her back in the crate and picked up Windy, with the white paws, and began taking her vitals. Storm pawed and meowed at the crate door.

"Those two are inseparable," Nora said. "They sleep curled up together and play even when Sandy is taking a nap. I'd hate to see them separated."

"Are you volunteering?" Gray asked, switching Windy out with Storm.

"Are you kidding? You've met my diva cat. She'd freak out if I brought another home. I tried once and lost a sofa over it. I warned you that I'd only be able to adopt one."

"Don't look at me," Gavin said, pulling surgical tools out of the autoclave. "Unfortunately, my dog's not cat friendly. That's why he ended up in a pound in the first place."

"I personally think our good doctor here ought to take Windy and Storm home to Mandi." Chanda grinned. "What girl would be able to resist a gift like that? Kittens are better than flowers."

"Hey. Flowers are fabulous," Nora said.

"Mandi isn't sticking around," Gray reminded them. "It isn't a good idea to give pets as gifts if you aren't sure the pet will be taken care of permanently. You know what happens to chicks and ducklings at Easter."

"You take them to her for now, and when she leaves, they become yours," Chanda suggested. "You have plenty of room for them to romp around, and Laddie would take his role as daddy very seriously, I'm sure. Mandi might even miss them and come back to visit them. Just saying." Chanda shook her finger at him before heading back to the front desk to check in an annual exam and shots.

"You're my office manager, not life manager," Gray called out after her. "Or relationship consultant," he muttered. He put Storm back and caught Gavin and Nora grinning at him. "Okay, she's probably right, but don't tell her I said that. I'll think about it. Right now, I have my hands full."

"He's totally going to take them home to her," Nora whispered to Gavin.

"I heard that," Gray said. He took the chart Chanda had just tucked in the wall holder and went past his office toward the first exam room.

This was his last patient for the afternoon, then he needed to spend a few hours with Mandi. Well, not with Mandi, per se, but working on the house. *Liar. You're wanting to spend time with her. Regular time. Not renovation time. Take the kittens to her. They'll soften her up.*

He backed up two steps and looked through the small window of his office door. Laddie was napping on the love seat. He was bored, poor guy. It was better than leaving him at home, and he got tons of attention from everyone between patients and at lunch, but Gray couldn't help but think that something was missing in his life. *Much like yourself.* Laddie needed a purpose. Smart dogs always needed work to do. A job. Maybe letting him bond with the kittens wasn't a bad idea.

Or better yet, what if he convinced Mandi to keep the kittens at Nana's place, since she was there most of the time and could keep an eye on them. If Laddie hung out with them, it would ease him into fatherhood and maybe help him get over Nana's loss. Dogs knew when someone passed away and Laddie had spent enough time with Nana to feel her absence. And having the kittens stay with Mandi, at least until her last day here, would give Gray even more reason to hang around Nana's with her. Wasn't that the point of getting her to spend time in Turtleback? To help her remember how special the town and its people were? To make her realize that the love they once shared had been a once-in-a-lifetime kind of love?

The bottom line was he knew he wanted her back in his life. The kittens were a long shot, but they were special to her. After all, she had saved them. Maybe they would help salvage any chance Gray had of ever winning her back again.

MANDI PUT A line through everything she had listed on the dry-erase board for today. She had gone through clothing, delivered donations and scrubbed and resealed the grout in all the bathrooms and the kitchen. She was hating grout like nobody's business at the moment. She even picked up new shower curtains and replaced the old ones. She didn't get much done outside, but there was always tomorrow.

She set a kettle on the stove for some tea and went into the living room in search of her watch. She'd taken it off and was sure she'd left it by the television, but it wasn't there. A rap sounded at the balcony door. Gray stood there holding a box with both hands. Laddie raised a paw and rapped at the glass again. That dog was uncanny.

She tried to temper the surge of excitement that coursed through her at the mere sight of them standing there. She opened the door and waved them in.

"Wait a minute. I heard something." She

looked at the box and the ragged holes cut into the top of it, then at Gray. "You didn't."

He set the box on the floor by the coffee table and opened it up.

"Surprise?" He gave her a pitiful, puppy-dog look and lifted the black and black-and-white kittens out of the box. "Look at these two. You know you want to hold them. They'll remember you…your scent. I'm betting they know you saved them."

She couldn't budge or talk as he held the adorable kittens out for her to take. She was cracking. She couldn't resist. She had to. *No. No. No.*

She gave in and cuddled them to her chest. The mewing and soft touch of their padded paws and fur was too much. Laddie stood at attention next to her, trusting, yet seemingly ready to take over parenting duty.

"You're killing me, Gray. This is not playing fair."

"Me? Not play fair? Technically, you're the one who started this."

"That's not fair either. I had to rescue them. And so did you. They've grown noticeably already. In just a matter of days. Where's Sandy?"

He reached over and freed a lock of her hair that Windy had snagged between her paws. Gray tucked it behind Mandi's ear for her. The gesture was sensitive and...too personal.

"Chanda took her home. These two were more closely bonded, maybe due to size and playfulness. Sandy was a lot smaller but she's gaining weight, too."

"But Gray, you can't expect me to adopt two kittens. I'm moving soon and they'd distract me if I take them to my apartment."

Gray laughed and took Windy from her. "Distract?"

"Yeah. Do you really think I'd be able to get work done at home with these two looking at me like they are right now?"

They wouldn't be as distracting as having Gray around here had been, but at least he knew how to fix a house. Kittens wouldn't be able to help her with projects assigned by the firm. Although, they would be nice to snuggle with. Gray was an excellent snuggler, too, but heaven help her, she wasn't going to think about that right now. Or ever.

"So, what you're really saying is that relaxing and playing with cute baby animals after a long day of work at the firm is not as appealing as bringing more work home with you at night? Man. Tough call."

Mandi plopped down cross-legged and Gray joined her. He leaned back on his palms and they let the babies explore the world between them.

"First, they won't be babies forever. Second, I do expect to work a little overtime. It's the nature of proving oneself at a new position. I'll be the underling. And it wouldn't be fair not to give them the attention they deserve."

"Cats are independent. They'll be fine spending time alone, once they're older."

Independent like her? Was that what he meant? That she'd be alone as she grew older?

"Are you setting me up to be an old cat lady?"

"That depends on how many you end up adopting. They're addictive. I hear New York apartment buildings are notorious for rodent problems. They'd earn their keep while staying entertained."

"Poor mice."

"Spoken like a true animal lover." That

earned him a smile. He shifted his weight slightly.

"Wish I'd brought my penlight," Gray said, off topic. He unhooked Windy's claws from the top of his shirt. That one was a climber.

"Oh. I can't find my watch. It was here somewhere. You could do a dancing reflection with it. It'll work almost as well as a penlight for them to pounce after. They'd love it."

Laddie walked right over to the console table by the door and came back with her watch dangling from his mouth by the band.

"Are you serious? What just happened? Your dog speaks English? Or are you really Dr. Dolittle? That must be why you hate talking about yourself. Special powers. We all know the government likes to kidnap and study people with special powers…like beings who land here from outer space."

"Yep, that's me. Trying to avoid lab testing at Area 51. You have found me out, dear Watson." Gray took the watch from Laddie. "Good boy." He angled the lens so a spot of light bounced on the floor. The kittens pounced on it as expected. "Honestly?

I don't know who his previous owner was, other than they passed away, but I think they may have needed the help of a service dog and trained him to do things like fetch the paper, the remote, a watch, etcetera. I realized a week into adopting him that he had a pretty impressive vocabulary."

"So you're not a Martian? Darn."

"You're into green men from Mars?"

"Why not?" she said, fluttering her lashes. A chuckle escaped her, but there was no humor in it. She stroked Storm's back and scratched under his chin. "You being from outer space would make more sense than the mere snippets of information you've ever shared with me about your past. Area 51 is all about keeping secrets."

"You make me sound like a vault. I'm not. You know all there is that's worth knowing about me. Besides, talking about the past is a waste of time. Learn to live in the moment."

"Our pasts are what shape us."

"In the moment, Mandi. Stop and be with me in this moment, right now. Just sitting here with Laddie and the kittens. Doing nothing but savoring each other's company, the way we used to. Give yourself this one moment."

Was he avoiding questions or was he right? She was always worrying so much about the past and future that, somewhere along the way, she had stopped enjoying moments like this.

Laddie lay down near them and let the kittens explore his belly.

"They're not going to find what they're looking for," Mandi said, keeping her eyes on the babies because she could feel Gray watching her. Everything felt right, though. Comfortable, the way hanging out with each other used to be.

"I don't think Laddie cares. Do you, Mr. Mom? I brought kitten milk, soft food and starter supplies. They're in my truck."

"Stepping out of the moment for a second, I really can't take—"

Gray held up a hand.

"I know. I don't expect you to take them to New York unless you want to. Laddie and I will take over after you leave. I just figured that with you here and me coming around daily to work on the place…"

"Okay."

"Okay?"

"Yeah. I'll watch over them while I'm here. You were right. They're hard to resist." He was hard to resist.

Gray reached out, took her hand in his, placed her watch against her palm and folded her fingers over it. She licked her lips and looked at him from beneath her lashes. It was such a rookie move, like a high schooler faking a stretch as an excuse to put his arm around a date's shoulders. Gray just wanted to touch her hands. She knew it…liked it… and let him. He leaned in and looked her in her eyes.

"I knew you'd say yes. You've always loved animals as much as I have," he said.

He was close enough to kiss her, but he got up abruptly and went over to her to-do list. Live in the moment? He was acting like that moment hadn't just happened between them. Mandi buckled the watch on her left wrist and joined him.

"You did all that today?" he asked.

"I told you having a list boosts efficiency."

"But what about stuff I'm planning to do?"

"I'm flexible. I moved painting until tomorrow and did the grout today instead. Take a look outside. How much painting are you really going to get done before dark?"

He raised a brow and studied the rest of the schedule.

"How about Laddie babysits, we order pizza for dinner, then we can do a few more things inside?"

It wasn't a date. Not even close. It was worse. It was casual and comfortable in a way only two people who shared a connection like theirs could experience. The whole thing had a married-couple-with-kids vibe to it. She remembered her father's warning. Would Gray have become a bored husband with a wandering eye? *You know he's not like that. Your dad set you up. Ask him. If he's a good man, he'll tell you the truth.*

"Pizza sounds great. Getting more done is a good idea. The sooner we finish, the sooner the house can go on the market." Mandi pulled her hair back, then twisted and clipped it in a messy bun. "I'm sure Coral would be happy to list it for us."

"No way. She's itching to make a commission but I'll find someone else." He started dialing the number off the pizza magnet on the fridge but hung up before finishing and cocked his head at her. "I thought she was dating John."

"Probably."

"Then why'd she come on to me today? She caught up with me in town, said she'd hurt her ankle but then went on about wanting to show the place to some guy. When I declined and insisted that I needed to get to work, she walked off without a limp. I had a weird feeling about the whole exchange."

Mandi's chest relaxed. Although she knew in her heart of hearts that the whole thing had been a setup, hearing it from Gray was reaffirming. She needed to hear it from him, considering how closed off he could be about his life. Hearing any truth from him was a reminder that he was a good man, though she still had that nagging feeling that he'd never learn to share his past with her. Things never felt 100 percent between them in the trust department. Nonetheless, she felt a little guilty for not mentioning that she'd witnessed the encounter, but she couldn't say anything now without him realizing she was testing him.

"Considering she approached me on the

beach about my dad wanting to buy, I'm sure they're working their magic together. My dad approached me today about it. I held him off, for now." Come to think of it, she'd never spoken to her father that boldly before. "Are you ordering?"

"Yes. The pizza. Do you still like extra green bell peppers?"

"Absolutely."

The kittens were curled up against Laddie, fast asleep. So amazing. Proof that blood didn't always define a good family. But sometimes, like with Nana, it did.

"Pizza's ordered. I'm going to get the pet supplies out of my truck before they wake up and need to pee. I brought a litter pan from work."

Mandi nodded and watched him leave. It wasn't until he closed the door behind him that she was able to exhale. She hated being confused. Maybe she needed another board…one to list the reasons why she left Gray versus the reasons he had been her first love. Her only love.

Was Darla right? Was she so insecure that she let things her father said make her doubt herself…then and now? Even as a teenager, she had sworn she'd never grow up to be like him, so why would she let him influence her so easily? Nana was the one she had looked up to and wanted to be like, not John.

She glanced at the dry-erase board. Advertising. Why had she studied it? Was it because her father told her when she was thirteen that she had artistic talent but that she'd never make money at it unless she went into advertising or interior design? He considered painting a hobby. Her grandmother had advised her to prove him wrong. She had told Mandi that if she was passionate about something, then she would be motivated enough to find a way to make money at it. Life had to be about passion.

Everyone she knew who was happy had their heart in their work. For Gray, it was all animals and nature. For Eve it was her bookstore and the kids who frequented it. Darla was clearly gifted and passionate about baking. And Nana…she actually wasn't sure what Nana did when she was younger, but she definitely loved living here, nature, animals…much like Gray. She used to say that she had traveled the world and had seen it all and had finally figured out that the only thing she wanted was to give comfort and watch the sunrise every morning. She gave through charity, opened her arms and home to Mandi, even if she had her dad around, and befriended Gray when he was new in town, long before anyone else welcomed him. But according to her journal, she'd lost people she loved before she ever settled down here in Turtleback. What was Mandi's life going to be like? Was she going to find success out there and finally settle down only to realize that her chance at love had been lost? Would she ever find something to fulfill her and fill the void the way Nana had?

Mandi did love that she could use her creative mind and artistic eye in advertising, and her ability to draw came in handy with presentations. But it wasn't like the oil paintings or watercolors she used to do when she lived here, and her New York apartment had no room for a hobby like that. Maybe someday.

But right now, staring at that obsessively organized chart, all she could see was her father. Was she more like him than she realized? Was her job in New York important because success freed her from him? Or because he had ingrained in her the need for success?

The look on his face earlier flashed in her mind. His tactics. His lying. Appearances. How was her career going to be different? Advertising was all about appearances and getting into people's minds.

"No. I can't be like him." She ran up to the board and started erasing everything. She rubbed the eraser in frantic circles.

"Whoa." Gray held her shoulders to stop her. His hands felt warm and firm and grounding. She tossed the eraser on the table.

"Tell me I'm not like my father."

"You're nothing like him."

She looked Gray in the eyes. They were a deep, soothing brown that made her want to sink into his arms and kiss him.

"For real?"

"Mandi, I don't know what happened when I stepped outside just now, but I assure you, being organized does not mean you're like John Rivers. You're your own person and always have been."

"But sometimes I wonder if I'm being selfish."

He lifted her chin.

"Taking care of yourself, discovering who you are and what your life's supposed to be about isn't selfish. If you think that I'm still angry about our wedding day, you're wrong. Maybe I was and, yes, I blamed you…for breaking my heart…but I now realize that you weren't selfish, you were scared. And I don't mean that as a weakness. It took a lot of courage to do what you did. It took incredible focus, determination and inner strength to bring you to this point in your life. The wedding? I was partly to blame. It was too much, too soon for you. I knew I'd be here the rest of my life, but you never got a chance to figure that part out."

"Thank you for that," she said, stepping forward. She rested her cheek against his chest and wrapped her arms around him. It was only a hug. Gratitude. Comfort. Maybe friendship. But a part of her would always know that she had paid a high price for discovering herself. He tucked her hair over her ear and rubbed her back.

"Mandi, I know what you said about the city being so mesmerizing and full of life, but I still don't get why you want to live there and have this job so badly. It doesn't jibe with the person you used to be. You were happy here. *We* were happy."

She stepped out of his arms.

"The person I used to be? That's rich. You feel equipped to judge who I was but you never like sharing who you were. You think you know better than I do if I was happy or not?"

"I take that back. I *thought* you were happy. You know who I've always been. I'm the same vet, animal advocate, motorcycle-riding guy you've always known."

"You forgot information management and control specialist."

"I'm not a control freak. That would be your dad."

"Maybe so. In some ways. But the woman you almost married was someone who figured it was her turn to be in control. I realized I don't have to answer to anyone. That's why I want to live in the city and start my career."

"As an underling."

"Gray, you have no right to try to bring me down."

"That's the last thing I want to do. Mandi,

I'd lift you up to the stars if I could. I thought you knew that. I thought you trusted what we had. I'm not trying to bring you down or minimize your accomplishments. I'm trying to understand why you'd trade living here, even if it means dealing with your father, for living in a different state and taking on a life where your daily schedule would be dictated by some stranger sitting behind a desk at a corner-window office."

"That's not how it is."

"I think it is. You had plans to run your own business and be your own boss and suddenly you're determined to be someone's minion. Everyone's afraid of something, right? I think you're afraid to do it on your own. I think you're afraid to fail in John's eyes, so you're hiding behind some prestigious company name. I'm not bringing you down, Mandi. I have more faith in you than you have in yourself. So did Nana. Think long and hard before you give some stranger that kind of control over your life. Trust me on that."

Mandi's nose stung and she bit the inside of her cheek. That wasn't true. She wasn't afraid. She left because she couldn't take this place anymore. She left because of Gray. She splayed her hands in frustration.

"Trust you on that? Why? Why, Gray? For heaven's sake, tell me. Who controlled your life? Were you abused as a child? Gray, I know something bad happened to you. All your excuses for not ever leaving town don't add up. Millions of people own doctor's offices or run companies or whatnot, where they are depended upon and on call almost 24/7, yet they find ways to arrange time off. You don't get nearly the number of patients that vets in more populated areas get. I'm not an idiot. Tell me, Gray, why, if you loved me so much, did you not even try to visit me after I left. You're trying to reconcile us now, so why didn't you do it then?"

"Because I didn't want to hold you back."

Mandi shook her head and finger at him.

"No, no. There you go again not making sense. You were just trying to convince me that this job in New York is all wrong for me."

"You're agitating the kittens and Laddie. Pets are sensitive to negative emotions."

"All the more reason for me not to have any in New York, then." He really had some nerve. Things were getting out of control. Maybe sending him home was a better idea than sharing pizza and working on the house.

The doorbell rang and he went to answer it, then returned with a pizza box.

"Can we have a truce long enough to eat? I'm starving."

She threw her hands up in the air.

"Sure. I can't stop you from eating in your own house. I'll take my slice into the kitchen."

GRAY WAS STUFFED. He leaned back against the sofa and stretched his legs out. The kittens were back to playing and Mandi, who had reappeared from the kitchen, was lying on her side on the living room floor, swinging a strand of yarn in front of them.

"You're right. We're never going to get anything done around here at this rate," Gray said.

"I warned you. Distractions. If we had my schedule up, I could have added in kitten playtime."

She had no idea she was his main distraction. Not the cats.

"That would take all the fun out of it. Should we bring a few boxes down from the attic and go through them here? That way we can keep an eye on these two," he suggested.

"Sure. But there's no light up there except for the window, and it's dark out. You'd need a flashlight." The attic was the one room in the house that Nana used to keep locked. She said that it was nothing but a storage room and she didn't want visitors or the occasional repair guy or gal going up there. She valued her privacy to the point that she would never hire cleaning companies. She did it all herself. But Mandi realized the key to the room upstairs was now in her possession. Was her other journal locked away up there?

Thunder rumbled and lightning followed within three seconds. The lights flickered but stayed on. Mandi sat up.

"Are we in a thunderstorm warning for the area? I didn't see anything on my phone's weather app," Gray said.

"Um, rummaging through a dark attic on a stormy night isn't my thing," Mandi said. "Let's call it a day. I don't think I've been sleeping soundly. It's catching up to me."

"Alright. I was planning to take Laddie home, but I remember how much you used to hate power outages at night. Will you be okay alone with the kittens? We can leave before the rain hits." He assumed that maybe given their earlier argument, she wouldn't want him sticking around.

Rain began pounding the windows and balcony door before she could answer. Her brow furrowed.

"I'm checking the radar and warnings. You can't leave in this weather," she said, motioning outside. "Lightning on an open beach? This house is half yours and big enough for both of us."

"I know but I didn't want to—"

"Gray, it's fine. You can stay." The lights went out. "In fact, now I'm begging you to stay. This place creaks in storms like this. I used to crawl in bed with Nana if I was sleeping over and the weather turned."

The room suddenly went silent. Gray guessed she was blushing.

"I didn't mean to suggest crawling in—"

"I know, Mandi. I understood what you meant."

He turned the flashlight on his cell phone

on and caught her frozen with her hand against her chest.

"You still hate storm power outages at night that much?"

"Keep that on a second. There's an LED lantern under the kitchen sink."

He followed her with the light and waited for her to turn the lantern on before shutting his. They went into the living room and set it on the coffee table.

"Here, help me set up this playpen ring around Laddie and the kittens so that they don't wander. I don't want to accidentally step on them." The click-in-place modules took mere seconds to set up. Laddie would be able to get over it but Windy and Storm would be trapped in a safe area.

"I think we should stay on the couch, so we can hear them if they cry," Mandi said.

"Sure." No argument from him. Thunder shook the house again. "I don't think the power is coming on anytime soon."

Mandi bypassed the playpen and curled up on the couch, searching her phone. Gray sat on the opposite end.

"No reception," she said, tossing it on the

table. She pulled her knees up to her chest. "This is going to be a long night."

He took the embroidered pillow from his side of the couch and tossed it over to her, then yanked the crocheted throw from behind him and passed it to her, as well.

"Go ahead and lie down," he said.

She studied him in the fading lantern light. The battery must have been old.

"You remembered the only way I could fall asleep on a night like this," she said.

He did. She used to curl up with that pillow hugged to her chest, the throw covering her legs and her head resting on his lap. They'd just sit there and he'd caress her arm until she fell asleep. She used to say she never slept as deeply as when she'd fall asleep on the couch with him like that. He wouldn't hold her tonight, but maybe his being nearby would be enough.

"Come on. Get some sleep."

She hesitated, then settled down with the pillow against her end of the couch. He adjusted the throw to cover her feet. It wasn't cold, but he knew the throw was her favorite because Nana had made it.

"Gray?" she whispered.

"Yeah?"

"I know we've been arguing and I realize we've hurt each other in the past, but I think Nana wanted us to understand that life is short. Please…promise me we'll always be friends."

He listened to the rain pour down like a dam had burst in the sky.

"I promise. Friends."

And there he had it. He'd never be more.

# CHAPTER NINE

"I ACTUALLY LIKE the yellow. It's not overly bright. Muted, clean and cheerful with a touch of elegance," Mandi said, standing back to judge the exterior paint. She wasn't a house flipper or designer, but there was a design element to marketing a place and she was sure buyers would love it. The color gave the cottage a welcoming beach-house vibe. Gray had been right about fixing things up before selling. They'd gotten pretty far in the past several days.

"Good. Because I don't have the time or inclination to start all over. This should help protect the wood until it starts peeling again." Gray dropped his brush in the bucket of dirty brushes that needed to be washed.

He had replaced a few rotting boards along the balcony while Mandi had nailed a new floorboard on the bottom step leading to the front door. The rest of the exterior was in pretty good shape. A little weeding and fresh flowers for curb appeal and they'd be done with the outside. The inside was another matter.

"I'll wash the brushes if you put the ladders and leftover paint cans away," she said.

"Deal."

"Are you up for checking out the attic?"

Gray threw his head back and cranked his neck.

"Not particularly, but you might be able to bribe me with food. Not pizza. I'm all pizza-ed out."

"Fine. We only have about a week before I'm due back in New York and Nana has so many boxes up there that I don't think have been opened in decades." She picked at the yellow paint that had dried on the back of her hand and mustered up some courage. "Why don't you go grab a shower at your place…your other place…and I'll shower and change here, then we can maybe grab a bite at The Grill."

It wasn't a date. She wasn't asking him out on one. It was a simple dinner because he was hungry. A non-date.

*You're lying to yourself.*

"Sure," he said, without looking up from folding one of the ladders. His tone affirmed that it wasn't a date. He barely sounded interested.

"Cool."

"You go ahead. I'll put the ladders away and meet you back here in thirty minutes. Does that work? Let Laddie out so he can come home with me."

Thirty minutes to get ready for a non-date. It wasn't much. If she wore her good jeans, as opposed to a dress or shorts, she wouldn't have to shave her legs.

"Sounds good. See you later."

She took the brushes inside and started rinsing them out in the kitchen sink as fast as she could, glancing once or twice at the paint-sprinkled face of her watch. Darn it. She'd forgotten to take it off. She'd be able to scrape the paint off the face, but her watch band was ruined.

She rushed the brush rinsing, then set them in a pitcher of water to keep them from drying out. She'd rinse them a little more later. Right now, she needed to shower and change. Why didn't she just tell Gray she needed ten extra minutes? Everyone knew long hair was harder to dry. She'd have to skip that part, too. She made sure the kittens had fresh food and water, then headed for the bathroom.

The shower was only lukewarm because she couldn't wait for the hot water to flow and the bedroom she'd sorted through yesterday was now littered with every item of clothing from her suitcase. She settled on the black jeans and silky, floral print tank-style top, clipped her hair up in a messy bun and dabbed some tinted gloss to her lips. The woman she saw in the mirror was average and, if she could see past the surface, insecure and confused, but she could pass as confident and sexy enough for a night out. Maybe. That's why her job interview had gone well. She knew how to fake confidence. Of course, it didn't really matter for tonight because it wasn't a date and it was only Gray. Gray, who'd seen her at her worst over the past five years, who knew what she looked like all sweaty after a morning jog...or dirty and cut up by kittens.

The doorbell rang and she jolted.

*Don't overthink this. Just go.*

She picked up her purse and keys on the way to the door.

"Hey," she said, opening it. Then she noticed his motorcycle parked out front, which wouldn't have been a big deal except for the fact that he was carrying an extra helmet. "I think I'll drive."

"Come on, Mandi. Just this once. I brought you a helmet and I have a jacket for you in one of the saddlebags."

"Motorcycles are death on wheels. In the years we were together, you were never able to convince me to get on that thing and now you think I'm suddenly going to hop on?"

"You make it through the streets of New York. What's one ride with me?"

"I walk in New York. Why don't we meet at the restaurant? I'll follow you in my car."

He took her hand and tugged her outside the door. He was standing so close. He smelled of fresh soap and shampoo and… and… She took a slow, deep breath. He had that special scent that was all Grayson and made her want to bury her nose in the side of his neck. She closed her eyes. She really needed to socialize more. He slipped

the keys out of her other hand and locked
the door for her.

"You kept the turtle key chain," he said.

*Shoot.* Heat spread through her cheeks.

"Uh, yeah. You know. It's a key chain. It
works." She couldn't read his expression. He
simply gave her back the keys and put his
hand to the small of her back and guided her
down the steps to where his bike was parked
next to her old car.

"It's a no-brainer," he said, pointing out
their choices.

She held her lower lip between her teeth
and shook her head.

"More people are killed on motorcycles
than are eaten by sharks," she argued.

"Sharks don't keep surfers from surfing."

*Because they're passionate about it.*

Where had that thought come from? She
frowned as he unzipped the saddlebag on
the side of the bike. He pulled out a leather
jacket in her size and handed it to her. She
had to admit, as risky as she thought motorcycles were, Gray had always been huge
on protection. He never rode without a helmet, gloves, boots and armor-plated jacket
for crash and skin protection. But she had

never ridden, so why did he have a spare of everything in her size? Eve's and Darla's faces flashed in her mind. Then every face of every girl in town. Taking someone for a ride meant they would be seated very close behind him with their hands holding his waist for balance. She'd seen it in movies, on TV and when bikers passed by on Route 12 for a scenic road trip.

"It's a very short ride to the boardwalk, Mandi. I won't go too fast."

He took his keys out of his pocket, and her lips parted at the sight of pewter catching the early evening sun. He still had his matching turtle key chain, too. What did that mean? He made no effort to hide it. He knew she noticed it because his eyes met hers and the corner of his mouth lifted ever so slightly at her reaction.

She cleared her throat and tried to keep the conversation from going there.

"How is it you happen to have a helmet and jacket for me?"

He chuckled.

"Mandi. I know what you're thinking but you're wrong. You know how I am about my bike. I've never taken a girl for a ride on *my girl*. You're the only person I know who is worthy."

She didn't know what to say. She'd walked right into that one. She'd set herself up for it.

"You're trying to butter me up. You're using psychology to get me on that bike."

"Nah. Psychology would be pointing out that you almost rode with me once, right after we met, but your father forbade it. You told me so at the time. He had warned you that he had police connections and he'd have them pull us over and bring you straight to him if they ever saw you on my bike or any other. Then he flooded your mind with graphic details of every motorcycle accident he could find. Now, don't get me wrong, that stuff can happen. You know how I am about preventing accidents and being careful. I take every precaution. A lot of the time, riders involved in accidents you hear about were being stupid, were inexperienced, lacked protection or were driving down treacherous roads with dangerous drivers or semitrucks. I don't fall into any of those categories and would never deliberately put you in danger. You must know that. One ride, Mandi. You can't head back to the city and live your life stuck in some office tower or cubicle without trying this at least once.

"Look, I'm not going to force you to ride. Encourage, yes, but not force. You have a right to make your own decisions and I can respect that. As for why I have a jacket and helmet for you? I've had this gear sitting in a closet for the past two years. I had bought it as a wedding gift for you. I figured that once we were married and you were out from under your father's thumb, you'd change your mind about riding. I never returned it because, for the longest time, I kept thinking you'd come back."

She'd forgotten about the warning her father had given her about motorcycles. When had his words and opinions become so embedded in her mind that she lost track of what he had "taught" her and what she believed or wanted of her own free will? Most parents influenced and shaped their kids' mentality about things, one way or another, but at some point an individual learned enough about the world to make up their own mind.

"I don't know," she said, actually contemplating putting on that helmet. A zing of energy zipped through her. The mere idea of getting on that motorcycle…of taking a controlled risk…made her pulse thrum with anticipation. Gray held up the jacket and lifted his shoulders questioningly. If she didn't want to ride, he'd put it away.

"Do you trust me, Mandi?"

That was a loaded question. Did she?

She paused, then took the helmet from him and put it on, then removed her hair clip. He helped her adjust and secure the helmet. She couldn't believe she was about to do this. She climbed on behind him and held on tight. Probably too tight. But the slurry of nerves and excitement transformed to a purely breathtaking sensation when he revved the engine and veered onto the road, then took off. The wind beat against her like a soothing massage and the speed…man, it was exhilarating…electrifying yet calming at the same time. This was a different sort of peace from what she got from doing things like kayaking or parasailing. There was more adrenaline involved in this. A more powerful rush. She felt freer than she'd ever felt before.

A lump rose in her throat and her eyes got damp, not in a fearful, bad way, but because so much of the tension that had been festering inside of her begged for release. Something about being on Gray's motorcycle, holding on to him with nothing but the wind against them, made her want to let go of any bad memories or bitterness between them. It made her want to break free and fly. And she was feeling all of this here, in Turtleback, where she never thought she would. She pressed herself a little closer to him and kept holding on because she knew the ride, the feeling, wouldn't last forever.

*He knew you needed this. He knew all along how badly you needed to feel this way.*

He understood her. Maybe, in some ways, Gray *did* know her better than she knew herself.

GRAY PULLED TO a stop in a spot reserved for motorcycles near the boardwalk. He took off his helmet and immediately slipped on his sunglasses, then he got off and helped Mandi remove her helmet. She looked absolutely gorgeous when she had opened the door back at Nana's, but right now…he was speechless, like some teenager on a first date. Sitting on his bike with her cheeks flushed, hair falling around her shoulders and eyes sparkling, she was beyond breathtaking. Her smile was more than he could have hoped for. It filled him with hope and joy. He had wanted her to ride with him for so long. To feel the freedom. Riding had been his savior. It had been the one thing that made him feel like he was rebelling against his past and having to live under protection. Having *her* in his life had made all the difference, too. He helped her get off and relished the way she held on to him and didn't let go.

"I'm sorry. My legs are shaking. That was amazing." She laughed and squeezed his arm. "Thank you for that."

"I won't say I told you so. Your legs feeling like that is normal. And no need to be sorry. You can hold on to me until you feel steady." *Hold on as long as you like.*

He scanned the area, out of habit, before they started for the boardwalk restaurant. Mandi's smile disappeared. He followed her line of sight about twenty feet down the boardwalk. John, with Coral by his side, had just stopped in his tracks near a gift shop. He was staring right at Gray and Mandi. His mouth hardened and face creased with disapproval. He tugged on Coral's arm and they walked away.

"Mandi, look at me," Gray said. She turned to face him. He hated that one look from her father still had the ability to fill her with guilt and unease. He brushed a lock of hair off her cheek. "You're an adult. A strong, beautiful, smart, independent woman. You're here with me, not him. We're going to have a nice time and nobody's going to ruin it. Got it?"

"You're right." She lifted her chin and smiled, but something in her brown eyes and the fact that she let go of his arm left him wondering if she really believed it.

"Come on. I made reservations." He preferred doing that, so he could request a table that wasn't in a high-traffic area. He felt more comfortable in corner spots. He held out the crook of his arm, as old-fashioned as it seemed, and waited for her to hold on. The road here had its share of weathering. He didn't want her tripping if her legs were still shaky.

"Let's do this. You're right. I'm not going to let him ruin our day," she said.

"You got that right." He just hoped that John wouldn't reappear and make a scene. Especially not here in a public area. These days, anyone could pull out their cell phone and start recording. People posted videos of public arguments and incidents all the time on social media. If that happened, WITSEC would have him pulled out of town within hours. Gone with no explanation...not even to Mandi. The thought of losing her permanently, when she had at least agreed to keep him in her life as a friend, killed him.

He hated self-pity, but sometimes he couldn't help but wonder why, of all people, he had to have been the one who had overheard classified information that impacted national security—navy and defense data on underwater strategies and plans involving the US Navy Marine Mammal Program—getting leaked to a Russian contact. It blew his mind that anyone would do that to their country...to their people, let alone a respected commanding officer. Criminal activity that he couldn't turn a blind eye to, or he would have been just as guilty. He had known that getting involved would entail some risks. It didn't end at reporting what he knew, though. He was asked to help secure bugs where the communications were taking place, then later, he testified and things went downhill from there. Before he knew it, he was sitting through witness protection briefings, awaiting paperwork supporting his new identity, then making his move to Turtleback Beach. A location WITSEC had chosen.

He lived every day knowing that his cover could be blown, which was why he didn't travel. He wanted to minimize the risk of anyone recognizing him, especially since he had found family and a new purpose here in Turtleback. Nana and Mandi. And protecting Mandi meant not telling her the truth, not only because he wasn't allowed to, but because if she accidentally slipped up, her life would be in danger, too. It was like he was caught in some catch-22 loop that he'd never get out of. Lose her by not being honest. Risk losing her by involving her in the truth.

He guided Mandi into the restaurant and let her go ahead of him as they were led to their table. They settled down and ordered drinks. Gray glanced casually around the canopied outdoor seating area and down the boardwalk to make sure no one was acting suspicious. It was a behavior he did automatically, but today he felt more conscious of everything. Maybe Mandi had awakened his senses. He could still feel her pressed against his back. Had she held on to him any tighter, he might have had trouble steering.

"I think I'll have the Mediterranean salad," Mandi said, putting down her menu.

"That's all? Are you sure?" He didn't want to point out that this was his treat because he didn't want to inadvertently offend her.

"I'm sure. I'm more thirsty than hungry. An iced tea sounds so good right now."

"Well, I'm hungry enough for both of us. If you change your mind and want to taste anything I get, feel free." He gave her a lopsided grin.

She used to love stealing bites off his plate whenever they ate out. He never minded. In fact, he liked it. Sharing like that was an intimate act and it made him happy to see her eat. Eating meant she was relaxed. She used to lose her appetite whenever her dad upset her. Or whenever she was irritated with Gray.

"You know me well. What are you ordering?"

"Let's see…the grilled salmon, a loaded baked potato, a side salad, iced tea with lemon and, if you'll share it with me like old times, the melted chocolate raspberry cake with extra whipped cream."

"You're not kidding about being hungry. And I won't say no to that dessert."

The waiter returned, took their order and hurried off. The poor guy looked exhausted with dark circles beneath his eyes, but he was on the ball with their order.

"You know what's tough?" Mandi asked.

"What?"

"That the only photo I have of you is in my mind. It didn't hit home until I had left town, but unlike most people in a breakup, since you never let anyone take or post pictures of you, I was deprived of looking you up online or scrolling through old photos of us just so that I could have the gratification of deleting them."

"You would have looked me up online? I'm flattered."

"Didn't you ever look me up online? I know you abhor social media, but weren't you curious enough to look me up at least once, just to see what I was up to?"

He thrummed his fingers on the table and narrowed his eyes at her. A truth. He'd give her this truth.

"More than once." He had wanted to be sure she was okay. There had been nights when he couldn't sleep and he just needed to see that she looked well or to read a tweet that indicated she was doing alright.

"Really? I'm flattered back at you."

"Nana used to slip in a comment about how you were doing, as well. I think she knew I wanted…needed…to know."

"She did the same with me regarding you, but still no pics, since you never let anyone take any. Let me ask you this. With my degree in advertising, would you trust me to help promote your practice? Maybe give you ideas on sprucing up your website?"

That was a tough one. She'd promote him too well, but she'd never accept that as a valid excuse to decline her services.

"I have no doubt you're brilliant at what you do, Mandi, but you know I'm the kind of guy who doesn't care for change. My website is fine as it is. Business is good."

*Or good enough.*

"Hmm."

"You don't believe that I'd trust you if I ever wanted a revamp?"

"Would you?"

He took her hand in his.

"I hereby swear that if I ever want to redo my website or design an ad for my clinic, you'll be the first person I ask. I only qualify that in case you're too busy with work to spare me the time. I'm small beans."

"I'd make the time." She sat back as the waiter put their dishes in front of them and asked if they needed anything else. "You may not want your photo on there, but a pic of Laddie on the beach would be gorgeous."

"That is a good idea."

"It's hard to imagine that at some point, you actually let the person behind the counter at DMV take your photo for your driver's license."

"It was pure torture." A lie. His photo IDs had been taken in private and put together by WITSEC. No standing in line at DMV.

He took a drink of tea and they both started eating.

"So, seriously, still no luck in getting this place and others to shut down their lights during a hatch?" she asked.

"No luck. Even Nana tried to get through to them, but the hatches can be unpredictable and no business owner wants to turn off lights, night after night, with revenue loss. Can't blame them, but at the same time, I wish they'd put the turtles first."

"I wish there was some way I could help."

"I honestly don't think they'll ever budge on it. The two who were willing to give it a few hours were Eve and Darla, but their shops aren't along the beach like this restaurant, so it wouldn't have the same impact."

"Well, we can try to add that stipulation to the family who wants to buy the cottage. Not that we'd have a way to enforce it."

"People don't like to give up their comforts in life. But money and comforts aren't everything. Lives are."

Mandi nodded slowly and, though he didn't press the matter, he hoped that she took that to heart.

MANDI HADN'T SLEPT so well in months. She lay there sprawled across her bed, muscles lax and mind rested. She turned onto her back and let the morning sun wash over her. She remembered the look on the waiter's face last night and smiled. Gray had left him a fifty-dollar tip for a sixty-dollar meal and when the guy pointed it out, thinking he'd made a mistake, Gray told him it was the best meal and service he'd had in a long time. The look on the waiter's face got her right in the heart. Gray told her afterward he had heard through the grapevine that the guy was a new father and had been working three jobs to make ends meet. *That* stole her heart. She then kissed Gray on the cheek and told him he was a good man. He brushed it off and said it was nothing. That wasn't true. Small acts of kindness made a difference. He did them all the time with people and animals. It was one of the reasons she had fallen for him. But then why had she lost sight of that side of him and run away?

She touched her fingertips to her lips. She could still feel his warm, unshaven skin against them. There had been no kissing beyond her peck on his cheek, nor holding hands. Not even when they took a walk to burn off their meal before riding back to the house. There had been no goodbye kiss, yet she was feeling pretty amazing right now. Blissful and carefree.

Her cell phone text alert dinged, ruining her moment. She hurried to the dresser to check the message. She didn't recognize the number it was coming from, but one look at the area code and first few words of the message and her temples tensed. It was from her future boss. She wanted to check in and make sure Mandi was on track to report to her first day as planned. She'd be there. She would be driving up the day before work started, which meant she only had five days left in Turtleback. Her stomach sank and she slumped on the edge of the bed. She looked around the room as if she'd never see it again. *But this is what you wanted. Don't lose your chance to make it big in the world. To prove yourself.* She answered the text, assuring her boss that she'd be there on Monday as planned. She set her phone down and fell back against the bed. If there was one lesson she'd gleaned from coming down to Turtleback, it was that nothing good lasted forever.

She took a fortifying breath and got up to make coffee. There was still work to do around the house. She couldn't leave it all on Gray's shoulders. With his clinic to run, he'd never get it done on his own and they'd end up sitting on the house indefinitely, which come to think of it, would not only keep her from making money on the sale, it would actually cost her in tax and insurance payments. She couldn't do that.

*Money and comforts aren't everything. Lives are.*

She recalled Gray's words, but the practical side of her brain couldn't ignore the fact that she needed the money. But Gray was right about not selling to John. Being around her dad, face-to-face, was a firm reminder that he always had his own agenda. She couldn't trust him. He was all about the money.

*Hypocrite.* Here she was worried about the money, too, but at least she had limits and boundaries. Her dad didn't care about Nana's house. All he did when she was alive was criticize it, pointing out the growing cost of repairs, the older-style floor plan and the waste of prime beachfront property. Nana had once told her during a phone conversation that John had been nagging her to sell the place. He had even shown her apartments and town houses in the state—likely searched for by Coral—that were a part of "fifty and older" all-inclusive, independent-living communities. They included workout facilities, a bank, doctor, craft classes and even a small library…all within close proximity of a hospital, "just in case" it was needed. Nana had been—in her own words—pissed. Her own son had been trying to slowly put her aside when, according to Nana, it was clear that his concern for her well-being was nothing more than a cover-up for his desire to have control. He'd even suggested more than once that she give him power of attorney and add his name as someone who could have access to her accounts in case of an emergency…like becoming mentally incapacitated or terminally ill. Nana had denied him, telling him she wasn't stupid and had taken care of everything with her lawyer and that he need not worry about it. What no one knew was that Nana had given Mandi power of attorney…because she knew Mandi would never abuse it.

Which only reinforced the fact that Nana simply didn't want John to have the house. This place was special in ways Mandi didn't have words for. It was as if, even in Nana's absence, it had a spirit that watched over the beach that lay before it and the turtles who would come to lay their nests there. It had history and Nana had filled its walls with love and good energy. It needed a family as much as it was meant to shelter one.

John would never comprehend that. And Mandi couldn't fulfill that need. As much as she and Gray had mended their friendship since Nana's passing, he hadn't changed. He wasn't being completely forthright and honest with her. He still didn't fully trust her, no matter what he claimed. Actions spoke louder than words and he was still holding back and carrying a figurative shield wherever he went. How could she possibly marry and build a life with someone whose past was so clouded? What if they ever had kids as they'd once planned? What would he tell them? What would she say if they wondered

why they didn't have photos with Daddy? Or
if he eventually came around and allowed
for a private family album, what would he
do if one of his kids used a photo from it for
school or posted it online without asking?
Kids did stuff like that, and most school-
work and assignments were done online
these days.

It would be impossible. He'd be keeping
secrets from her and his children and eventually grandchildren, the same way Nana
had kept her own secrets. Mandi remembered the missing journal.

The coffee maker gave a beep to signal it
was done. She poured a cup and went to sit
on the floor in the living room, within the
kittens' safety playpen, so that Windy and
Storm could play with her toes and give her
some love.

Nostalgia spread through her with the
warmth of her first sip of coffee. Today,
after cleaning the litter box, she would fix
the garden beds around the house, then she
was going to tackle the attic room and see
if the journal was up there. Gray said he
wouldn't be able to come around until late
afternoon. He was dropping off Laddie at

Castaway Books because Eve was doing a dogs-in-books theme this week and thought having him around would draw a crowd, especially for reading time. If Mandi could get through all the boxes and separate memorabilia from things that could be tossed or donated, then Gray would be able to help her carry the boxes and piles downstairs. They'd almost be done and could carry out their plan to find someone other than Coral to list it. And if her father made an offer, she and Gray would have the prerogative to decline it, in favor of one from a family with kids and pets who would make the cottage a home again.

She prayed they'd get an offer like that. It was their only hope.

GRAY PINCHED UP the skin on the bulldog named Bison and inserted the subcutaneous injection. That made three shots for the old guy, whom he'd been seeing since he was a puppy.

"He's all set," Gray said, lifting the sixty-pounder off the exam table and setting him on the floor. Bison started licking his owner's shoes. Mr. Krink also owned the hardware store, and Gray had warned him numerous times to be careful about what was on the floor or anywhere Bison could reach with his tongue. Hardware stores were full of items that were dangerous for pets, like nuts, bolts and poisonous substances. Bison had an indiscriminate, scary appetite. "Just follow what I said about his diet. He's got to come down five to ten pounds or he's going to end up with problems, and we don't want that." Gray stuck his head out in the hall. "Hey, Gavin, can you grab a couple samples of the weight-loss food that rep brought around?"

"I swear I measure what I put in his bowl," Krink said.

"I don't doubt it. But since he hangs around the shop, if I were you, I'd hide whatever trash bin you or your employees throw lunch leftovers in."

Krink's eyes widened and he shook his head at Bison.

"That's gotta be it."

Gavin brought the food samples and Krink was on his way.

"Dr. Z, we have an emergency." Chanda

hurried over and handed him a chart. "Nora is taking her back right now."

Gray flipped the chart open and rushed to their emergency intake and surgical area. The name on the chart was Petra, a one-year-old Labradoodle here on vacation with her owners.

"Did you speak to her family?" he asked, putting a stethoscope to her chest, then palpating her abdomen. Petra whimpered and struggled to escape. "Whoa, there." He held her in place with Gavin's and Nora's help.

"They think she might have swallowed a fishing lure. One with two hooks on it. All they know is that it was missing from their fishing box while they were out on the sound early this morning and she started acting sluggish and whimpering soon afterward," Nora said.

Oh man. Not good.

"Okay, we need an X-ray and I want her on something for pain. Do we have permissions?"

"Yes, I had them sign. It's all in the chart," Nora said. Of course she did. She was always on top of things and had enough ex-

perience to know they were going to need
X-rays and that Petra was in pain. Appeas-
ing pain was a priority. They didn't want
any of their patients suffering.

It didn't take long to get a good digital
image up on screen. It confirmed the family's suspicion. The fishing lure was lodged
halfway down. Gray cursed.

"Start prepping her. I'll go talk to her
family."

Signed papers for emergency care or not,
he needed to check in with them to make
sure they knew what was going on and that
surgery was required. They'd have to sign
for that and blood work. He hoped they
would. There were some people in the world
who would spend money for years on lot-
tery tickets and cigarettes without a second
thought, but in a lifesaving situation, would
balk at the cost of medical care for their pet.
He had a feeling, considering they'd gone
out of their way to rush Petra in here, that
she had a good family who would put her
well-being above all. However they decided
to proceed, it was going to be a tense few
hours.

He stepped into the exam room Nora

pointed him toward and froze in the doorway, but only for a second. He immediately recovered and tried to act as normal as possible, but his heart raced erratically. He'd seen this family before he entered witness protection. He didn't recognize their last name on the chart, but he knew their faces. He scrambled to place them in his mind but he couldn't. The look on their faces told him they'd recognized him, too. This wasn't good. He cleared his throat.

"Hello. I'm Dr. Z. I just met Petra and wanted to let you know that we're running X-rays on her." He rattled off the intended procedure and lab work that might be necessary and they told him to do whatever needed to be done to save her.

"You look familiar," the wife ventured.

Gray shrugged and shook his head as if he'd never seen them before.

"I don't think we've ever met. Have you been in here before? Maybe with a different pet?"

"No, she's our first dog. But my wife's right. I think I've seen you before, too. Were you by any chance with the army? We used to live on a base. Maybe you were a vet there?"

"Not me. I'd remember if I had joined any military branch," he said, laughing off the idea. "I have been told, however, that I have one of those faces. The kind that looks familiar."

"That must be it, then," the wife said. "Because I could have sworn I'd seen you somewhere, and Tyler's 's right, I think it was on base before we ever had kids."

"Like I said, one of those faces. I'm going to check on Petra and scrub for surgery. You'll be more comfortable waiting in the front room. Let Chanda know if you need anything."

"Thanks."

He fled the room and pressed his back against his office wall. He needed to catch his breath and think straight. This was okay. He had things under control. They were a nice family with a sick dog—not hit men. He took a deep breath. He needed to save their dog. That was the most immediate life in danger. Then he'd reassess. He wasn't turning his own life upside down on account of a nonthreatening family passing through. He'd let Carlos know to keep an extra eye out without notifying the marshal. The marshal would overreact. He had this. It was a close call, but everything was going to be okay. It had to be.

## CHAPTER TEN

MANDI TIED HER hair into a high ponytail, scooped up Windy and Storm and took them up to the attic with her. She hated leaving them alone too long, even if they had a penned-off area, especially since Laddie wasn't around today to babysit. Besides, she couldn't resist them. There was nothing cuter than a kitten. She was really going to miss them. Taking them to New York with her and having them spend all day in her tiny apartment, alone, wouldn't be fair to them. They would be happier and healthier here with Gray and Laddie.

*You'd be happier here, too.*

No. That wasn't possible. She didn't know where that voice in her head kept coming from but it had to stem from nerves and insecurity. New job. New life. She was doubting herself. Everyone went through that, didn't they? Wondering if they were good enough and if they could make it in the world or at a new job? It was normal.

*But you had cold feet and backed out of a commitment before.*

She nibbled at the inside of her cheek. That was different. Marriage and career were different things. Weren't they? She remembered Gray accusing her of trading her father's control for a stranger's and how she was settling for not building her own business and being her own boss. Did she want that? He didn't understand that without a reputation getting a new business off the ground would be hard. It was a competitive market. By working for a reputable firm, she'd be building recognition. Clients would associate her with quality service. Didn't he understand that names mattered? That hers wouldn't carry as much clout without the firm standing behind her?

She reached the attic and placed the kittens in a wide, foot-high box she'd found earlier and filled with an old soft blanket and some cat toys. That would keep them out of trouble while she sorted through the place. Sunlight streamed through the one small window she'd opened earlier to air out the room. There were at least ten boxes and several bags Nana had stashed up here.

She was about to delve through the past and she was feeling almost as nervous as embarking on her future.

*How do you know your future is meant to be in New York? Did Nana know when she was your age that she'd end up spending the rest of her life in Turtleback?*

She carried the first box closer to the window where there was more light and sat on an old wooden, kid-sized chair she recognized as the one she used to use in elementary school, when she'd color in her coloring book at Nana's coffee table. She opened the box and waved away the dust motes that escaped. If the first journal was in here, she'd have time to look through it before Gray arrived.

"Hey, Mandi. It's me. Where are you?"

She nearly jumped out of her chair but pressed a hand to her chest when she registered Gray's voice. He'd let himself in, which was absolutely fine, but she noticed how they'd gone from knocking to being more casual. *Hey, honey, I'm home.* She pressed her hands to her head. Yes, his calling out to her kind of reminded her of the clichéd husband calling out to his wife, but they weren't married. She'd made that choice long ago. She needed to get back in control. She'd make a list if she had to, emphasizing her goals, her loans, her job and the fact that she should be focusing on her career right now. If she had it in notes on her phone, no one else would ever see it, but if Gray didn't stop entering her mind, she'd make herself read through it until it knocked her upside the head and set her straight.

"I'm upstairs in the attic," she called out, grabbing her phone to start the list before he reached the room. She could type fast. Just starting it would be enough. She typed in "Focus" as the list name and went to the next line. She could hear him taking the first steps. A breeze came in the window, fluttering a paper in the box, then, before she could type another word, her phone went dead.

"Seriously?" It had at least a 15 percent charge remaining only five minutes ago and she had just picked it up. Another breeze ruffled her hair. She frowned and looked around the room. *Nana?* Okay. Now she really was losing it. Yes, she was afraid of attics and dark spaces, but it was broad day-light, not midnight, and Nana's ghost was not messing with her. There were *no* ghosts in the attic. The steps creaked again and she exhaled when Gray appeared.

"YOU OKAY? YOU look spooked," he said, grinning. "All I did was walk in. Didn't mean to scare you. I haven't seen that look on your face since the time I snuck up on you in the lighthouse on Halloween the year after we met."

"Don't you laugh at me. You know how I am. I should have waited for you before coming up here." She put her phone in her pocket. "Remind me to charge this thing when I go downstairs. How was your day?"

"A day in the life of a vet. All good. Gavin's taking a night shift to watch over a post-op dog with a fish identity crisis. Don't ask. She's going to make a full recovery." He frowned and got that dark look in his eyes. The look he got when he wasn't telling the full story.

"Wow. That sounds scary even without the details."

"Have you gotten far, here?" he asked, reaching down and petting the kittens.

"Just started."

He walked over to the stack of boxes.

"Why would she label a box 'junk' and then keep it?" he asked.

"Beats me. This one was marked 'baby clothes,' so I thought it would be mostly for donation, but it's all papers and notebooks. It looks like there's a photo album near the bottom, too."

Nana had been pretty organized. At least enough to label storage correctly. Gray carried the "junk" box next to her and sat cross-legged on the dusty floor.

"Maybe we'll find your baby booties in this one, then." He used a pocketknife to open the several layers of tape that sealed the top seam. "Hmm."

"What's that one have in it?' Mandi craned her neck.

"Looks like manuals, language books… I didn't know Nana spoke Spanish, French, German…and Vietnamese, Swahili and Arabic? Really? Unless she was in the habit of starting a language and quitting it. One doesn't typically learn Vietnamese or Swahili on a whim."

"I didn't know she was multilingual. I did know she had been to Africa—it's where she first got hooked on Kenyan coffee, she told me—but I thought she'd gone on a vacation or something. Maybe she studied languages before traveling. You know…like knowing how to ask where the bathroom is."

"I don't think so." He flipped through one of the books. "This isn't like those quick, everyday-lingo type of travel books."

She was discovering more about Nana every day. She was feeling like an outsider who didn't know everything about a person. What was with Gray and, now, Nana? She pushed a lock of hair off her forehead and glanced at him. Maybe it was time she told him about what she'd found. He was going to discover things about Nana up here anyway.

"Gray, I need to tell you something. I found a journal in Nana's bedside drawer. It was labeled as the second of two, but I never found the first. I think it might be up here."

"Okay. Do I want to know what it said?"

"There were only two entries in that one. One from the day my mother left us and the other from the day I left you. It was strange. And the first one mentioned two people who had been dear to Nana but who'd died. I'm not sure how. I'm not sure if one was my grandfather or not. She didn't list names. It sounded a little cryptic, as if she didn't want anyone to fully understand who or what she was talking about if it were ever found. And on top of that, she had some strange things in her drawer, including a multitool pocketknife that I'd never seen her use before.

Gray stared at her, listening. His forehead creased.

"Well, maybe we'll find the other journal in these boxes."

"Yeah, hopefully," she said.

Mandi took out a thick hardcover notebook from her box. It had nothing on it to indicate it was a journal. She opened it. There inside the cover was "Journal #1" written in faded pencil. The pages were blank, though. She turned toward the middle in search of entries.

"No way." It had a cutout in the center, the kind of old-fashioned, hide-something-in-a-book secret compartment. There were two black-and-white photos in it, one of Nana, who had to be in her twenties at the time.

"Holy—let me see that." Gray took the photo and studied it. She wore a traditional Middle Eastern kaffiyeh scarf around her neck and covering her mouth, but her eyes gave her away. She was standing next to two servicemen. "Those are US Marines uniforms from the fifties. And look at the background. The landscape. I'd bet money this photo was taken during the 1958 Lebanon Crisis. What the heck was Nana doing in Beirut with the US military?"

"Let me see." Mandi took the photo and looked at it again. "I can tell it's an old war photo, but that's about it. How can you be sure it's Lebanon?"

GRAY SCRATCHED THE BACK of his neck. His parents had been high school teachers. His mother taught science and his father taught world history. But telling her that would lead to more questions, like about where they taught. Questions he wasn't supposed to answer.

"Military history was a hobby when I was a kid. You know how teenage boys can be about war. In 1958, President Eisenhower ordered Marine troops to land in Beirut during what was called Operation Blue Bat, to help control political unrest and protect the regime from Soviet influence. That's just the basics, but the point is, your grandmother was there. I'm still trying to wrap my head around this photo of her."

"So am I. Did you ever talk military history with her? Did she know you were into it? I never knew this about you...or her." He quickly directed the conversation back to the photos.

"Forget me. It seems your grandmother was the one who didn't like talking about her past. Look at this other photo."

Mandi scooted closer to him. In this one, Nana looked worn and thin but there was steel in her eyes. She stood with her arm around another woman and a man against a lush, jungle backdrop.

"Do you know who they are?" he asked.

"No. I don't recognize them, but her journal referred to two people who were her most loved, trusted friends. The man..." She looked more closely. "I think he might have my dad's eyes but I'm not sure. John looks so much like Nana."

"Look around them, Mandi. The tent they're in front of. The stuff around them and military markings. That guy back there with the helmet, standing near the jungle." He looked away from the photo and then at Mandi, as if trying to fit the pieces of a puzzle together. "Mandi, this photograph… this was taken during the Vietnam War. I'd bet my life on it."

Mandi's lips parted and she went pale.

"They're definitely in a jungle. It reminds me of pictures I've seen of Vietnam or scenes from movies," Mandi said, "but you have to be wrong. I mean, I see the photos, but there's no way she served in the military. She would have told me. Besides, she was a woman. They wouldn't have sent her to the front lines back then. Unless she was a translator or something? She always encouraged me to be a strong woman and to go after whatever I wanted in life, so why wouldn't she have told me about her past if she could have served as an example for me? Why not tell me the truth?"

Gray took a deep breath.

"Because maybe she couldn't, Mandi."

*Who were you, Nana?* Gray's temples were beginning to pound. He wanted so badly to tell Mandi that he had been living a secret, too. That he understood at least part of Nana's reasoning for keeping her past in the dark. But he couldn't. Acting on a whim was what got people like him in trouble. He handed Mandi back the photos and pulled out a flat velvet container from the cardboard storage box. Would Nana have told anyone about her past? Maybe not. Gray knew firsthand that sometimes a person's past stayed in the past. He opened the container. His head buzzed and his mind churned at warp speed. A service medal inscribed with the years *1966–1967* and an accompanying note lay there. He read the paperwork as Mandi lifted the medal and examined it.

"She wasn't in Vietnam the whole war, Mandi. She was in Bolivia. Look at this newspaper clipping from 1967. Nana really got around."

He handed the newspaper to her, then wiped his hand across his mouth and jaw. Was this why Nana had taken him under her wing? She wasn't listed as someone who knew about him…a contact like Sheriff Ryker…but something told him that she must have had a sixth sense about what was going on. Someone with a past like hers would have picked up on the slightest details. She'd have known how to read body language and detect incongruities better than the average person. She would have understood how critical it was to keep his true identity a secret.

"This clipping is about the capture and execution of Che Guevara," Mandi said. "I don't get it."

"Mandi. The CIA played a major role in that operation, as with the other operations she seems to have been a part of. Nana wasn't serving in the military, directly. Your grandmother worked in intelligence. I believe our sweet little Nana was a government spy."

Mandi lowered herself to the floor, lay back and held her head.

"Just give me a second," she said, closing her eyes. "This is too much. It's you all over again. Keeping secrets from me. The two people I have opened my heart to more than anyone else in my life are the very two who kept secrets close to theirs. I say *kept* for Nana, because she's gone now and I won't ever have the chance to ask her questions and she won't ever get the chance to tell me her full story. But you, Gray? You're still keeping them. Aren't you? I can feel it but I can't understand why. What are you? Ex-CIA like my grandmother? Did she know this about you?"

"Heck no. I'm not CIA and never was. I'd swear that on her grave. Mandi, you have always had not only my heart but my soul, too. All of it."

He didn't deny the secrets, but he was telling her the truth. It didn't matter what his name had been in the past or where he'd lived or what he'd done, his heart and soul were constant. His soul was the one part of him that was his true self no matter what. The part of him that had never changed, other than to let her in.

It was a lot for both of them to process. He still couldn't tell her about his past. It wasn't safe to do so, especially after his close call today. But what if someday she found out like this? After his death. After a life of not sharing the whole of him with her. He'd asked her if she trusted him. This whole thing reeked of the Red Riding Hood and Big Bad Wolf story, even if he hadn't harmed her grandmother. He'd lied to them both. Worked his way into their lives. Put them at risk, nonetheless. Sure, Nana had kept secrets about her life, but they were all in her past. Gray was actively, consciously living a lie and letting them get tangled in it. He swallowed back the bitter taste of guilt then reached into the box again. Mandi just stared at him from where she lay.

He rummaged through more evidence and held up a love letter with names he didn't recognize. It was one of many between someone named Blue Bird and Spider Lace. Code names. He held up the letter for Mandi to see. "Do these code names ring a bell?"

She sat up, looked at the note and shook her head.

"No, but that's Nana's handwriting."

There were still more boxes. He was thinking there was a pretty good chance that the one marked "doll collection" didn't really contain dolls. *You sneaky woman, Nana.*

"Gray." She sounded worried. He put the letter back in the box.

"Yes? You sure you're going to be alright?"

"I know I've seen my birth certificate and I even saw my dad's once, but I can't help but wonder—"

Gray got on his knees and rubbed his hands on her ankles. He knew where she was going with this, and he knew how easily the government could issue a fake birth certificate if they wanted to. He had one. But he was sure that wasn't the case here.

"Mandi, have you looked at your dad and Nana? And yourself? Trust me, you're related. Even strangers would know that at first glance."

"Yeah, I guess you're right. It's hard to take this all in, though. And I'm still wondering if the man in the photo was my grandfather."

He patted her ankles and stood, then offered her a hand and pulled her up.

"I know," he said. "There's more stuff in this box. We can keep looking if you're up to it."

She started looking through her box as he

went through his. Some of the items were just old magazine editions, a vintage sweater or two and what looked like old souvenirs from various countries.

"If she was a spy, why would she have all this stuff saved?"

"Most of it isn't classified anymore. Maybe it was given to her later on. Maybe, for safety…just in case…she decided to keep it quiet. Who knows? Sometimes it's hard to part with memories that are an integral part of you…of your history. Or perhaps, since you said she lost people she cared about, maybe she was torn between memories and letting go."

"Maybe. I still can't help but wonder about my grandfather…the father John never knew. I have a strong feeling he was the man in the photo with the other woman. I just know these have to be the two friends she spoke of in her journal. The two she considered to be family."

Gray pulled an envelope from between the pages of an old calendar and opened it. He held up a photo of Nana and her same two friends sitting around a bistro table with smiles on their faces. Nana sat in the middle and both of her friends were pointing at her belly. Mandi took it from him, then glanced at the backside. A note was written in faded ink in the upper corner.

*Our last photo before I was sent home pregnant. They were supposed to follow after a few more months in Vietnam. They never made it out alive. My child will never know his father. Of all the things I've done in life, I don't know if I can go on without them in my life or if I can raise this child alone.*

Mandi covered her mouth and went to the window. She stared outside for a few silent seconds.

"So that was my grandfather. Nana did share something in confidence, Gray. I was eighteen at the time. I don't think she'd care if you knew at this point and I don't know what my father knows or doesn't know. Nana said she never got married, which I can understand after seeing the life she led. But not being married, according to her, made life hard for a while because she was older than most women raising kids at the time and she was doing it alone. She told people her "husband" died at war to avoid gossip and stigma. That's all I knew until recently. I feel like we should still respect that part of her history. Keep it to ourselves because, although times have changed, I don't know what the community knows and I want people to remember her the way she wanted them to see her. She was private. She wanted her actions…advocacy…to be what stood out. Not her personal life."

He nodded and put a hand on her shoulder.

"Don't worry. I won't say anything. We'll need to move all of this somewhere else, though." He went over and got the box labeled "doll collection." "This might have more answers in it."

Mandi turned and joined him.

"Oh. I did have a lot of dolls in elementary school. I got rid of them by the seventh grade. I thought they were given away."

Gray raised a brow at her.

"Didn't you notice the other clever box labels? I guarantee you there aren't dolls in here." He cut the tape and looked inside.

"I told you," she said. "That was my favorite baby doll because you could give her a baby bottle of water and it would actually pee out into her diaper. Oh, and the horse figurines. I was so into them because of the wild horses of the Outer Banks."

Gray shook his head. There really were dolls in the box.

The doorbell rang and then someone knocked loudly.

She put the dolls down and they both looked at the room and open boxes.

"Were you expecting someone?" Gray asked.

"No. Let's lock up. We can come back to deal with all this later." She closed the window and they each picked up a kitten from the box they were napping in. Mandi followed him, stopping briefly at an upstairs hall window to look outside.

"Gray, it's my dad. I don't want to deal with him right now. I'm sure it's about seeing us last night on your motorcycle and this house and who knows what else."

"Keep quiet and follow me." They reached the living room and placed the kittens in the playpen, then he filled their food and water while she ran upstairs and locked the attic door. The doorbell rang twice, back-to-back.

Gray took Mandi's hand. "They'll be okay," he whispered.

Windy and Storm snuggled on the blanket and fell asleep. Gray slid the balcony door open and held a finger to his lips. He pulled her outside and closed the door behind him, quickly locking it because he didn't trust John not to snoop.

"What are we doing?" she asked.

"Isn't it obvious? Just like when I first arrived in Turtleback and you were twenty. We're ditching your dad."

MANDI HELD ON to Gray's hand and ran as hard as she could. They didn't dare laugh until they were halfway to his place and out of earshot. She stumbled in the sand and couldn't stop cracking up.

"No, no. We can't stop yet. Hurry, he's behind us," Gray said.

"Is he really?" She looked over her shoulder as they cleared the grassy dune to his property and headed for the lighthouse. "I don't see him," she panted.

"He's not, but I got you to go faster," Gray laughed. She looked at him in shock, then broke out laughing again. He unlocked the lighthouse and let her duck inside ahead of him, then bolted the door behind them.

Mandi leaned forward to catch her breath. The air was damp and salty. Thick stone walls lined the small entry and a spiral iron staircase wound its way past whitewashed masonry walls clear to the top. There were chips in the black-and-white-tiled floor that needed repair and the walls bore the signs of aging, but it was all perfect. Exactly as she remembered it. She went to the stairs and touched the cold, iron railing, then looked over at Gray. He was leaning back against the door watching her. The space was silent but for the faint break of waves coming through the walls and the sound of their heavy breathing. Not a word, yet so much was being said in the way he looked at her. She took one step up.

"He might hear us through the door. Are you coming?"

Chances were her dad had given up when she didn't answer the door and had gone home, but the excitement was real. The thrill of the escape and adrenaline still coursed through her, the way it used to when they would meet secretly. Forbidden love. She remembered how powerful and deep and undeniable it was. They weren't able to ignore it back then. She wasn't so sure they were successfully ignoring it now.

He pushed off the door and joined her at the stairs.

"Race you to the top," she squealed and took off.

"You're not going to last. Did you forget how many steps there are?"

"Two hundred and eight," she called out.

"You're killing me."

"You run on the beach all the time. I'm the one who's out of shape. This is pure adrenaline."

"This is running vertically. You complained about not being able to move after one day of painting. You're going to regret this."

He caught up to her and she slowed down, though she didn't want to admit her thighs were burning like a campfire.

"I'm slowing down so that you can keep up," she said.

"I thought we were racing."

"Did I say that?" She smiled and started hanging on to the railing more to pull her weight. "Okay, fine. Maybe we should head down."

"I don't think so. You made me climb this far. We're more than halfway. You can't leave in less than a week and not spend a few minutes at the lookout."

Her chest pinched and it wasn't the exhaustion. The closer they got, the faster her last day seemed to approach. Life could be so twisted. Neither of them said much the rest of the way up. She cleared the last step and just stood there. The glass-enclosed lookout circled the level, giving them a 360-degree panoramic view of the Atlantic, the Outer Banks stretching north and south of them and the sound side of the island.

"It's unreal. You stand up here and everything looks like a painting, frozen in time," she said, under her breath. She felt his fingers lace into hers.

"You said almost those exact words the last time we hid in this lighthouse," he said.

Had she? She rubbed the pad of her thumb along the rough surface of his palm.

"I don't remember saying that, but I do remember that afternoon. We sat here and watched the sunset. By the time I made it to Nana's, she was furious with both of us, but she still covered for us when my dad called, angry because I hadn't come home or returned his calls."

"She did. She also had a firm talk with me the next day," Gray said. "She was so composed, it almost made her scarier than your dad and his threats."

"You never told me that," Mandi said, elbowing him. "You were my first kiss that evening, you know."

"I don't remember that part," Gray said.

Mandi turned and scowled at him.

"You don't remember? It was our first kiss and my first kiss ever. How could you forget?"

Gray pulled the hair band from her ponytail gently along its length. Her hair fell loose down her back and he touched it. He remembered. He remembered everything and he was going to kiss her again. She knew it. She wanted it. One last kiss.

"Remind, me, Mandi. What happened?"

He stepped closer, until the tips of their sneakers touched. He let go of her hands and held her face. Their lips were a breath apart and she rested her palms against his shirt. Her heart rate raced out of control.

"We stood in this spot, just like this, then you kissed me."

"Like this…" He pressed his lips against hers and kissed her with the same longing that had consumed them the first time. She met him with equal intensity, holding on and letting her heart spiral in a dangerous free fall. He wrapped his arms around her and threaded his fingers through her hair like he wanted to hold on forever…as if this time, he wouldn't let her go. She held on, taking his lips in hers, afraid that it was going to end. A tear escaped the corner of her eye because she knew it would. He rested his forehead against hers and wiped her face, then gave her one last tender kiss. A soft, whisper of a kiss that promised neither goodbye nor forever.

"We should go. I have to pick Laddie up," he said.

She nodded and rubbed her fingertips

against her swollen lips. She couldn't look up. She was afraid to read the message in his eyes.

She didn't want it to be goodbye.

But how could she stay and make it work when he was still as closed off as he'd ever been?

## *CHAPTER ELEVEN*

JOHN HUNG UP the phone and took a sip of his scotch. He was on to something and the power fired him up and gave him purpose. His contact further up the ranks in the political world, from John's days as mayor, had come through. It took some pressure, but in the end, no one with serious political aspirations wanted incriminating dirt on their campaign finances or personal life getting in the hands of reporters. Especially not before an election season. This guy knew that getting the information John wanted carried the risk of getting fired, but that only served as extra incentive for him to keep quiet about it. The PI John had hired also contacted him just a few hours ago and simply said that he was sending a file that John would find very interesting. He assured John it would be worth every penny he'd paid him.

He took another sip, then opened his

emails. He tapped the end of his pen on the desk waiting for the spotty internet service to work. It had to be another storm coming through. That always broke up the signal, an issue most of the Outer Banks had to deal with. He was counting on the information. He needed to stop that Grayson Zale from getting his paws on Mandi again.

He wiped the sweat on his temples against his sleeve and refreshed the page. It still wasn't loading. He wasn't a stupid man. He understood business and finances. He'd built himself up. Sure, his mother had put him through school, but he had made use of every bit of his education. Nothing had been wasted. And when it came to people, he had learned from experience. He had been only halfway through college when he had married Audra, but he made it work for as long as he could. He finished his degree and put all he had into being the best provider he could be. And where did it get him? She had abandoned him and, eventually, divorced him. People did not understand love or life at that age. Period. All the stories he'd heard from people around town about how they had met in high school and were still happily married thirty years later? He didn't believe it. Married, maybe. Happy?

He snorted out loud. Grayson Zale wasn't going to ruin his daughter's life the way Audra had ruined John's. Mandi needed to pursue her career and be successful because love didn't last, but money did. If a person was smart about it and knew how to invest, then when people turn their backs on them, at least they'd still have a home and bank account.

He needed Mandi to listen to him. That girl was born stubborn. Maybe he lied a little about what he would do with the cottage, but only to get her to listen. She didn't understand money the way he did. What he could do with the property would be an investment in her future. It would put her in a position where no one could mess with her. She'd have something to fall back on. And Grayson wasn't going to get any of it. Not a dime. He saw those two yesterday. Grayson was getting to her. He could see it in Mandi's face. She was falling for the guy again and getting confused. It was the motorcycle. What was it about guys with motorcycles? He didn't get it.

The page loaded and he logged into his emails. There it was in a secured file. He opened it and scrolled through the scanned documents and some old photos.

"Well, I'll be." He tapped the pen faster. "I knew you were a liar. Dr. Zale, I believe I finally have you right where I want—and need—you."

MANDI PARKED IN front of The Saltwater Sweetery. She had insisted on driving. She needed to feel in control.

"I won't take long," Gray said. He got out and crossed the street to pick up Laddie from the used bookstore. Mandi hurried into the bakery. She needed someone to talk to and, with Nana gone, the only person she could trust with this was Darla.

She opened the door and was relieved that there weren't any customers in the bakery. Darla wasn't up front, which meant she was probably in the kitchen pulling out something fresh from the oven. Mandi went around the counter and through the swinging doors to the kitchen and was caught off guard for the umpteenth time today. She held up her palms apologetically.

"I'm so sorry. I didn't mean to interrupt anything."

Darla and Nora were near the back door to the bakery standing quite close. They let go of each other's hands and Darla quickly grabbed a chocolate ganache cake with a Will You Marry Me sign stuck in it off the counter and put it in a box. Nora's face was beet red.

"You're not interrupting," Darla said in too singsong a voice. "Come on in. Nora just came by to pick this cake up for Gavin."

Nora gathered herself.

"Yes. Don't say anything because it's supposed to be a surprise," she added.

Mandi was confused.

"You're proposing to Gavin?"

Nora looked aghast.

"Gosh no. Gavin is proposing to his girlfriend tonight and didn't have time to set it all up, so Darla made the cake and I offered to pick it up for him."

"Oh, okay. That's really sweet."

It was. So was the fact that Darla and Nora clearly cared about each other. How long had that been going on? Had she really disconnected herself from Turtleback so much that she didn't even know what her friends were going through or how their lives had been changing? Was it hypocritical for her to have come here needing to talk to a friend about what was happening between her and Gray, when she had not been around for Darla to confide in? And since Darla had never mentioned anything on the phone or in a text message, that meant Mandi really had left a rift between herself and the people in Turtleback. The truth was, two years ago, she had wanted to do just that. She thought or felt that she needed to shut her past off in order to embrace her future. No regrets? Forget that. She was beginning to regret everything.

"Are you okay, Mandi?"

Darla looked at Nora, who joined her in ushering Mandi to a metal kitchen stool to sit down. All Mandi could do was shake her head. She was getting choked up. She didn't want to cry. Gray was going to meet her here and she couldn't let him see her like this. She could feel the ugly cry face coming on.

"Oh, girl, what happened?" Nora said, handing her a wad of paper towels.

A sob escaped and the ensuing tears showed no shame. She wiped her face and blew her nose but the sobs still came in hiccups.

"I kissed Gray." More tears and hiccups.

"Okay," Darla said, processing what she'd said. "How is that a bad thing?"

"I'm leaving! Darla, I can't stay. We had our chance. What am I doing? I hurt him once and now I'm going to put him—and myself—through the same thing again. Everything is wrong about this. I don't even know if we trust each other enough or communicate well enough to ever be together that way."

"But I don't understand," Nora said, rubbing Mandi's back. "Do you love him?"

"Does it matter anymore?"

"Honey. It's all that should ever matter," Darla said softly, exchanging looks with Nora.

Nora handed her more paper towels and Mandi dried her face and tried to compose herself.

"That's what my grandmother used to say. Love was all that mattered. I do understand and believe that, but I don't know if I can make it work or if he really feels the same way. A kiss is one thing, but now, his job is here and mine isn't."

That's the only explanation she could

give them. She couldn't tell them about everything in Nana's attic or how it only reminded her of how Gray never really opened up about his past with her. Her own grandmother...the one person she trusted more than anyone in the world...had kept an entire life from her. She wanted to trust Gray...she *did* trust him to some extent...but she didn't think he would ever fully trust her. How could two people build a life on that? Love *was* all that mattered, but with love came trust. Maybe that meant he simply didn't love her enough.

"What are you really afraid of, Mandi?" Darla asked.

"I don't know." She got up and threw the paper towels in the trash and washed her hands. "I should go. Thank you for listening. I think I've been holding so much in since the funeral I just got overwhelmed. Especially today. And... I'm so sorry for barging in here earlier."

Nora's cheeks flushed again. Mandi didn't know her as well, but she seemed like a shy one.

"Um, about that," Darla said. "It's a small town and, unfortunately, not everyone is—"

"You don't have to say another word. I get it. I respect privacy." She thought of her dad and how he disapproved of her and Gray and interfered from the start. "And you know what? Our relationships are nobody else's business. But remember, when I'm gone, that I'm only a phone call away. Don't be strangers. And hang on to what you have. You two deserve to be happy together."

They both closed their eyes and only then did Mandi realize that Gray had pushed open the kitchen door behind her and, from the looks on Nora and Darla's faces, must have heard her last words. *Shoot.* She turned and smiled at him. His face wasn't readable.

"Hey, ladies. I didn't want to bring Laddie into the kitchen. When you own a rough collie, dog hair becomes a condiment. I don't think you want that."

"I'll be right out," Mandi said, turning back around and mouthing "sorry" to her friends.

"Oh, and Darla, I was hoping to get a bag of saltwater taffy but I think I smell something burning in here," Gray said.

"No! My batch of almond croissants," Darla lamented. They all rushed about,

Darla opening the oven, Mandi tossing her oven mitts and Nora opening the back door to keep the alarm from going off. The croissants looked okay on top but their bottoms were charred.

"It's my fault," Mandi said. "I kept you from your work. I'm so sorry. I'll stay and help you with another batch if you need me to. Gray can take my car home."

"I'd stay, too, but I have to get this cake delivered," Nora said.

"Tell me you're not chucking those," Gray said. "Save the tops, like people do with muffin tops. Cut the bottom off and you have a smoked croissant. Great with cheese."

Mandi, Nora and Darla stared at him.

"That's why you're a vet and not a chef," Darla said. "They're all yours, Gray. On the house. I'll throw in some saltwater taffy as a thank-you for putting them to good use."

Mandi scrunched her nose at him. The things one could still learn about a person even after years of knowing them. Smoked croissants. Just, wow.

GRAY PICKED UP speed and Laddie kept pace at his side. Twenty-five minutes and counting. He needed the run. He needed to sweat and settle his nerves and think. The morning sun had already cleared the horizon, but he didn't have surgeries scheduled this morning and his first appointment wasn't for an hour.

He adjusted his ball cap and pushed his sunglasses higher on his nose. Neither was that comfortable with as much as he was sweating, but he had decided to avoid passing Nana's house. The whole point of the run was to purge his mind and if he so much as got a glimpse of Mandi, that wouldn't happen. She'd be leaving in just a matter of days. He was having a tough time accepting that fact. He had already run down the beach from his place, up a side trail not many knew about and around the outskirts of town, stopping only once, briefly, to give Laddie a drink of water. They were on the road leading out of the central part of town and toward the side street that wove its way to the lighthouse and access to other beach houses. Ten minutes and they'd be home… but his thoughts weren't any clearer than when he'd set out running.

That kiss…

It had floored him. He should never have

let it happen because now there was no turning back for him. There would be no denying that he still had feelings for her. He may have hidden them…stored them away like Nana had done…but that kiss proved that nothing had changed. His feelings for Mandi were the same, if not stronger.

*You love her. You've never loved anyone else. Don't let her walk away this time.*

But how was he supposed to manage that? His situation was limiting. And he already had a practice here in Turtleback. People didn't walk away from something like that. Medical practices of any kind were tough to get off the ground and in the black, and he had already started his life over once. He couldn't do it again even if he told Mandi the truth and she agreed to throw her life away and relocate with him through WITSEC… with new identities. He couldn't abandon the animals—pets and wildlife—that he cared for. His work here was his life. The problem was that Mandi meant the world to him, too, and he couldn't expect that kind of a sacrifice from her either.

She'd left him with a hole in his life once and she was going to again. God help him, he could still smell her hair and feel her lips on his. He could still feel her in his arms and he wanted to hold her like that forever. But he wasn't sure she felt the same way. He could tell, back at the bakery, that she had told her friends what had happened. It showed all over her face. She was torn.

He thought about Nana's past. There was something of her spirit in Mandi. The need to explore, maybe. Nana had gotten that need out of her system in a big way, but she had eventually settled down. Or she'd lost her drive when her friends had been killed. He wasn't sure if Mandi was ready for settling down and he had no right to hold her back. Maybe they just weren't meant to be in this lifetime.

Sometimes, true love was about letting go.

Laddie slowed his pace slightly, so Gray did the same. Loyalty and trust. There was so much people could learn from dogs. Sticking with your pack…your family. Facing the odds together.

*Keep it all close to your heart.* Nana must have known they'd find her secrets tucked in those boxes after her death. Maybe her message wasn't just about the house. Maybe she knew he'd catch on and understand that she had suspected he was in the protection program. Was she telling him to keep his past a secret? To not tell Mandi or anyone else? Because she understood the dangers involved firsthand in having an undercover identity revealed?

He slowed to a cooldown walk. Love. Keep *love* close to your heart. Maybe she was trying to let him know why she had bequeathed him half the house. He was right. She really was giving him a second chance. She was telling him not to throw what he and Mandi had away. Just because WITSEC strongly urged witnesses to never tell anyone—not even a new spouse— about their past for safety reasons didn't mean he couldn't show Mandi love and trust in other ways. He needed her in his life. He needed to tell her that he loved her. Maybe if she had no doubts…

He glanced behind him at the sound of a car engine. Laddie circled him. No dog would have nervous energy after a run like that, but he couldn't blame him. He recognized John's car. Laddie never liked the guy.

Gray kept walking at a brisk pace. John

drove up, slowed alongside him and rolled down the passenger window.

"Want a lift?"

"Nope. We're good." He kept walking. Odd that he asked. John would have a fit over dog hair in his fancy car.

"Hop in, Grayson. We need to talk." John kept rolling at his pace. The guy had nerve.

"It might come as a shock, John, but not everyone drops what they're doing when you snap your fingers. I know what this is about. Mandi's old enough to make her own decisions now and I don't take orders from you." Gray kept walking. Laddie insisted on walking between him and the car.

"Well, I think you'll take one from me this time. I always did find it curious how you sometimes wear those shades of yours on the beach or around town, even when it's cloudy. Or how you're known as the guy who always offers to take the photos but is never in them."

Gray stopped in his tracks. His sweat turned cold. Adrenaline instantly shot through him. His pulse buzzed in his ears. It was happening. His world was caving in. His life in Turtleback would all be gone.

Grayson Zale would have to disappear all over again and reappear as someone he didn't know. Someone dropped off with a month's stipend in a new town and left to start over.

"I thought that would mean something." John chuckled and the sound made Gray want to grab him by the collar, but he didn't. John wasn't worth a scene or arrest. John patted a stack of paper copies on the passenger seat. Gray didn't have to look long to know what was happening. Between the copy of his diploma sticking out from the stack and that of a yearbook page with his senior photo on it, he knew. "Get in, Gray."

"You get out. You have something to say? Come stand in front of me like a man and say it."

"As you wish." He sounded confident and condescending. The hairs on Gray's neck prickled.

John gave his gas a short spurt and pulled over ahead of them. He got out, hoisted the waist of his pants up and walked over as if he owned the street, grass, sand and Gray. Gray folded his arms and waited. His pulse sped up instead of slowing down. This wasn't good. What had John done? Was he bluffing? Maybe he didn't know everything. But he was implying he *knew*. If he did, that was it. It was over. He had the power to force Gray into an entirely new life. New name. New identity. Leaving everything and everyone behind. Including Mandi.

"Grayson Zale. *Doctor*. Sorry, I forgot your title. I shouldn't, considering it's one of the only real things about you. That and your first name. Am I right? Funny how classmates talk and post things on social media. There are a limited number of vet schools in America. It didn't take long to track you down and check posts from that school. Look at this old photo." He brought it up on his cell phone and held it so Gray could see. "I have a print of it in the car. I have duplicate prints and photos of everything, so don't bother trying to take that pile you saw. Look." He held the phone closer. "Right there under your vet school class photo it reads 'Dr. Grayson *Killian*.' I counted across the row more than once, so unless you have an identical twin…"

An icy wave spread through Gray's chest. Of all the people who could find out about him, the one he trusted the least *knew*. This would mean reporting him to the marshals, who in turn would give Gray thirty minutes to pack up and disappear. His life was over. Again.

"Do you have any idea what you're doing? What do you want, John?"

"I want you to leave my daughter alone. She doesn't need some lying criminal in her life."

Criminal? He wasn't a criminal. He'd helped to put away a government traitor. What had John actually found on him?

"What makes you think I'm a criminal? Or not good enough for her?"

"Because I know enough to know that you're hiding something. The name change? On credit cards, too. I'm betting your ID is fake. What was it? Embezzlement? Scam artist? The perfect murder?"

"I assure you, I haven't killed anyone."

"I don't think you did. There's no such thing as a perfect murder. You would have been caught by now. My contacts said nothing indicated you were a killer, but I wanted to see the look on your face. A man's eyes say a lot about him."

Had John looked in the mirror lately?

"There are plenty of reasons a person chooses to change their name. Sometimes it's personal." He needed to think. He couldn't reveal classified information, even if John had something on him, but maybe if he gave John just enough to get him off his back, he'd stop digging and leave well enough alone.

"Family is as personal as it gets. The welfare and safety of my daughter is important to me," John said.

"I'm not a criminal and you know that. But I will say that there are some vindictive people out there who don't like me and if they find me, they'll try to hurt anyone I care about, too."

"What are you? Mafia?"

"No." Jeez. Gray rubbed the sweat off his face with his T-shirt. "Are you listening to me? People I care about includes your daughter. If family is so important to you, then you wouldn't want to endanger her. Let it go, John. Whatever you think you're going to dig up on me? You won't find anything worth Mandi's safety. Her life or mine."

John narrowed his eyes and contemplated what Gray had given him. It had to be enough.

"I think there's more to it," John finally said.

Gray flexed his knuckles and raked his hair back.

"Have you told anyone who knew me by Killian where I'm living?"

John grinned and it made Gray feel sick inside.

"Have you?" Gray realized his voice was loud enough to carry. He took a deep breath and lowered his voice. "Have you?"

"You really are nervous. None of that arrogant, macho motorcycle guy left. Huh?"

"John, don't push me."

"No. I didn't tell anyone. I was getting information, not giving it. So obviously that means a couple of contacts know, along with my PI, if that counts."

A fraction of the tension in Gray's chest eased, but only a fraction. *Anyone* knowing posed a risk, but at least John's sleuthing was limited to a few people. For now. It hadn't been blasted across media channels. Yet. He could still put a stopper in the bottle if no one in town or in general knew. If he could shut John up, he'd at least be able to keep his life as it was, here at Turtleback Beach.

"What do you want from me? I just told you that you might put Mandi in danger and you're still at it? You're a sick man."

"Maybe. Anyway, here's how it's going to work. First, you're going to distance yourself from Mandi. She'll be gone soon and I don't want her throwing her future away for you. Secondly, you're going to convince her to sell her share of the house to me. Tell her you changed your mind and think that it's the best choice you two have."

"You're blackmailing me."

John ignored him and went on. He was a man with blinders on. He couldn't see anything beyond what he'd set his mind to do, regardless of the consequences.

"You're going to be selling me your share of the house, too, by the way. That whole clause about the two of you having to agree on the sale and all that? Let's just agree that it's not going to be an issue. Got that? Don't think I didn't notice how you two have been fixing the place up to put it on the market. She wouldn't have been doing all that on my account because I told her I'd buy the place as is. So, the sale goes to me. It's that simple. After that, we can each keep to ourselves and live happily ever after. And I know you'll do all of this because you've made it clear that you care about Mandi and don't want her in any danger, on your account. But if you ever reconnect with her or lead her on or tell her or anyone else about this conversation, I'll have the authorities investigating you and I'll make sure the whole world knows who you really are."

## CHAPTER TWELVE

MANDI CHECKED THE lasagna in the oven and set the timer for an extra ten minutes. The cheese on top needed to be a dark golden brown. Eating lasagna any other way was a sin.

"Smells good, doesn't it, kiddo?"

Laddie panted and his brows quirked up. He had somehow escaped Gray's place earlier today and showed up at her balcony door. The second she let him in, he went straight for Windy and Storm. Poor guy. Their adopted dad had missed them. She called Gray's clinic immediately to let him know and he said he would come around after work to pick him up. It was kind of odd that he didn't mention hanging out or even helping with boxes. He sounded preoccupied and said it was going to be a long day at work and that he'd be late. It was to be expected. He was a vet and the only one in Turtleback, which meant he was always on call. It *was* getting closer to a full moon. Maybe vet clinics suffered the same full-moon phenomenon that human emergency rooms did.

"Don't look too hopeful. This isn't for you. Gray would kill me if I upset your stomach."

She was also pretty sure onions and garlic were toxic to dogs and cats. Cartoon versions could eat all the pizza and junk food they wanted, a fact she didn't quite get. Kids watching those shows would think it was okay and go feed their pets things that would make them sick.

She took the lettuce, tomatoes, cucumbers and feta cheese out of the fridge and grabbed a large salad bowl and a jar of kalamata olives and some extra-virgin olive oil and balsamic vinegar from the pantry.

Forget burned croissants. She was making a special dinner for Gray tonight. A surprise, partly because he was having a long day and partly because she had the urge to do something nice for him. If he wanted to think of it as a date, she was okay with that. She tugged the hem of her shirt down, then rubbed her palms nervously against her jeans. No, really. She was okay with it being a date. After yesterday's kiss and talking to Nora and Darla, it hit her. There had to be a way to make this work. If they both wanted to…if they were passionate enough about it…about each other…they'd figure out a way. Even if she had to be the one to travel for work or commute out of state, she'd consider doing it. For him. For them. All she knew was that she couldn't run away this time. She had to see where this would go and hope that eventually he'd trust her enough to open up. When he had told her his soul was hers, everything seemed to click into place. Their souls were meant to be together. The rest was…noise. Sensory pollution that confused things the way light pollution confused turtles and other wildlife.

After seeing how Nana had lived her life, Mandi was beginning to realize she was stronger than she thought she was. Nana had proved her bravery and courage against the odds. She'd proved herself in what was predominantly a man's world at the time. And not just in one town, but all over the world in different cultures. The constant was an individuality and strength that had come from within, not from those around her. She took it with her wherever she landed…even here in Turtleback.

Mandi didn't need to fear living under her father's domineering attitude, and she could now see how different Gray really was. She had been projecting her father on him, and that was so unfair. Gray was his own man. Honest. Compassionate. Loving. And maybe she had been too hard on him because of her own insecurities. If there was something in his past too painful to bring up, then if she loved him, she'd give him that space and the time he needed. Nana had her reasons for keeping her past to herself. Like Gray had said, she had suffered loss or maybe even some other event that was too painful to relive.

A lump rose in her throat at the prospect that Gray might have suffered in his past… his childhood. Had he been abused? She covered her mouth and shook her head. She couldn't think about it. She couldn't let her imagination run wild like that, dwelling on scary thoughts. All that mattered was the truth and he'd tell her when he was ready.

If ever. She would have to accept that. She was the one who needed to trust him.

For now, she wanted to show him that she was ready. Ready to come back to him. She only had three more days left in Turtleback before heading back to New York. She had to report to work in five days, but she could talk to her supervisors. Maybe she could do some telecommuting or even alternate weeks—one here working via the internet and one in New York. The travel would cost her, but she'd figure something out. She could get a roommate in New York to cut rental costs.

It was just that, when she walked through the house this morning, it felt different. All she had left was to paint the living room and touch up the paint in the hall and bedrooms—which she planned to do tomorrow... In fact, she and Gray were going to move the kittens to Gray's because, even if she used paint low in volatile organic compounds, she didn't want them breathing any odors or fumes. They were too little and vulnerable. But it wasn't the fact that things were repaired or updated that had changed. She and Gray had worked on the place together to get it ready for sale, but the very act of doing so had made the place feel like a home for them. She realized that Nana was right and the two of them belonged there with Laddie, Windy and Storm.

Butterflies flitted in her stomach the way they used to when she first laid eyes on the new vet in town. They were getting a second chance.

*Thank you, Nana. I love you.*

The oven timer went off and she set the pan on the stove top, then finished the Mediterranean salad. She glanced at her watch. The sky was beginning to dim. He said late but this was much later than he'd worked other nights.

She went to the living room and looked outside. The only people on the beach were a couple taking a walk in the direction of town. What if something happened to him? What if he was on his motorcycle and—

She shook the thought away. She couldn't think like that. She had no reason to worry. He'd be here. Likely in his truck, since he'd planned on picking Laddie up. Except that he didn't know that this morning. So he could have ridden to work. Maybe he went home first and was walking over. That's why he still wasn't here. She looked down the beach toward the lighthouse but there was no sign of him. Okay, then. Maybe he was coming straight here and planning to leave his bike here and walk home with Laddie after dinner. Or…stay over and crash on the couch.

Laddie let out a bark and ran to the front door wagging his tail. He was here. She straightened her shirt and lit the candle in the oversize votive on the kitchen table. Gray let himself in.

"Hey, you. I hope everything was okay at the clinic," she said, meeting him by the door. She kind of expected at least a quick peck on the lips. There wasn't one.

"Hey. Yeah, everything was fine. I mean, the patients did well. There were just a lot of them and a few walk-ins. As tourist season builds up and people bring their dogs along, things happen. People don't think ahead and plan right. I mean, when there's a duplex rental with a shared yard and one family brings along their dog and the other kids bring their guinea pig, it's not a good scenario. Especially when the kids forget to close doors."

"Oh, no. The guinea pig?"

"She made it but was terrified. Luckily her heart held out. They intervened in time and the dog couldn't get under the planter where the guinea pig managed to hide. They wanted the dog checked, though, because they pulled so hard on his leash he kept gag coughing."

"Wow. I bet they were glad you were nearby." Turtleback Beach needed him. He was saving lives here. All she was doing with her career was coming up with fresh ways to push products on people.

Gray didn't acknowledge her compliment, but then, he'd always been humble. He looked over at Laddie, who was now lounging with the kittens playing on his back.

"That must feel like a great massage," Mandi said. She could offer Gray a neck rub after dinner. She'd wait and see how things went.

"Come on, boy. Time to go," Gray said, patting his thigh. Laddie whined like a toddler not wanting to leave the playground.

"But…you can stay. I made dinner. Lasagna. Nana's recipe. I figured you'd be hungry and there are only so many smoked croissants a guy can eat."

"Aw, man. It smells good. Really. But I'm wiped out and have some cat spay and neuter surgeries early tomorrow morning, so I need to get home."

Any butterflies in her stomach fluttered to her feet like dried leaves falling from a tree in autumn. He looked tired. Distracted. But her gut told her it wasn't because of work. He was retreating again. She had scared him. He was regretting their kiss. She shrugged.

"Of course. You're busy. How about I pack you some to take with you?"

"That would be great. If it's not too much trouble."

So formal sounding. She went to the kitchen to rummage for a couple of containers and filled them with salad and lasagna. He didn't follow her. Instead, he was lifting the kittens off Laddie and trying to coax him to get up. She took the bottle of Pinot Noir off the counter and shoved it in a cabinet, as if it were to blame, then bagged the containers and left the kitchen.

"Here you go. Oh, did you bring the truck? Remember about the kittens? I was going to try to paint tomorrow."

He rubbed his forehead and pointed at the kittens.

"Yes. I almost forgot, but yes, I have the truck. I'll take them. That'll get Laddie moving and hopefully he'll stay at home tomorrow. He's never done that to me before—escaping and running off. I need to reinforce the window screen he knocked out."

"Where there's a will, there's a way. Look at the three of them."

They looked like an inseparable family. It was heartwarming, yet the thought saddened her.

"Do you think you'll be by tomorrow to help empty the attic?" He had suggested yesterday that they store Nana's boxes at his place, temporarily.

"Um. Actually, tomorrow's another busy day. Look, Mandi. I know this isn't what I said before, but maybe we don't have to move her boxes. Maybe we should just sell to your dad and be done with it."

"But you were so against that. *I'm* so

against that, now. The turtles, the beach...
everything."

Where had his change of heart come from?

"I know. But with work and...stuff... I'm
realizing that I've taken on more than I can
handle."

"More than you can handle? I stayed,
Gray. We've been working together. We
were on the same page. We had a plan."

"Yeah, well. Plans change. Don't they?"

"Wait. Is this about the cottage or us?"

He averted his eyes and put his hand on
the doorknob.

"You're leaving. There is no us."

And there it was. She was such an idiot.
Why? Why did she let herself think that he
could forgive her for leaving him the first
time? Why did she let her guard down? *Because you still love him. You can't erase
love.* But what she felt for him didn't matter. She had been reluctant to trust him, but
she was the one who had left him at the
altar. Why should he trust her? She couldn't
blame him for wanting out. *There is no us.*
Fine. If there was anything she was experienced at, it was leaving. This time, it would
be for good.

"SHE SAID YES." Gavin waltzed into the clinic bright and early the next day, his face beaming. Chanda and Nora squealed and congratulated him.

"Congrats, man." Gray shook his hand. He was happy for Gavin, but he had to stop himself from warning the unsuspecting fellow. He was dying to tell him not to throw the ring receipt away or not to get his hopes up until she actually said "I do" and they were pronounced man and wife. Because even seconds before that moment, everything could change and turn his world upside down.

Gray took some charts that he needed to update from last night and went to his office. Within minutes Nora came in and closed the door.

"What's up?" he asked, without looking over. He kept filling in his notes. Probably not all necessary details, but he needed to be busy and left alone.

"Can we talk? It's important."

He hesitated, then set his pen down and gave her his full attention. Had she heard something? Had John reneged on his promise to stay quiet if Gray held up his side of the deal? Nora shifted her weight and fidgeted with her necklace.

"I need to know if you don't want me working here anymore. I mean, I know my rights, but I don't want to be anywhere I'm judged or not wanted."

"What? What in the world are you talking about, Nora?"

"You've been in a mood since yesterday and I know you walked in and overheard what Mandi said at The Sweetery…" She pressed her lips together and he could tell where she was going with this and that she was trying to find the courage to talk to him about it. Society was really messed up if a person had to feel that way. "…when I was there with Darla. If you're trying to figure out how to fire me because you disapprove or something, without my suing you, then don't worry. I can give you my two weeks' notice right now. Technically, I could sue you, but I'm not like that. I just want everyone to be happy." Tears were welling in her eyes.

Gray scrubbed his stubble and leaned forward on his elbows.

"Nora. Listen to me. You are the best

vet tech anyone could ever have. Don't tell Gavin I said that. He's good, too, but you can read my mind. You're smart, skilled and one of the nicest, best people I know. Why in the world would I give a you-know-what about anything else, other than, like you said, your happiness? That said, don't you *dare* quit on me. I count on you too much. If I'm not paying you enough, say the word."

She dabbed the inner corner of her eyes and stood a little taller.

"Thank you, Dr. Z. I just thought with how serious and grumpy you've been... I kind of got nervous and thought it was about me and Darla. You still read news about people getting fired for all kinds of personal reasons."

He knew that. The world was still a backward place in so many ways. When were humans going to learn from the past and stop repeating the worst parts of history?

"I know, but that's not happening on my watch. You, Chanda and Gavin are like a second family to me here at the clinic. Don't forget that. My mood has nothing to do with you. I swear it."

"Okay. Thanks again. You know, you

and Mandi are so lucky to have each other. It makes me happy to see two, super nice, great people together."

"Yeah, well. The day after tomorrow's her last day in town. Sometimes things don't work out, but as they say, everything happens for a reason."

Nora tucked her hands in the pockets of her scrubs.

"I'm sorry. I knew she wasn't staying but the way you two looked at each other at the bakery, I thought maybe you had worked something out. I guess, with Gavin proposing and all, my head was in a romantic place."

His had been, too. There was no greater fall than coming off being high on love. But love was about giving. It was about the other person. It wasn't selfish. And that meant, for Mandi's protection and the people and critters that counted on him in this new life of his, he needed to let her go. He'd never forgive John for what he had done.

"Well, um. Why don't we go get started on our surgeries? At least there are some things we can fix in life. No pun intended."

That was not a smooth change of subject but he wasn't in his best game.

"Sure thing, Doc."

She gave him a bittersweet smile and left the office.

Gray sat back and closed his eyes. It would be easier when Mandi left. Like the first time, it would eat away at him day after day, but eventually, he'd think about her only in the dark of the night or during his sunrise walks. Except last time, he still felt like there was a thread connecting them. Nana had been that connection. This time, there was nothing holding them together.

THE HOUSE PAINTING was done and the furniture was back in place, but she had done it more to preoccupy herself than anything. After what Gray had said last night, everything seemed like a futile waste of time.

*You were wrong, Nana. We weren't meant to be. You tried, but I think you understand about leaving some things in the past.*

She finished cleaning the brushes, then she lay down on the couch and stared at the ceiling. The place was too quiet. No mewing or talking or laughing. No music playlist from Gray's phone. It felt as empty as she did.

Her phone dinged with a text from Darla.

Nora told me something was wrong with you and Gray. He's being a grizzly bear at work. Text or call me.

Did nothing stay private around here? It was a major testament to how long Nana had maintained her privacy. She must have been one smooth spy.

I'm fine.

Two seconds later.

No. You're not. I'm coming over for my lunch break in ten.

Mandi pushed her hair back and sat up. Did she want to talk? Not really. She needed to pack her suitcase and car and get ready to leave in a few days.

Fine.

She got up and tied her hair back, then went around closing the windows she had left open from painting. Things were dry enough and she didn't want her voice carrying outside when Darla came. She had already made the mistake of being overheard when Gray walked into the bakery kitchen. When would she learn? Her grandmother used to say "the walls have ears." Was that what they taught people in the CIA?

She answered the door on the first ring and Darla came bounding in.

"Okay. I don't have much time. I have someone helping at the register but I'm running low on cookies. Come sit."

She tugged Mandi back to the living room, sat next to her and looked at her expectantly.

"What gives?

"I told you I'm fine."

"*Fine* is a bad word when you use it like that. Especially when less than forty-eight hours ago you were in love."

"Well, he's not."

"Baloney. I saw him looking at you."

"But I heard his words. He's given up on this place. Last night he said to just let my dad buy it so he can focus on work and I can go start my new job. He was cold, Darla. No kiss. Not even a touch. He was distant."

"Maybe he was cold, but not in a bad way. Just cold feet. Did you tell him how you feel, or have you two been handling this like high schoolers?"

"How could he not know after what I told you happened at the lighthouse and all the time we've been spending together?"

"Mandi! You have to tell him outright. Not to be sexist, but men can be dense about this stuff. Our brains are different. I get couples who walk into my shop and the woman will comment on how she loves the decor and design of the place and all the guy will notice is the food and the smell of cinnamon. They always ask if they're smelling cinnamon. It's weird. It's like catnip or something. I can prove it. Ask Gray if he likes the painting I have hanging on the back wall and he'll probably say something like, 'What painting? There's a painting there?' But I guarantee you he knows exactly how many of what pastry I'll have baked on each day of the week."

Mandi laughed. "Okay, maybe. I get it. Our brains work differently. That still doesn't mean it can work out."

"All I'm saying is that you both have good reason to be nervous about the future. I mean, you were a runaway bride and all. You need to talk to each other. Communication is key in a relationship. Tell him the truth about how you feel and how it could work out. No euphemisms. Be clear and blunt. Promise me you'll talk to him before you leave."

"Okay, fine. I promise."

"I'll let that *fine* slide because you're promising. I gotta run. Give me a hug."

She gave Darla a big squeeze.

"You're the best. Thanks for coming here."

"I'm hoping it all works out and I'll get to see you here a lot more in the future. Let me know what happens."

Mandi smiled and nodded, then shut the door behind her.

Darla had a point. Maybe not all was lost. She'd try to talk to him. Directly and bluntly, as her friend had suggested. But the problem was that Gray was about as smooth at evading questions and changing subjects as Nana had been at keeping her past under wraps. Chances were, this time, he wouldn't be any different. But there was only one way to find out.

## CHAPTER THIRTEEN

JOHN WATCHED AS Coral opened her birthday gift and relished the way her face lit up when she lifted the multicolored gemstone bracelet from the box and laid it across her slim wrist.

"John! It's gorgeous, but it's too much. It's only my birthday."

"And worth celebrating. Besides, I have news, too. The house? Get ready to list it. And that developer you mentioned? I'm ready to talk."

"That's amazing. What made them change their minds?"

He knew she was referring to Grayson and Mandi. She didn't need all the details. Just enough to satisfy her.

"Let's just say that I finally convinced him not to pursue anything with her, and without Mandi around, he really has no need for the place."

"That almost sounds too easy." Her eyes widened. "He must have the hots for someone else if he was that willing to drop her. I bet it's what's-her-face at that bookstore."

"Maybe so."

"But wait," she said, hanging the bracelet on her wrist and holding it out for him to help her with the clasp. "Then why was he headed to her place the night before last? I know because I passed him on the road and he didn't take the turn to the lighthouse. He went straight and we both know where that leads. Oh, and I ran into her buying food earlier at the organic mercantile. Supplies for an Italian meal, plus a bottle of wine. A good one, too. That doesn't sound like a breakup to me. Are you sure they aren't toying with you to try to get a bidding war going on the place?"

John's ears felt hot. He should have known that Grayson would defy him. But he also knew how to up the pressure. He had done it in plenty of business dealings before. Successfully, too. He just needed a little more information and, this time, he wouldn't bother with Grayson. He would take it directly to Mandi. He'd get her on his side and it would be him and Mandi against Grayson Zale. His daughter was about to get a hard, tough-love lesson in why family stuck together.

GRAY TIED OFF the suture on the retriever's ear and gave Nora the nod to bring her off anesthesia. He took off his sterile gloves and rolled his shoulders. Poor thing had gotten in a dogfight with some other canine with territorial issues that needed to be on leash and wasn't. According to her owner, the trigger had been the perfect blade of grass to do their business on.

"That ear needs to be bandaged flat against her head, Gavin. You'll have to bring the bandage under her chin tight enough to keep her from shaking it loose. And she'll need a cone." Gavin had done plenty of bandaging, but they hadn't had a split-ear injury like this before and Gray wanted to be sure he knew how to handle it."

"I'm on it," Gavin said.

Gray glanced at the heart rate and blood pressure monitor. She was doing alright. And Nora was doing her thing. All good.

"I'll call in the pain prescription and talk to the owner."

He left the room before anyone could ask how *he* was doing. He didn't want to talk about it and had deliberately tried to put on a more pleasant face since Nora had approached him yesterday. His neck, however, was tighter than a bowline knot on a ship and a migraine was threatening to take hold. The look on Mandi's face, when he had brushed her off and told her there wasn't an "us" was still tearing him up inside.

He saw the candle she had lit on the table. She had clearly been hoping for time with him and he had wanted more than anything to spend it with her. She had gone out of her way and had opened her heart. That wasn't easy for her, and what did he do? He stomped on it. He'd reminded her of all she used to love about Turtleback—the cottage, the turtles…him—and then he flipped everything on its head and told her to sell the place. That he didn't care. She'd never forgive him. All this on account of her father blackmailing him. He took a swig of cold water from his bottle in the small office fridge, gathered himself and resumed his clinic duties.

He managed to reassure the family in the waiting room, got through an annual exam and, at that point, knew if he didn't lie down, he wouldn't last the rest of the day. His head was really beginning to pound.

"Hey, Chanda, how's the schedule for the afternoon? I'm gonna take lunch at home, but if we don't have anyone booked, I'll just come back if you call me with a walk-in."

"You look terrible, Dr. Zale."

"Why, thank you, Chanda. I can always count on your honesty." He gave her a lop-sided smile. He wasn't mad. He was used to her way of putting it all on the table. So used to it, in fact, that he was surprised she was the only one who hadn't commented on his mood or asked him about Mandi.

"I can't help it. It's my sign. I'm an Aries. Brutally honest to a fault."

"You keep being honest. I like it. Lying never ends well," he said.

Boy, didn't he know it. Lies had a way of growing more complicated. He rounded the counter to see her schedule screen on the computer.

"Just this one here at four. Should I call and move it?"

"No, I'll come back for it."

"Sounds good," Chanda said. He started to leave but she kept on talking. "Dr. Z, while you're at home, you might want to call and talk to her. It would probably clear up that headache. Just sayin'."

He gave her a pointed look before slipping out the door. His staff knew him too well. He knew their butting in came from a place of caring and not gossip. They definitely were a second family. One he didn't want to lose. Possibly, the only one he'd ever have here on out, since Nana was gone and he was losing Mandi, too.

*Brutally honest...talk to her.*

His temples were throbbing.

*Don't put her at risk. If you love her, then keep your messed-up life and the danger it comes with away from her.*

He geared up, put his helmet on and headed home. The sounds of the engine and his tires against the road were like jackhammers to his head and the helmet seemed to trap his thoughts in a loop.

*Tell the truth to out a lie. End up living a lie because of it. Tell lies to protect those you love. Get blackmailed for lying and get threatened with the truth. The truth puts everyone in danger, which brings you back to the original lie. Because the truth, in this case, can't set you free.*

The words looped through his head again. Whoever went around saying that the truth would set you free had never been in the witness protection program.

*Brutally honest. The truth will set you free.*

He pulled up to his place and killed the engine.

That was it. *The truth will set you free.* The truth was what got him living this lie in the first place, but the only way to deal with blackmail was to not let the blackmailer have anything to hold over you. His life here had a purpose and he loved Mandi so much the thought of losing her again was torture in its sickest form. And the pain in her eyes the night before last was no different. He couldn't do this to her. None of it was fair. To turn your back on the love of your life, to walk away from love and live the rest of your life without it…without her…it wasn't right. He had been trying to keep her safe, but letting her father manipulate him—and her—like this was the kind of betrayal she would definitely never forgive. She had done everything she could to keep her father from controlling her life and here Gray was letting him do just that to her.

He unlocked his front door and went in. Laddie came up to greet him and the kittens pounced all over his sneakers, swatting playfully at his laces. How had they escaped the playpen? Was Laddie training escape artists? He picked them up and put them back in the pen where they'd be safer and able to access their toys and food.

"Keep an eye on them, Laddie. Good boy."

He went to the kitchen cabinet by the fridge, found his migraine medicine and took a couple of capsules with a glass of milk. He'd feel better in an hour and he'd have his thoughts together. If he told Mandi the truth about what John was doing and the truth about his past, but made her understand that she couldn't ever breathe a word of it, then maybe things would be okay. He'd fill the sheriff and marshal in on what John knew and let them know Mandi was in his life for good.

No. That wouldn't work. If he told them what John had done, they'd consider him a weak link and Gray didn't want to take that chance. He was still Mandi's father and Gray didn't know or trust what officials might do in the name of keeping witnesses safe to someone who was threatening them. If her father disappeared or had an "accident," how would Gray ever be able to face Mandi?

He could sell his share of the house, though. He'd explain to Mandi why and they would keep John quiet by giving him what he wanted. And John wouldn't know any more about Gray than he had already let on, but Mandi would. Gray would tell her everything. He'd beg her to forgive him for keeping his secret. Worst-case scenario, if their lives were threatened and WITSEC had to relocate him, she could come with him. He didn't want to put her through that, but things were beginning to unravel. Black-mailers rarely stopped at one attempt. So if that's what it came to, at least she'd be safe and alive. They would have to leave Turtle-back Beach forever, though. WITSEC would find a way to cover their tracks. They always did. Maybe they'd say that they had drowned out at sea while boating…like his parents had. And he and Mandi would start over with new identities. Somewhere. They'd lose everything they had here, but at least they'd have each other.

"DAD, I'M BUSY. I can't come over right now.

Mandi put her phone on speaker and set it on the counter. She was busy baking home-made cookies instead of more lasagna. Not that she was taking what Darla said too lit-erally, but she figured snickerdoodles with extra cinnamon couldn't hurt. She wasn't going to leave for New York after tomor-row without trying one last time. She had called Chanda at the clinic to see when Gray would be done for the day and Chanda had told Mandi that he'd gone home for a bit but had one more appointment at four. That gave her two hours. She still had a final batch in the oven that had another eight minutes to go. She technically had time to swing by her father's house and then loop back to Gray's, but she didn't really want to see her dad. She was fired up and ready to lay the truth on Gray. To tell him she loved him. Her father would kill the mood.

She had the words ready in her head and had an answer prepared for anything Gray might say. By the time the sun set tonight, Gray wasn't going to have cold feet. And if he did? Well, then at least she would have put her heart out there the way Nana had been trying to get her to do for so long.

"It's important, Mandi," John insisted. "Sweetheart, listen to me, there's something you need to see."

"Then just tell me what it is. I'm that busy." She used a spatula to transfer the previous batch of cookies onto a cooling rack.

"I can't." He sounded somber. Hesitant. Like someone had died.

"Dad, what happened?"

"It's… I just can't tell you over the phone. It's serious and confidential. Life-changing, Mandi. You need to come here before you speak to anyone in town. Especially Zale."

"Really, Dad? This again? Can't you just let it go? You need to get a life instead of obsessing with mine and Gray's. I should have known that's what this was about. More games." She wiped her hand on a towel and was about to end the call.

"Mandi, he's not who he says he is. Zale

isn't even his real name. I have it here. Everything about his past. Everything you ever wanted to know. Everything he has kept from you. It's on my desk. If I'm not here when you get here, use the spare key. It's the blue metal one in Nana's console. I know we have issues, Mandi, but this is for real. I was right to worry about you."

He hung up but it took a minute for Mandi to move. Gray's past? His name wasn't real? The oven alarm startled her. She turned it off and set the tray on the counter to cool. The aroma of cinnamon had lost some of its appeal and her excitement over taking the cookies to Gray's place had dropped a notch. Her dad had a way of doing that to her. She loved him as her father, but he practically defined "toxic relationship." Nonetheless, this time she couldn't ignore what he was saying. Everything she ever wanted to know about Gray's past? Maybe it was another one of his manipulative tricks, but his voice sounded urgent. The same way he sounded when he had called her in New York to tell her that his mother had passed away.

Mandi looked at the container lined with paper napkins that she was planning to fill with cookies. She left it, took her keys, found the exact blue one her dad had told her about and walked out to her car. She'd come back for the cookies. First, she needed to see what was on John's desk and deal with whatever her dad was up to. She wouldn't be able to tell Gray all she had planned to tell him if this call from her father was weighing on her mind. She didn't want anything ruining the moment. And if John was telling the truth, then she'd deal with it, but after he pulled the Coral setup, she needed to see whatever paperwork he was talking about with her own eyes.

She drove faster than usual and hoped Carlos or one of his officers wouldn't ticket her. Her dad's place was only a few minutes away. She parked out front, noting that his car wasn't there. He must have planned not to be here. He had told her about the key for a reason. Where had he gone? To Gray's? She rang twice, then unlocked the door. Coral's perfume lingered in the air.

"Are you here, Dad? Coral?" she called out. No answer. He had mentioned his desk. She crossed the dark wood floors of the open-design living area and went to the small room on the far left that he used as a home office. His heavy mahogany desk sat at an angle facing the window that overlooked the marsh. There was a bottle of scotch sitting on the corner and an empty glass. She tilted it. Any residual liquid in it was dry. Thank goodness. If she found out he had a problem and was drinking and driving, she'd need to ask him about it. Chances were, he didn't have the scotch recently. The stack on his desk had a sticky note on it with her name. Next to it was a note that read, "Went to confront the scumbag. Talk to me later."

Oh, no. That wasn't good.

She quickly flipped through the contents of the file on top. It was all about Gray. Newspaper clippings, document copies and a few photos fell out. She picked them up and looked at each one. Gray in a uniform? He had been in the army? Why wouldn't he have told her something like that? Especially when they had found photos of Nana during all those wars. He could have brought it up then. Lots of people did college through the military. Why would it have been such a big deal?

One article featured breaking news about a captain who had been charged with treason. He looked like an older fellow in the photo. How did this relate to Gray?

A separate lined sheet of paper had a handwritten and titled "witness notes." She scanned them. They were from people who said that they had recognized his face in the background of a social media photo. That they had known him in high school but thought he had been killed in a car accident. At least that's what their school alumni magazine had reported. Another statement mentioned running into him at a grocery store while vacationing in the Outer Banks, but that Gray had insisted he had one of those familiar faces and wasn't who they thought he was. And yet another…someone from veterinary school who claimed Gray's last name wasn't Zale. Just like her dad had said. But how could that be? Mandi's pulse went into overdrive and her chest tightened. She had seen his Doctor of Veterinary Medicine certificate hanging in his office at the clinic. Was that fake, too? What was going on here?

Her legs felt weak. She sat down in her

father's desk chair and tried to process everything she was seeing. She flipped back through the evidence. She wasn't an expert at fake documents, but everything here certainly looked legitimate. There was even a copy of an old class photo he was in with New York landmarks in the background. The state he claimed he'd never visited.

She pressed her fingers to her eyes and tried to think straight. Was he a scammer? A catfish, preying on older women like Nana, getting their money—in his case half of a house—then disappearing and reappearing with a new identity? Had her father been right all along? All these years?

*No. This can't be. Calm down. There has to be some sort of explanation.* Communication was everything. Wasn't that what she'd just been told? *Talk to him.*

She took cell phone photos of each sheet and left the file on his desk. Her eyes burned and mouth felt dry. On one hand, she knew her father was a master manipulator, but even this was beyond anything he'd ever come up with before. This wasn't getting Coral to flirt or telling a white lie. This was big. Hard-core stuff.

Yet, Mandi knew Gray. Sure, he'd never been fully open about his past, but she never once imagined that the kind of things he had been keeping from her included a fake identity. This wasn't about sharing something like a childhood trauma. This was about potential criminal activity.

Her stomach churned. She stood and willed her legs to carry her down the front steps and to her car. She got in and pulled out of the driveway, just as a drop of rain hit her windshield.

She didn't know what to think. She had almost married him. She had just been thinking about marrying him now. Maybe her instincts had been right when she'd left him at their wedding. She would have married someone who wasn't even using their real name. And in leaving town, she had left her grandmother alone with him. Someone who had the entire town fooled. She gave her head a shake. *No. Gray would never hurt anyone. Whatever is going on here, I can't believe that about him.* The photos of Nana in the attic flashed in her mind. Her Nana with the secret past.

"No way."

Was Gray working for the CIA? He had denied it, but was he an agent or something? Had Nana known all along? No, that didn't make sense either. Nana had clearly spent time in dangerous areas. Turtleback Beach was the last place she'd describe as dangerous, except for when a hurricane passed through. The town wasn't newsworthy. Nothing like the things she'd seen in action-packed, double agent thriller movies happened here. If Gray were CIA, he wouldn't be doctoring animals and counting turtle nests. Would he? What was he really thinking that day when they went through Nana's boxes in the attic?

A few more raindrops hit her windshield as the lighthouse came into view. Was her father there yet? She didn't even want to imagine the confrontation between him and Gray. Her mind was spinning. Gray had kept many things from her. It had been the very reason she had doubted their relationship in the past. Right now, it seemed that the three most important people in her life—Nana, Gray and John—had all lied to her one way or another. And even if Gray finally came clean about whatever was going on, the fact would remain that, even if she had loved him, their relationship lacked honesty and trust. Love wasn't enough. And she wasn't sure she'd ever trust anyone again.

GRAY'S EYES SHOT open when Laddie started barking and jumping at the door. He still had remnants of his headache but it was at least 50 percent better. The barking didn't help, though.

"Enough. Good boy." Laddie would bark like that only if there was an intruder. He stopped at the "enough" command but stayed close to the door growling. Gray immediately hit the button to light up his surveillance screens.

"John Rivers. Now what?" Within seconds, Mandi's father was pounding at the door.

"Laddie, over there. Stay."

Gray opened the door and Laddie disobeyed, coming back and placing his body between the two men.

"Grayson. We need to talk." John walked in without invitation. Laddie let out a soft guttural growl but didn't attack. He just wanted to protect Gray and his cat babies. Gray shut the door.

"I thought we already had and you made yourself clear."

"Apparently not clear enough. I happen to know you were at the house the other night, after we had our little talk."

"What, are you spying now? I was picking up my dog and cats."

"Right. I don't buy it. You think you're invincible, don't you?"

"Spit it out, John. I have a patient to go see soon and a headache you've just worsened."

"As of right about now, Mandi knows everything there is to know about you and now she'll never let you back in her life again," John said. "You won't hurt us the way you hurt others in the past."

Gray's blood rushed to his feet and adrenaline fired his pulse.

"What did you do?" he demanded.

"I found out a little more. My investigator spoke to someone named Bruce Keenan. The guy said you had harmed his family. Took his brother, Richard, from them."

Damn. Richard Keenan. The captain he had helped to indict. Gray covered his face.

"You don't know what you've done."

"I warned you plenty of times not to mess with me," John said.

"You're crazy. You've endangered her. Don't you get that? I was a freaking federal witness, John. Bruce Keenan is the brother of the guy I blew the whistle on in the name of protecting our government from a traitor. Your PI spoke to his brother, Bruce, who is determined to take an eye for an eye. Loved one for loved one. They'll go after Mandi to get to me. You son of a—"

He couldn't even get the words out. He raked his hair back. Anger singed every vein and nerve in his body. He needed to get out of here. He had to alert the marshal and Sheriff Ryker. He needed to find Mandi and warn her.

John just stood there, half pale and half pissed and looking distraught. He loosened his tie and sweat trickled down his temple.

"How do I know you're telling me the truth?" John asked, suddenly not so sure of himself.

"I don't care if you do or don't. You want confirmation? Ask the sheriff."

John's face fell. "This was all your fault," he said. "You could have told me."

"I wasn't supposed to tell anyone. It goes along with being in the witness protection program, if you haven't clued in. And you're the last person I would have trusted."

How was it his fault? John Rivers had lost his mind. Gray dialed Mandi's cell again. No answer. He dialed Ryker's direct number.

"Carlos. It's happening. I can't find Mandi. She's not answering. She's in danger. She *knows* and so does her father. He's here with me at the lighthouse."

"I'm on it." Carlos hung up and Gray immediately called his WITSEC contact.

"Get to your agreed extract location. Go straight there. Got it? You know the rules. No stops or goodbyes. Thirty minutes and we'll have you out of there. Be ready."

He disconnected. Gray knew the rules but this time was different. He had to be sure Mandi was okay. Laddie sat, ears perked and eyes tense, near the pen where the kittens were.

"Laddie, boy. This is the part you didn't sign up for. You take care of Windy and Storm. If you need anything, you go to the clinic. They'll look after you. And…if I'm gone but somehow Mandi is okay and still here, take care of her for me."

He wasn't sure if she would come with him and the marshals or not. Laddie barked once, then made a concerned whimpering sound. Gray pressed his face to Laddie's head. The marshal would never agree to Gray bringing a dog like him. He stood out too much. He was too recognizable. *I'll never have another friend like you, Laddie. Be good and safe.*

John wiped his palm across his mouth.

"She's got to be alright. I didn't know. How could I have known things were this complicated? I was trying to protect her. Can you blame me? A father who finds out the man after his daughter has a fake identity?" He paced the room. "What do I do now?"

How quickly John had gone from pompous and aggressive to pitiful and defensive.

"It's too late for that. Next time, try thinking of others before yourself."

"I would never intentionally hurt Mandi. I told you I was trying to protect her and to give her a better life than I've had. I love my daughter."

Gray unlocked a cabinet in the corner of the room, took out a Glock and loaded it at lightning speed. "You, John, don't even know the meaning of the word."

MANDI PULLED UP to Gray's fence, next to her father's car, and ignored the light sprinkle as she made her way around the gate and past the laurel tree.

"Dad? Grayson Zale? Or whatever your name really is. We need to talk. Now," she yelled. She was still a good twenty feet from the cottage but she knew she could be heard. Not being able to hear their voices worried her, though. Were they fighting or arguing in there? John did have a temper, although he was no physical match for Gray. Gray didn't have a temper, but what if her father had pushed one too many buttons with this file? "Dammit, Gray! I need answers. For once in your life, you're not going to hold back. I need to know the truth."

The door to his place swung open.

"Mandi. Get over here. Now."

That stopped her in her tracks. She glared at him from the center of the clearing.

"I don't take orders from you or anyone

else, including my father. I'm sick and tired of lies and games. I know he's in there and I'm sure he's told you everything he knows. Is it true? The fake identity? Fake life? The witness statements and birth certificate? All of it? The truth, Gray."

He raked his hair back and looked restless.

"Yes, Mandi. It's true."

Raw disbelief enveloped her. Her feet felt as though they'd been weighted down by anchors. An admission of guilt? This wasn't happening.

"How could you? Five years. *Five.*" She shook her head. "I almost *married* you. Under a different name." Every cell in her body ached. She wanted to die.

"I can explain, but first, you need to get inside. You're not safe out here."

"I can't believe you anymore. Truth, Gray. You promised honesty and truth. It makes so much sense now…how you always held back, never opening up. I should have listened to my gut. I knew something was off."

"Mandi, hear me out. I've been in the Federal Witness Protection Program. I couldn't tell you even if I had wanted to, and believe me, I did. It was too dangerous. But I was going to today because it was the only way to get out of your father blackmailing me. You have to believe me. We're in danger. John blew my cover and that puts you in danger, too, because anyone out there seeking revenge would have figured out that you mean everything to me.

"You know the real me, Mandi. The new name and documents? Those were about appearances. My outward identity." He jabbed a finger at his chest. "The real me is still in here. He's really a vet who loves animals and pizza on a rainy night. You know the real me, Mandi. The guy who fell in love with you and who still loves you."

She shook her head and took a step back. She couldn't stop the tears or the rain that was getting heavier or the pain. She had loved the man she thought he was. A man who didn't exist.

"I don't know anymore," she said.

The sound of a vehicle speeding down the road grew closer. No sirens. Just the engine getting louder. It sounded like a motorcycle. Someone was taking a risk driving that fast in the rain. She glanced down the road and back at Gray.

"Mandi. You can't stand there like that. It's dangerous." He started to close the gap between them. She took a step back.

"Where's my dad?"

"He's telling the truth, Mandi," her father said, appearing in the doorway of the care-taker's house. "I think I made a mistake. I'm so sorry, Mandi. Listen to him. Hurry."

The afternoon clouds thickened and blan-keted everything in a foreboding shade of gray. The sound of the engine revving got closer. Her dad was the one who had all the evidence against Gray. He was the one who never liked Gray. And yet, here he was admitting fault and backing Gray up? It was true? Gray had been in the witness protection program all this time? Memo-ries from their times together…small bits of conversations…it was all coming back in a new light. The pieces were falling into place. Tears stung the rims of her eyes. She walked toward him, unable to speak but wanting to say so much.

The headlight of a motorcycle appeared through the rain at the end of the road and aimed right for the gate without slowing down. The look of horror on her father's face…the intense fear in Gray's eyes…the headlight beaming right toward them. It was all registering at once. Then a second bike sped up behind the first.

"Mandi! Now!"

GRAY BOLTED FORWARD and lunged at her. Whoever was approaching clearly wasn't on their side. The marshals wouldn't have come for him on bikes. They wouldn't have approached so aggressively. WITSEC made people disappear. They didn't draw attention to those under their protection. Where were his contacts? Or Carlos? *Now would be a good time to get here, Sheriff.* The rain started coming down even harder.

"John, get inside and lock the door!"

His priority was to protect Mandi and the safest place he could get her was the lighthouse. Its walls were impenetrable. It had height. It was his WITSEC designated safe place in an emergency. There wasn't time to get John, Laddie and the kittens there, but maybe he and Mandie heading for the lighthouse would also serve as a decoy and buy them all time.

Gray grabbed Mandi's arm and ran toward the lighthouse as fast as he could, trying to shield her with his body, but the helmeted intruders crushed the picket gate and sped across the clearing, aiming straight for them. The first one swerved to block their path and the other circled like he was corralling sheep. The rider pulled out a gun and aimed right at them.

"Gray!"

He shoved Mandi to the ground, pulled out his own gun and aimed straight for the chest of the motorcycle driver, but in a flash, Laddie appeared in his peripheral vision, faster than he'd ever seen him run. The dog bolted into the air and knocked the rider off his seat. The rider's gun flew off to the side and landed a few yards out of reach. The bike fell to its side and did a one-eighty, spraying wet sand with it. Laddie wrestled the guy and kept him pinned down. The other driver swerved around and started for them. John, of all people, ran out of the house and began waving his hands in the air and yelling curses to bait him.

"John, no! Get back!"

John ignored him. The man was going to get himself killed. Gray could hear vehicles approaching in the distance. Hopefully the right ones this time. They needed to buy time. He knew the motorcycle riding jackets worn were embedded with armor to protect in an accident, but he wasn't sure if they'd stop a bullet or not. He aimed and shot the tire on the bike first, to slow the guy down. The rider lost control but jumped off his seat, rolled out of his fall, then tackled Gray. Gray's gun skidded out of reach. The attacker had managed to hang on to his. Gray grabbed the guy's wrist, jammed his knee behind his leg and flipped him over, pinning his arm behind him. The gun fired. John buckled to the ground.

"No!" Gray screamed.

"Dad!"

"Mandi, take these keys, run for the lighthouse and lock yourself in. Go, now!" He threw her the keys just as his attacker used a similar combat move to escape the hold Gray had him in. Gray took a punch to the face. If only he had his helmet on, too. He twisted the man's wrist, forcing him to drop the gun, put his knee behind the attacker's and flipped him back down. He grabbed the gun off the ground and aimed it at his chest.

"Move and I'll shoot."

The first rider had gotten out of Laddie's hold and started running at Mandi, who had ignored Gray's orders. Instead, she ran for the first attacker's gun that was lying in the sand not far from where Laddie had first pinned the guy down and aimed it at the man. Laddie jumped him again, this time latching on good with his teeth and pinning him down. Mandi's hands were shaking, but Gray somehow knew she wouldn't shoot, because of Laddie, unless she had to. She had to be okay. If she got injured—or worse— he'd never forgive himself or survive it.

Everything was happening in microseconds. From the corner of his eye, he saw a black SUV swerving into the clearing and slamming its brakes. The sheriff's car and Carlos. *Finally.* Laddie yelped and the man he had by the arm started to run. Someone yelled "down" and shots rang out at the same time that Mandi hit the ground.

"Mandi!"

Gray's attacker took that moment to leg

flip him in the mud. The man made a run for it. Gray aimed the gun at him but shots rang out again before he fired. The man went down.

Gray's breath caught in his chest. He recognized the marshal running toward him through the rain. There were teams fanning out to secure the area. Ambulance sirens nearing. He couldn't see Mandi. He could only see the sheriff kneeling down where she'd fallen. Panic consumed him. His pulse was erratic. If she was hurt…if he'd lost her…his life would be over, too.

MANDI SAT UP with Carlos's help. She couldn't keep up with each breath. She started gasping. She couldn't control her breathing. She saw her father go down. She didn't know if Gray was hit. Where was Laddie?

"Slow down. Slow breaths. You're hyperventilating. It's all over. You're going to be alright." Carlos signaled for a medic, then moved out of the way when Gray reached them. Laddie was glued to his side, looking up at him repeatedly to make sure he was okay.

Grayson. She didn't care what his last

name was or had been. He was her Gray and he was alive. Tears began streaming down her face uncontrollably. She could feel them, but the moment was surreal. She could feel Laddie licking her hand. Voices were everywhere but they sounded muffled in her ears. All that really mattered was Gray.

She tried to say his name but only heard her heavy breathing and sobs.

"Mandi." He took her in his arms and held her tight against his chest. His warmth and the beating of his heart helped soothe her pulse and breathing to a steady pace. As steady as her pulse could ever be in his arms. He stroked her hair and pressed desperate kisses to her head, face, then lips. "I love you."

"I love you, too." She kissed him back, then buried her face in his shoulder. "Gray I'm scared. My dad…"

Gray kissed her forehead again.

"He's going to be alright. A bullet grazed his shoulder. They're walking him to the ambulance right now. Come on, I'll take you to him. You need to get checked, too."

"I'm okay. Just shaken. I've never held a gun. I couldn't shoot because I didn't want to hit Laddie, but I was afraid that guy would get it or get away. And then I heard the shot and I dropped to the ground for safety but I also saw him fall and I don't know if I did it. Did I kill a man?"

"No, but you sure were ready to. So was I. The marshal got him first. I was scared to death for you, Mandi. But the fact is, you were amazing and you and Laddie teaming up against that guy made all the difference."

"Laddie made the first move. He deserves a medal. Don't you?" She gave Laddie a hug and Gray gave him a good rub.

"He'll get one even if I have to make it myself. But first, he'll be getting a thorough check at the office. No cuts, but I think he's limping slightly on his back leg. You'll be okay, though, boy. Let's check on John before the ambulance leaves."

"Wait." She took his hands in hers and held them to her chest. "I'm sorry, Gray. I'm sorry that I doubted you for even a moment. I knew deep down you were a good man…someone I'd never stop loving. I know how my father can be and I knew there had to be some sort of explanation for what I was seeing in the file he had on you. But when you first said it was all true, I let my insecurities and emotions get in the way. Please forgive me. For everything. For not trusting you enough about your 'secrets,' for abandoning you on our wedding day and for doubting you today. I love you with all my heart, Gray. I trust you with all my heart. You have to believe that."

"I do." He rested his forehead against hers. "I love and trust you too. And I can't blame you for your reaction. Falling in love when you're in the witness protection program isn't exactly the typical dating scenario for either party." He gave her a lopsided grin and she smiled.

"Very true," she said, before sharing a kiss.

"Let's go check on your dad, now."

He put his arm around her and walked Mandi, with Laddie at their side, to the ambulance. John's eye was already turning black-and-blue and a paramedic was pressure bandaging his shoulder wound. Mandi ran up to him and held his free hand in hers. A tear escaped the corner of John's eye.

"Oh, Dad. You're hurt badly."

"I'll be fine. I'm just glad the two of you are alright."

"John. You may have triggered what happened today, but what you did back there was risky, insane…and courageous. Thank you, from both of us, for trying to distract that rider."

"I can't take any credit. I got you both into this mess. I put you both in danger. I'll never forgive myself. Mandi, you mean the world to me. You do, whether you believe it or not. I think I was trying to hold on too tight and messed up along the way. I didn't want you to suffer the way I did when your mother left me."

"Dad, you can't keep trying to relive your life through me. I'm not your do-over. I'm my own person and so is Gray."

"I know that now. I was trying to fill a void and lost sight of what was important. Showing how much I love you and am proud of you, for one thing."

Tears welled up in Mandi's eyes again.

"Thank you, Dad. I'm going to need some time to get over what happened today, but we'll talk. Focus on getting well for now."

"The fact that either of you is still willing

to talk to me is more than I can hope for. I'll live every day here on out trying to make it up to you. I know it's not enough, but I mean it when I say that I'm sorry. You deserve to be happy. Forever. Both of you do. Life's short. Don't waste it apart."

The medics apologized for interrupting, got him in the ambulance and closed the doors.

"Gray, Mandi," Carlos said, walking up to them. "I have another ambulance on the way for the two of you. I know 'you're fine' but after what just went down, you're not arguing with me."

"We're fine," they both said, exchanging looks.

"Sheriff's orders," Carlos said.

Mandi rested her head on Gray's shoulder.

"Carlos, did you know all this time?" she asked. "About Gray being in witness protection?"

Carlos looked at Gray.

"I'll let him fill you in. I believe the US Marshals will want to talk to you both, before more is said or done." He motioned over his shoulder as a marshal approached.

"Mandi, this is US Marshal Brenda Finn,"

Gray said. "Brenda, fill me in because I can't do this again. I can't start over. And I can't do that to Mandi, but at the same time, I want her safe."

"You had a close call here, Zale. My intel said that as far as they can tell, these two guys were the only ones who had tapped into Rivers's info search on you and passed your location on. I can't give you guarantees and you know we usually recommend staying in the program, but we've ID'd the bodies. They were the two we suspected might come after you—Keenan's brother and his friend—and Rivers inadvertently drew them out of the woodwork. And let's just say they're no longer an issue. One of your attackers today was Keenan's brother."

"You're saying I'm a free man?"

"I'm saying, I'd keep your current identity and play it safe, but if you want out, I believe the threat has been neutralized.

"Understood. I'm not going anywhere. This is my life now. My choice."

The marshal nodded, said something about paperwork and went back to her team. Mandi wrapped her arms around Gray and felt her body melt into his when he held on to her.

"So, are you keeping the last name Zale?" She looked up at Gray and linked her fingers in his.

"I guess I will. Everyone here knows me by that name. My practice is built around it. Changing all my legal papers would be a pain. But at least I'll have my past...my history...back, too. Does it still matter to you? The name? The fact that I kept it from you?"

"I love you, Gray. Not a name. *You.* And the only reason I'm asking is because I'd like to know what I'd be changing my last name to."

Gray's brow twitched and his lips spread into a slow, lopsided smile.

"Are you saying what I think you're saying?"

"If you'll give me a second chance, I promise I won't run away this time," she said. Her pulse was racing all over again. What if he said no? She wasn't even sure how it would work out. All she knew was that she couldn't picture life without him. "Grayson Zale... I don't want to *almost* marry you. I want to *marry* you."

"Mandi, all I ever wanted was for you to be my bride, so that I could wake up every sunrise by your side and love you every minute of my life. Marry me, Mandi."

She brushed her lips against his and he held her face in his hands, then kissed her like there was no tomorrow, but with the promise of forever.

## EPILOGUE

THE LIGHT FROM the full, strawberry moon glistened across the Atlantic. Gray turned off the house lights, then made his way down the steps from Nana's cottage, carrying a thermos of coffee and a couple of mugs. It was going to be a long night, but Mandi was with him and that made all the difference. She sat there, silhouetted against the moonlit sky, waiting for him…and the turtles. He walked over, set the thermos down and sat behind her in the cool sand, spreading his legs so that she could rest her back against his chest.

"Hey, you," she said, looking over her shoulder at him.

"Hey," he gave her a kiss, then held her hands. "Laddie's taking not being down here with us a lot better now that he has Windy and Storm. All three are sleeping on the new dog bed we got him."

"They're so sweet together. I'm so glad that Laddie's leg is okay."

Gray brushed his lips against her ear.

"I think we're pretty sweet together too," he whispered. "I can't wait to get married, grow our family and have kids to tuck into bed."

"I'm ready for it. I don't want to wait. And as soon as we are ready to walk down the aisle, my dad said his shoulder won't stop him. He wants to walk me and give us his blessing. It's going to be a long time before I can really trust him, but this will be a good first step toward healing our family."

"Let's not wait. The end of summer will be here before we know it. Let's have a beach wedding before fall arrives and it gets too cold."

"That sounds perfect. Nothing big or fancy. Just natural and comfortable like I want our life here to be."

"I know I asked before, but are you sure? I can't ask you to give up a job you worked so hard for. It won't be easy, but now that I'm no longer in WITSEC we can alternate weekends visiting each other."

She put her fingers to his lips.

"No. This is the right decision. I feel that in my gut. This is where I belong and where I want to be. I don't want to work under anyone or have anyone control my life like that. You were right about that. I can make this work...open my own business here and hopefully help the town economy in doing so. Even help businesses along the entire Outer Banks. And I want to help with advertising for nonprofits, too, like the Native American museums and turtle and wildlife rescue groups."

They had already talked about restoring the lighthouse and turning the keeper's cottage into a ranger station to help oversee turtle and other ocean life rescue along this stretch of beach, while living in the house that would always be known as Nana's place. But he wanted to be sure that Mandi wasn't having second thoughts.

"You're the best. You know that?" He nudged his foot against hers in the sand and kissed her hair.

"It's like Nana always said. Find passion in what you do," Mandi said.

"She'll be missed."

There was a moment of silence, broken

only by the sound of the surf and the music coming from the boardwalk restaurant down the beach."

"How long until the babies hatch?" Mandi asked.

"No telling. I just hope most of them make it."

There were two separate nests due to hatch tonight—one loggerhead and one Kemp's ridley—which meant pretty soon there would be a couple of hundred baby sea turtles scrambling through the sand to find safety beneath the waves. Nature would take its course once they made it there, but until then, Gray would help any that needed assistance in reaching the water. He knew interfering with nature wasn't always recommended, but he figured man was already affecting the turtles' natural environment with artificial light and sound pollution. He was trying to make up for it in a small way. Mandi and he were babysitting one nest, and farther down the beach, Nora and Darla were watching over another.

The music from the boardwalk suddenly stopped and Gray looked off to his right to see what happened. All the town lights went out. Every single one of them.

"Did you see that?" Gray asked. "Did we have a town-wide power outage?" He looked down the other side of the beach toward cottages in the distance.

Mandi stood up and brushed the sand off her rear. She extended her hand and pulled Gray up next to her.

"A deliberate power outage."

"What are you talking about?"

Deliberate? As in a shutdown to help the hatchlings? A shutdown like the one he had been trying to get folks to do with no success?

"All the town businesses agreed to it, at least until the babies make it to the water. I promised some free web advertising with custom designs and convinced them that, if we help the turtles, they'll help us back by drawing visitors willing to sign up as nest hunters and sitters. I suggested the town use a catchphrase like Hatch Watch for tourists to ask about and sign up for. I also told them that doing it tonight would be a nice way to honor Nana and her contributions to Turtleback Beach during her lifetime."

"You did this?"

"Consider it an early wedding gift."

"Mandi. You have no idea how much this means to me."

She leaned into him and wrapped her arms around his neck and kissed him.

"Oh, I don't know. I think I do."

Darla gave a big arm signal without calling out.

"Their nest is hatching," Mandi said, looking over his shoulder to where Nora and Darla were.

Gray and Mandi slowly approached their nest. There was movement in the sand.

"It's happening." Mandi texted Carlos so that he'd let the town know the babies were hatching and to keep their lights off until they got the all clear.

The sand shifted and began to cascade away from the hatching eggs. Hundreds of baby turtles started breaking free from their shells and headed toward the water, only a few needing help along the way. They were embarking on a journey that, for them, would be long, hard and not without obstacles or danger. But they pushed forward and didn't give up because they knew where they needed to be and where their future awaited them.

Just like Gray and Mandi knew that they belonged together and that Turtleback would always be home.

\* \* \* \* \*

# Get 4 FREE REWARDS!

## We'll send you 2 FREE Books plus 2 FREE Mystery Gifts.

**Love Inspired®** books feature contemporary inspirational romances with Christian characters facing the challenges of life and love.

FREE Value Over $20

---

**YES!** Please send me 2 FREE Love Inspired® Romance novels and my 2 FREE mystery gifts (gifts are worth about $10 retail). After receiving them, if I don't wish to receive any more books, I can return the shipping statement marked "cancel." If I don't cancel, I will receive 6 brand-new novels every month and be billed just $5.24 for the regular-print edition or $5.74 each for the larger-print edition in the U.S., or $5.74 each for the regular-print edition or $6.24 each for the larger-print edition in Canada. That's a savings of at least 13% off the cover price. It's quite a bargain! Shipping and handling is just 50¢ per book in the U.S. and 75¢ per book in Canada.* I understand that accepting the 2 free books and gifts places me under no obligation to buy anything. I can always return a shipment and cancel at any time. The free books and gifts are mine to keep no matter what I decide.

Choose one:  ☐ **Love Inspired® Romance Regular-Print**
(105/305 IDN GMY4)

☐ **Love Inspired® Romance Larger-Print**
(122/322 IDN GMY4)

Name (please print)

Address                                                                                    Apt. #

City                                    State/Province                          Zip/Postal Code

### Mail to the **Reader Service:**
**IN U.S.A.:** P.O. Box 1341, Buffalo, NY 14240-8531
**IN CANADA:** P.O. Box 603, Fort Erie, Ontario L2A 5X3

**Want to try 2 free books from another series? Call 1-800-873-8635 or visit www.ReaderService.com.**

*Terms and prices subject to change without notice. Prices do not include sales taxes, which will be charged (if applicable) based on your state or country of residence. Canadian residents will be charged applicable taxes. Offer not valid in Quebec. This offer is limited to one order per household. Books received may not be as shown. Not valid for current subscribers to Love Inspired Romance books. All orders subject to approval. Credit or debit balances in a customer's account(s) may be offset by any other outstanding balance owed by or to the customer. Please allow 4 to 6 weeks for delivery. Offer available while quantities last.

**Your Privacy**—The Reader Service is committed to protecting your privacy. Our Privacy Policy is available online at www.ReaderService.com or upon request from the Reader Service. We make a portion of our mailing list available to reputable third parties that offer products we believe may interest you. If you prefer that we not exchange your name with third parties, or if you wish to clarify or modify your communication preferences, please visit us at www.ReaderService.com/consumerschoice or write to us at Reader Service Preference Service, P.O. Box 9062, Buffalo, NY 14240-9062. Include your complete name and address.

LI19R2

# Get 4 FREE REWARDS!

## We'll send you 2 FREE Books plus 2 FREE Mystery Gifts.

**Love Inspired® Suspense** books feature Christian characters facing challenges to their faith... and lives.

FREE
Value Over
**$20**

---

**YES!** Please send me 2 FREE Love Inspired® Suspense novels and my 2 FREE mystery gifts (gifts are worth about $10 retail). After receiving them, if I don't wish to receive any more books, I can return the shipping statement marked "cancel." If I don't cancel, I will receive 4 brand-new novels every month and be billed just $5.24 each for the regular-print edition or $5.74 each for the larger-print edition in the U.S., or $5.74 each for the regular-print edition or $6.24 each for the larger-print edition in Canada. That's a savings of at least 13% off the cover price. It's quite a bargain! Shipping and handling is just 50¢ per book in the U.S. and 75¢ per book in Canada.* I understand that accepting the 2 free books and gifts places me under no obligation to buy anything. I can always return a shipment and cancel at any time. The free books and gifts are mine to keep no matter what I decide.

Choose one:  ☐ **Love Inspired® Suspense**
Regular-Print
(153/353 IDN GMY5)

☐ **Love Inspired® Suspense**
Larger-Print
(107/307 IDN GMY5)

Name (please print)

Address                                                                    Apt. #

City                              State/Province                    Zip/Postal Code

### Mail to the Reader Service:
**IN U.S.A.:** P.O. Box 1341, Buffalo, NY 14240-8531
**IN CANADA:** P.O. Box 603, Fort Erie, Ontario L2A 5X3

Want to try 2 free books from another series? Call 1-800-873-8635 or visit www.ReaderService.com.

---

*Terms and prices subject to change without notice. Prices do not include sales taxes, which will be charged (if applicable) based on your state or country of residence. Canadian residents will be charged applicable taxes. Offer not valid in Quebec. This offer is limited to one order per household. Books received may not be as shown. Not valid for current subscribers to Love Inspired Suspense books. All orders subject to approval. Credit or debit balances in a customer's account(s) may be offset by any other outstanding balance owed by or to the customer. Please allow 4 to 6 weeks for delivery. Offer available while quantities last.

**Your Privacy**—The Reader Service is committed to protecting your privacy. Our Privacy Policy is available online at www.ReaderService.com or upon request from the Reader Service. We make a portion of our mailing list available to reputable third parties that offer products we believe may interest you. If you prefer that we not exchange your name with third parties, or if you wish to clarify or modify your communication preferences, please visit us at www.ReaderService.com/consumerschoice or write to us at Reader Service Preference Service, P.O. Box 9062, Buffalo, NY 14240-9062. Include your complete name and address.

LIS19R2

# BETTY NEELS COLLECTION!

Buy 3 and get
**1 FREE!**

**Experience one of the most celebrated and beloved authors in romance! Betty Neels will delight you with her signature brand of storytelling: happy romances, memorable couples and timeless tales of lasting love. These classics have been combined in 2-in-1 books for your reading pleasure!**

**YES!** Please send me the **Betty Neels Collection**. This collection begins with 4 books, 1 of which is FREE! Plus a FREE gift – an elegant simulated Pearl Necklace & Earring Set (approx. retail value of $13.99). I may either return the shipment and owe nothing or keep for the low members-only discount price of $17.97 U.S./$20.25 CDN plus $1.99 U.S./$2.99 CDN for shipping and handling per shipment.* If I decide to continue, I'll receive two more shipments, each about a month apart, each containing four more two-in-one books, one of which will be free, until I own the entire 12-book collection. Each shipment is mine to keep for the same members-only discount price plus shipping and handling. I understand that no purchase is required. I may keep the free book no matter what I decide.

☐ 275 HCN 4623          ☐ 475 HCN 4623

Name (please print)

Address                                                                                    Apt. #

City                              State/Province                    Zip/Postal Code

**Mail to the Reader Service:**
**IN U.S.A.:** P.O. Box 1341, Buffalo, NY. 14240-8531
**IN CANADA:** P.O. Box 603, Fort Erie, Ontario L2A 5X3

*Terms and prices subject to change without notice. Prices do not include sales taxes, which will be charged (if applicable) based on your state or country of residence. Canadian residents will be charged applicable taxes. Offer not valid in Quebec. All orders subject to approval. Credit or debit balances in a customer's account(s) may be offset by any other outstanding balance owed by or to the customer. Please allow 3 to 4 weeks for delivery. Offer available while quantities last. © 2019 Harlequin Enterprises Limited.

**Your Privacy**—The Reader Service is committed to protecting your privacy. Our Privacy Policy is available online at www.ReaderService.com or upon request from the Reader Service. We make a portion of our mailing list available to reputable third parties that offer products we believe may interest you. If you prefer that we not exchange your name with third parties, or if you wish to clarify or modify your communication preferences, please visit us at www.ReaderService.com/consumerchoice or write to us at Reader Service Preference Service, P.O. Box 9049, Buffalo, NY 14269-9049. Include your name and address.

MBN19

# Get 4 FREE REWARDS!

## We'll send you 2 FREE Books **plus** 2 FREE Mystery Gifts.

**FREE** Value Over **$20**

Both the **Romance** and **Suspense** collections feature compelling novels written by many of today's best-selling authors.

**YES!** Please send me 2 FREE novels from the Essential Romance or Essential Suspense Collection and my 2 FREE gifts (gifts are worth about $10 retail). After receiving them, if I don't wish to receive any more books, I can return the shipping statement marked "cancel." If I don't cancel, I will receive 4 brand-new novels every month and be billed just $6.74 each in the U.S. or $7.24 each in Canada. That's a savings of at least 16% off the cover price. It's quite a bargain! Shipping and handling is just 50¢ per book in the U.S. and 75¢ per book in Canada.* I understand that accepting the 2 free books and gifts places me under no obligation to buy anything. I can always return a shipment and cancel at any time. The free books and gifts are mine to keep no matter what I decide.

Choose one: ☐ **Essential Romance**  ☐ **Essential Suspense**
(194/394 MDN GMY7)      (191/391 MDN GMY7)

Name (please print)

Address                                                                Apt. #

City                          State/Province                Zip/Postal Code

### Mail to the **Reader Service:**
**IN U.S.A.:** P.O. Box 1341, Buffalo, NY 14240-8531
**IN CANADA:** P.O. Box 603, Fort Erie, Ontario L2A 5X3

Want to try 2 free books from another series! Call **1-800-873-8635** or visit www.ReaderService.com.

*Terms and prices subject to change without notice. Prices do not include sales taxes, which will be charged (if applicable) based on your state or country of residence. Canadian residents will be charged applicable taxes. Offer not valid in Quebec. This offer is limited to one order per household. Books received may not be as shown. Not valid for current subscribers to the Essential Romance or Essential Suspense Collection. All orders subject to approval. Credit or debit balances in a customer's account(s) may be offset by any other outstanding balance owed by or to the customer. Please allow 4 to 6 weeks for delivery. Offer available while quantities last.

**Your Privacy**—The Reader Service is committed to protecting your privacy. Our Privacy Policy is available online at www.ReaderService.com or upon request from the Reader Service. We make a portion of our mailing list available to reputable third parties that offer products we believe may interest you. If you prefer that we not exchange your name with third parties, or if you wish to clarify or modify your communication preferences, please visit us at www.ReaderService.com/consumerchoice or write to us at Reader Service Preference Service, P.O. Box 9062, Buffalo, NY 14240-9062. Include your complete name and address.

STRS19R2

# READERSERVICE.COM

## Manage your account online!

- Review your order history
- Manage your payments
- Update your address

*We've designed the Reader Service website just for you.*

## Enjoy all the features!

- Discover new series available to you, and read excerpts from any series.
- Respond to mailings and special monthly offers.
- Browse the Bonus Bucks catalog and online-only exclusives.
- Share your feedback.

*Visit us at:*
**ReaderService.com**

RS16R